# A Flash of Lightning

# A FLASH OF LIGHTNING

by
Tony Drury

*A Flash of Lightning*
Copyright ©2013 Tony Drury
Published in 2013 by City Fiction

City Fiction
c/o
Sue Richardson Associates Ltd
Minerva Mill Innovation Centre
Station Road
Alcester
Warwickshire B49 5ET
T: 01789 761345
www.cityfiction.com

A CIP record for this book is available from the British Library.

ISBN paperback: 978-0-9572017-9-8
ISBN hardback: 978-1-910040-0-0-3
ISBN ebook (epub): 978-1-910040-0-2-7
ISBN ebook (mobi): 978-1-910040-0-1-0

Printed and bound in Great Britain by TJ International, Padstow,
Cornwall

Have you ever watched a storm approaching on a hot summer's day? It's especially spectacular in the mountains. At first there's nothing to see, but you feel a sort of weariness that tells you something is in the air. Then you hear thunder – just a rumble here and there – you can't quite tell where it is coming from. All of a sudden, the mountains seem strangely near. There isn't a breath of wind, yet dense clouds pile up in the sky. And now the mountains have almost vanished behind a wall of haze. Clouds rush in from all sides, but still there's no wind. There's more thunder now, and everything around looks eerie and menacing. You wait and wait. And then, suddenly, it erupts. At first it is almost a release. The storm descends into the valley. There's thunder and lightning everywhere. The rain clatters down in huge drops. The storm is trapped in the narrow cleft of the valley and thunderclaps echo and reverberate off the steep mountain sides. The wind buffets you from every angle. And when the storm finally moves away, leaving in its place a clear, still, starlit night, you can hardly remember where those thunderclouds were, let alone which thunderclap belonged to which flash of lightning.

**Extract from *A Little History of the World* by E. H. Gombrich (2008): Yale University Press**

## Also by Tony Drury

*Megan's Game* (2012)
*The Deal* (2012)
*Cholesterol* (2013)

# PART ONE

*If you miss the train I'm on, you will know that I have gone*
*You can hear the whistle blow a hundred miles.*
*A hundred miles, a hundred miles, a hundred miles,*
*a hundred miles,*
*You can hear the whistle blow a hundred miles.*

**'Five Hundred Miles' (1962), Peter, Paul and Mary**

# Chapter One

Matthew Orlando Buckingham, obviously known as 'Mob', was angry, very angry. He was also fed up with feeling cold. There had been a bitter, chilly easterly wind blowing in from the Russian Tundra, which was threatening to spoil the oncoming Easter holidays. Where were the early spring rainstorms? Why was there still snow on the roads?

His angst was based on two factors. First, he was guilty. Second, he could not think of anybody to blame. That stopped him in his tracks. He was never wrong about anything. That was what his former wife had claimed.

In fact there was a possible culprit: her name was Tattalia and she came from New Zealand. He had met her two weeks earlier at the Dorchester Hotel off London's Park Lane. They'd had coffee together. He'd thought she was gorgeous but that did not mean much because Mob thought that of most women. She'd seemed oblivious to the temperatures outside and had been wearing a chiffon dress which really didn't cover very much. Her body was glowing from the winter sunshine and the three holidays she'd had in the last five months in Brazil, Florida and Thailand.

During their meeting, which was to discuss her possible role as his Public Relations Adviser, she'd crossed and uncrossed her legs at least three times. On each occasion she'd showed him her virginal white panties. She had never worked for a stockbroking firm despite her efforts to convince Mob otherwise. She'd realised she was fighting a losing battle and so resorted to the oldest trick in the book.

Men the world over vary in their choice of the ideal colour for ladies' underwear. Fashion Houses earn a fortune offering alternatives. For Mob, as for many males, white was the colour that boiled the testosterone the most. The vision and intimacy of those crossings had occupied much of his thinking since they'd parted, having agreed to meet again. He suspected that they never would, although he was unable to rid himself of the thought of removing her underwear.

It was a pity because, as he was driving his Mercedes-Benz S-Class along the A505 southern relief road bypassing Leighton Buzzard, he should have been thinking about the speed limit. It was a dangerous stretch whose construction had been held up by a wealthy landowner for many years. It was three lanes with no central barrier. It invited fast speeds. The authorities had countered this by building a short 50 mph divide through which Mob drove, he thought, at 56 mph. That was the speed he registered as the camera flashed.

The letter had arrived that morning. He was clocked at 60 mph. He already had six points on his driving licence. He tried to excuse his indiscretion. He had wanted to leave for London as soon as possible after seeing his daughter.

He could remember clearly why he and his former wife had decided to live in Bedfordshire. It was because moving from the north, and being new to the south of England, they had discovered that the first house they liked, and could afford, was in Leighton Buzzard and the trains to Euston seemed to run efficiently. They both commuted for four years until Olivia arrived, whereupon his wife found that she enjoyed domestic life, especially when it was enriched by her solicitor. She'd decided to claim against a local furniture shop whose goods proved faulty and their attitude unhelpful. Matthew tried to hold things together but she was smitten. Not only did John Sneddon persuade the retailer to replace the goods and pay compensation, he also began their affair.

She accepted his suggestion that he should arrange member-ship for her at the local golf club and was flattered when she found that he had paid her joining costs. Almost inevitably, the legal eagle was a single handicap player. He introduced her to the club professional with whom she spent some attentive, and at times, tactile hours on the practice ground. She was a natural and was soon chipping and putting with some style but she could not master using the more demanding clubs: the woods

4

off the tee and the long irons. One day, when sitting with John in the club lounge, her frustration became apparent.

"What's the use of being sodding Tiger Woods around the greens if I can't reach the fucking things in the first place?" she asked.

He spoke privately to the club professional who remained perplexed. He suggested a second opinion and recommended a colleague at the local driving range. After three lessons the fault was diagnosed. As Anne Buckingham prepared to hit the ball her left leg was too near the tee. That was the obvious problem which had already been identified and worked on. However, what had not been spotted was that she was bending her left leg too quickly on the downswing. This produced the classic 'inside out' shot which not only lost distance but sliced the golf ball from left to right. In the case of Leighton Buzzard golf course that inevitably meant into the trees.

Within weeks her game had improved and she was able to put her name down for the competitions. She came last on her first three attempts and then in the bottom three and then she started climbing the ladder. Her game continued to feature the high handicapper's nightmare: a good round and then, from nowhere, an 'eight' or 'nine' or a lost ball, so ruining the score card.

On a summer's day in August she and John were playing in a mixed 'better ball' match and it was becoming rather competitive. He was a handsome man who usually wore an all black outfit whatever the weather. Anne had selected a white top and a green skirt. Her tanned legs reached all the way down to her matching golf shoes. She was not wearing socks.

It was essential that they did not lose the last hole, in order to retain their slender lead and so win. John hit his drive out of bounds. Their opponents played decent shots but were both short. This meant neither had a second shot on to the green on the difficult dog-leg par four finishing hole.

Anne hit a three wood off the tee and reached the top of the apex. She was the last to play the second shot which, in her case was, thoughtfully, a five wood which she held with her hands positioned down the shaft. The ball landed in the centre of the green and her two putts secured their victory.

After the handshakes she and John embraced. They had been sleeping together for many months but today was different. Her moist lips devoured him and he held on to her with a passion she had never before sensed. She went home and told Matthew that their marriage was over.

He had left home seven years ago, when Olivia was two years old, and moved into a one bedroom flat in Clerkenwell. His career took off almost immediately and now he was running a large stockbroking firm based in the City of London. He visited his daughter every two weeks. She enjoyed shopping in Milton Keynes, ice-skating sessions, visits to Whipsnade Zoo, trips on the Grand Union Canal and going for meals at the various eateries in the area.

By now Anne and John had moved to Ledburn, in the parish of Mentmore, just on the southern edge of the town. They purchased a farmhouse on one of the two roads and Anne quickly became involved in its renovation. John worked long hours and she became restless. Then Thomas was born after many false alarms and visits to the fertility consultant. He had recently celebrated his first birthday and Matthew was puzzled that Olivia rarely spoke about her half-brother. He had not been allowed to see him.

He now disliked Leighton Buzzard probably because his wife seemed to have discovered happiness with her new husband. What was worse was that she retained the good looks for which he married her in the first place. As he drove away he would sneer. "Trying to pretend they're French," he would scoff.

In fact 'Leighton' was from the old English word meaning a 'farm in a clearing in the woods'. The derivation of 'Buzzard' was weird. In the twelfth century the Dean of Lincoln wanted to differentiate two towns in his parish both of which started with 'Leighton'. So he added Buzzard from the name of his local representative Theobald de Busar which gave him 'Leighton Buzzard'. Had he bothered to look it up he would have found that neighbouring 'Ledburn' came from the Anglo Saxon word for 'stream with a conduit'.

Mob would try to fathom out why anybody would want to live there: in fact thirty-eight thousand people did. The rail services were good to London, Birmingham and Manchester. The M1, M25 and M40 motorways were close by and Luton Airport housed EasyJet. There had been a Conservative Member of Parliament for decades.

* * *

Detective Chief Inspector Sarah Rudd clung to her husband. She felt a kaleidoscope of colourful emotions. She was having relations again with her husband Nick after her loss of libido following awful facial injuries suffered during a hostage rescue. Then her former lover had reappeared. This was trumped by her award-winning act of supreme bravery which resulted in her receiving the Queen's Gallantry Medal.

On leaving Buckingham Palace, having collected her medal, she told her boss that all she wanted to do was to return to serious crime investigation in Islington. The civic lunch was abandoned. Nick's parents had taken her two children off for a picnic and she and her husband had walked, and talked, in St. James's Park.

She always tried to remember that as a headmaster he also had his own challenges. But somehow the life of a police officer seemed overpowering and eventful.

She rolled off him and lay back on their bed. Sarah Rudd was forty-three years of age and they had two children. She and Nick had named them for obscure reasons. They both agreed that family names did not work for them. In Sarah's case it was because her parents had been dedicated to their church and not to her. Nick wanted his kids to have ones which worked in the modern environment. He had seen too much bullying in the class room of girls christened Madonna to take any chances.

Their son was now thirteen. He was called Marcus. Susie was really Susan but, to Nick, she was Susie. She was named after the doctor who delivered her. For her ninth birthday Nick had bought her an iPad and their relationship was secured forever.

Sarah's doctor had told her that she was around a stone overweight. She was, however, a woman who carried the surplus flesh to great effect. The curves somehow added to her sexuality.

7

From the first occasion he had seen her naked Nick found her unbelievably seductive. When they made love she had this ability to use all of her physical attributes to good effect.

They also talked about, and worked on, their relationship. After a particularly alcoholic dinner together Nick had told her that he found her police uniform a compelling aphrodisiac. The next night she had come out of the bathroom wearing lacy black underwear, stockings and suspenders, carrying a pair of handcuffs and her truncheon.

She announced that she was arresting him for being a pervert who prayed on innocent women. She locked his arms around the top of the bed and removed his pyjamas. She then sat astride him and took nearly seven minutes to remove her clothing. She left her panties until last.

As she recalled those early days Sarah reflected that, for her, the best times were their walks over the hills. Following their police-style sex they had, the next day, climbed together for over two hours. She knew that she could not manage to live her life without Nick. If anything was ever to happen to him, for DCI Sarah Rudd, life would be over.

* * *

Historically only one event really mattered to Matthew's former home town. On 8 August 1963 The Great Train Robbery took place at Bridego Bridge near to Cheddington, not far from Ledburn and close to Leighton Buzzard.

At ten minutes to seven on the evening of 7 August that year, a Travelling Post Office train left Glasgow with five carriages, added four more south of Glasgow and three more at Carlisle. After stops at Preston and Warrington it halted at Crewe. It was here that the replacement driver Jack Mills and the fireman David Whitby joined the train. It continued to Tamworth and Rugby and was due to arrive at Euston at around four o'clock in the morning.

The train was carrying a hundred and twenty-eight mailbags which were being sorted by over eighty post office workers. In the High Value Package coach there was the cash which was being transported to the East Centre District Post Office in King Edward Street, London EC1, for delivery to the Head Offices of various banks.

Just before three o'clock in the early hours of Thursday 8 August 1963, the Travelling Post Office train passed the signal box at Leighton Buzzard station. The driver, Jack Mills, then spotted an amber light and saw in the distance a looming gantry showing a red signal. He stopped the train a mile further on at Sears Crossing. He and the fireman David Whitby were over-powered and manhandled by the robbers. The first two carriages, comprising a brake van and the High Value Package coach, were uncoupled and a replacement criminal driver attempted to drive the train forward but failed. Jack Mills and his firemen then drove the train south and stopped it at Bridego Bridge.

The Great Train Robbers then stole about £2,600,000 in used five pound, one pound and ten shilling notes. Significant amounts of Scottish and Irish currency would be later discarded. They made their way to Leatherslade Farm in Buckinghamshire, twenty-eight miles by road from the scene of the crime.

* * *

Mob enjoyed his Sunday with his daughter. They went to the cinema in Milton Keynes to see the new blockbuster movie.

Afterwards, to his delight, Olivia started talking about her step-father: she was finding him irritating. She decided that he was pompous and he seemed to have little time for Thomas.

Mob reached his flat in John Adam Street in Covent Garden, in the West End of London, and went to bed early. He would not lose any sleep over its cost at above £1 million and the huge mortgage he had managed to obtain just before the recession really took effect.

The next morning he called in at his bank in Moorgate. He wanted to pay in several cheques. He noticed, not for the first time, that the branch premises were quiet. There were seven cashiers in position and two had no customers. He completed his transaction when the bank official suggested he could save him some money. Mob raised his eyebrows. The cashier explained that he could see from his screen that his client had a credit card issued by the bank.

"Mr Buckingham, you have a personal loan about to complete. We could reschedule the balance of your credit card and save you £800 a year. Would you like to meet one of my colleagues?"

A few moments later he found himself in a private office, the door of which announced 'Jessica Lambert: Personal Banker'.

Twenty minutes later the transaction was finalised, his credit card balance was repaid and the new personal loan, at a fixed rate, would run for four years.

She was dark-haired, olive-skinned, serious and attractive. When she smiled her eyes twinkled and her face lit up.

As he collected the personal loan papers together he asked her if he was allowed to thank her with a gift. She told him that bank rules allowed no more than £25.

"That's a pizza," he laughed.

She said nothing. She looked at him, slightly raising her eyebrows with a quizzical look, giving him that smile again. He wilted.

"You're doing rather well to be a personal banker at your age," he said with a certain desperation.

She looked him up and down. He noticed she was wearing a dark blue business suit and a white blouse. Her black hair was cut short so emphasising her classical features. She rationed her smiles.

"How old do you think I am?" she asked.

"Er… well…" he stuttered. "You're… senior but you seem… hell… you're twenty-nine."

The restriction on displays of emotion remained in place.

"I'm thirty-seven and my mum says it's time I had a baby."

Matthew Orlando Buckingham was rarely, if ever, short of a response. But on this occasion he was defeated. He looked at his watch. "It's eleven-thirty. I'll come back at twelve-thirty and take you for that pizza."

"Make it one-fifteen and Japanese food and I'll accept."

Two hours later she was eating her sashimi.

"I have no intention of calling you 'Mob'," said Jessica. "Perhaps 'Matt' but I don't like shortened names. I'll refer to you as Matthew," she said.

It only took another eight minutes before he managed to upset her.

"Don't patronise me Matthew. My mum is concerned that I'm nearing forty and I don't have a child. Nearly 48 percent of babies are now born outside marriage. The average age of new mums is around thirty. There were thirty thousand babies born to women over the age of forty over the past twelve months."

He paused as he poured her some water.

"How do you have a baby without a partner? You said that you live on your own."

"Don't be naive. I've had three long-term relationships, two of them with males like you, and all three have failed. I'll have a baby and skip the man."

He decided to concentrate on his tsukemono and then focused on the bottle of wine. She was sipping the fizzy water.

"How?" he asked.

She thanked him for a generous lunch and left. He did not hear from her again until after the Easter holidays.

* * *

Mob slumped back into the sofa. He had taken a girlfriend to France and it had not worked out. The sex was up to standard but their row in Montmartre over impressionist painting had resulted in a parting of the ways at Charing Cross Station. Did it really matter whether Claude Monet had painted outside the Basilica of the Sacred Heart? Perhaps the real damage was done in the nightclub when Mob had become transfixed by the Parisian girl who was wearing a transparent dress.

It had been a difficult day at work. He had dealt with nearly forty emails on his home computer including one from his ex-wife saying her monthly payment needed to be increased. He was listening to Classic FM when he received a text message. It had been over two weeks ago that they'd met.

*Thanks for lunch. Sorry I was rude. Jessie.*

He thought carefully before replying. Should he wait until the next morning? He was smitten.

*Can only accept texts from Jessica.*

There was an interval of around ten minutes before the red light pulsated on his mobile phone.

*Cool and impressed. To save mobile bill will call u 'Matt'.*

This time he thought carefully before keying in his response.
*Jessie. Apols re personal question.*

This time the response was immediate.

*I was inviting you to ask.*

The reply caused him to think carefully. What was her angle?
*U don't know me.*

She was obviously considering her reply or was she making him wait until the next morning? The red light signalled that she had sent a response.

*You're 41, divorced, CEO of brokerage, live in new flat and earning a lot.*

*Banker confidentiality?* he texted back.

*U mustn't tell anybody,* she replied. She then followed with a second text.

*Would u like to know what I'm wearing?*

He could not understand where this last question came from. Should he ignore it?

*Bankers' briefs?*

She replied immediately. Had she been testing him?
*Now that made me laugh.*

He became nervous. He was enjoying this exchange and did not want it to end. He delayed his reply and then saw that the red light was flashing.

*What are you thinking about?* she texted.
*You.*

*No point. You've had all the credit I can give you. Come back in six mths: I'll do you another loan.*

He liked her response. She did want to continue.
*You're FCA regulated?*

*Yes.*

He was referring to the regulatory body, the Financial Conduct Authority, which controls everybody in the financial services industry.

*So you had to complete 'know your customer' procedures on me.*

Her response was immediate.

*I think we know all about u.*

He chuckled to himself.

*What if I admit that I'm a Russian secret agent?*

*No problem Sir. I'll convert the loan into roubles tomorrow. Spuhkoi-nai no-chee.*

He quickly googled it.

*And goodnight to you Jessie.*

\* \* \*

At one o'clock in the early hours he received some good news. He was having trouble sleeping. He arose and went to the kitchen where he made himself a pot of tea. He decided to read the police prosecution letter. They said they had photographic evidence that he was travelling at 60 mph in a 50 mph speed limit area. Reading further on he was liable to a £60 fine and three points on his licence, which would take him to nine points. It would also mean an extra £80 annually on his car insurance.

In completing the 'Driver's Statement' he noticed that he might be eligible for a 'Speed Awareness' course. This, so the papers said, could mean he would not be fined and the points would not be added to his current total. He discovered that as he had been travelling at less than 64 mph (in a 50 mph area) he could qualify for this concession.

He ticked the box to indicate that if that option was offered he would accept it.

He went back to bed, closed his eyes and thought about Jessica.

\* \* \*

The four directors of Six Weeks in Summer Production Limited were booked into single rooms in a hotel just west of Bloomsbury Square. They were having dinner together in order to prepare for their meeting with Silverside Brokers in the City.

The producer of the film, Amanda Adams-Smythe, was taking the lead by explaining that she had great faith in Mark Patterson-Brown to raise the funds they needed.

"Mark is going to introduce us to the best brokers in London. They will sell our shares to their clients," she said.

"But I'm already putting in £3 million," said Osama Al-Kabal. "What's the problem?"

"The film will cost £6 million, Osama darling. We need to find another three."

"So what are we doing at these… what's a broker?" asked Martine Madden.

It was explained to the casting director that it was an old-fashioned word, referring to individuals who buy shares as cheaply as they can, and then sell them for as much as they can make.

"Sounds like a film to me," said Richard Rochards, the director. "Mind you there have been enough. 'Wall Street' comes to mind and there was the recent Kevin Spacey movie 'Margin Call'. That was brilliant."

"What about 'Rogue Trader' about Nick somebody who brought down a bank?" suggested Osama.

"Nick Leeson and it was Barings Bank," interjected Amanda. "Here's a presentation I have prepared for us. We need to be on good form. They're sharp cookies these traders."

"I'll sell the film Amanda," said Martine. She handed round a proposed casting list with the five main parts and at least three well known names against each.

"She'll take the lead?" asked an amazed Amanda, pointing to the name underlined.

"It's conditional," replied Martine. "A fee of £300,000, profit share of 7 percent and her agent wants two of her other clients in the cast list."

"Cheap at the price," said Richard. "I've directed her before. She's fussy but very good."

Amanda looked around her at the three others.

"The problem we have is that too many investors have lost too much money in films These tax schemes that the Revenue are questioning have done enormous harm. We are going to have to be rather convincing."

"Bring the brokers on, I say. Leave 'em to me." Martine chuckled to herself and decided to go into Soho for some fun.

\* \* \*

She was listening to ballet music and thinking about him. She was angry. She re-read every text message that they had exchanged. She was continually letting herself down. She shuddered as she re-read *Would u like to know what I'm wearing.* She was actually dressed in a rather tired track suit. Perhaps she was imagining the sensual scene in 'Get Carter' when Michael Caine telephoned Britt Ekland and she proceeded to entertain him over the telephone. She decided to re-read the article from the evening newspaper she had collected at the railway station.

*Donor Dads win right to see their children.* She shuddered as she realised the impact on her life of the implications of the report of the court judgement. A ruling by the Family Division in the High Court decreed that a sperm donor need never have had a sexual relationship in order to have rights to the child's upbringing. The case itself involved three gay and lesbian civil partnership couples and she could barely follow the details.

She was thirty-seven and nearing her next birthday. She desperately wanted a baby. Her mother, although she hated to admit it, was right: time was running out for her if she was to enjoy motherhood. She had a successful career and was well paid. Her mother would one day leave her a serious amount of money. She refused to see her father who was in Portugal.

So how did she have a baby? Her first relationship was many years ago and simply fizzled out. Oscar, who lasted four years and left her when she was thirty, was her closest ever friend. They simply could not convert that into a lasting coupling. Oscar left the night he discovered she was not taking precautions. Ian was tall, good looking and Mr Right. A year ago she realised she could never trust him. She would have thrown herself under a train for him. He was generous, loving, caring and racing ahead in the media. He just could not stop falling in love with other women. They ended their relationship when they were in The Ritz in Mayfair one evening and she was telling him about a difficult bank customer when she realised he was following a rather demure woman around the lounge with his eyes.

"The trouble was, Ian, that the customer had one leg, three eyes, no nose, had no clothes on and spoke Polish."

"Really Jessie. You've had an interesting day."

She no longer wanted a partner. She was lucky that she enjoyed her own company. She was not too bothered about the lack of sex although she knew, given the right man, that could change.

Matthew seemed a good man. She knew all about his financial affairs and his career was going well. He was a little stretched financially and on another day she would have refused to provide the personal loan which had been agreed. She convinced herself that his prospects were good and decided to override the adverse credit score which he registered. She was able to use her initiative on borderline cases.

He was good-looking and she enjoyed their lunch together. The exchange of text messages had been amusing. He had reacted well when she told him about her mother's comments.

"No," she shouted out to herself, "you're not going to."

But she did.

*U asleep?* she texted.

She jumped up with joy when the red light flashed within two minutes.

*Working out Russian for 'will u have dinner with me?'*

*Try it in English,* she immediately responded.

*Will u have dinner with me Jessica?*

He simply loved her reply.

*But I don't really know you Mr Buckingham.*

*Bring your mum then.*

*I think I'll take the risk.*

He telephoned her the next morning. They decided to meet at Oxford Circus the following evening and explore the area. She anticipated that Matthew was going to be fun.

She lay back and began drifting off to sleep thinking about what she should wear. It was early May and getting warmer. She knew she had a near perfect figure. Men never stopped telling her. Her olive skin favoured light colours. She was five-foot eight inches tall and so she could wear heels comfortably as Matthew was over six foot. As she fell asleep she chose an off-white dress.

# Chapter Two

The word was out on the streets of Islington in North London. Detective Chief Inspector Sarah Rudd was back on duty. There was to be no mention of the award following her saving the life of the Duchess of Cambridge in The Mall. In the station they all respected her wish to return to active duty. In the community she would have to accept the bunches of flowers and the occasional applause which she did with a silent acknowledgement of gratitude.

There had been a reorganisation of the Metropolitan Borough police force which was centred round two stations: those of Holloway and Islington itself in Tolpuddle Street near to the Culpepper Community Centre. The five thousand seven hundred and fifty square miles provides homes for around two hundred thousand people. Nearly 60 percent are white British: there is a range of other ethnic groups including Caribbean and African families. There is a sizable Irish presence and over four thousand Chinese inhabitants.

The streets are wide and filled with life: retail centres, bars, jazz clubs and restaurants. There is some magnificent architecture including the Town Hall in Upper Street. This is the A1 main road and dominates the community. It runs from Angel Tube station at the City end up to Highbury Corner. Later in the year there would be a celebration of one hundred years of Arsenal Football Club in Islington although the Emirates Stadium was situated further north off the Holloway Road.

Sarah walked the short distance from the car-park to the front of the station. She looked up at the old-fashioned blue light which would remind pensioners of the television programme 'Dixon of Dock Green'. Jack Warner played Constable George Dixon over four hundred times before completing his final walk round the fictional East End borough in 1976. She walked in for her first day back.

The force was controlled by the Borough Commander, Detective Chief Superintendent Max Riley, a distinguished career officer. Under him was Superintendent Monica Moses and beneath her Detective Superintendent Majid Khan. There were two DCIs and a Chief Inspector. Because of her unusual circumstances Sarah was a DCI with additional responsibility for public protection. This high profile position linked in to the Borough partners which included The Mayor's Office for Policing and Crime, The Safer London Foundation and Crimestoppers.

DCI Sarah Rudd was becoming aware of the increasing incidents of 'hate crime assault'. This was the label being given to the violence practised by Islamic extremists. Vigilante patrols were targeting abortion clinics and betting shops. A group calling itself the 'Muslim Patrol' was operating in the Whitechapel area and undertook revenge attacks including harassing a white woman for wearing a short skirt. It confiscated alcohol from young revellers.

In a trendy area of Shoreditch a group of white youths was attacked and one man was beaten up. Footage of the 'Muslim Patrol' appeared on YouTube. Another group called the 'Sharia Project' was carrying out attacks on prostitutes.

Whilst attacks happened in her area DCI Rudd was not yet aware of any racially motivated violence. She suspected however, that it was only a matter of time. She was also puzzled by an anonymous telephone call she had received within hours of reporting for work.

A voice said, "Watch Rashid" and rang off.

Her officers had tried every possible link, searching both the Internet and the police database, but so many individuals of that name were known to the police they simply had no way of making any sense of the call. They reported back to Sarah that it was an Arabic name meaning 'rightly guided'. Their lack of progress was unfortunate because an extremist group had decided to explode a number of bombs.

The Planner wanted to cause maximum devastation, disruption and loss of life. The London Underground offered the best option but, despite popular myth, his 'brothers' were not readily agreeing to commit suicide. The memory of 9/11 and the terrorist attacks was fading. The Americans were less aggressive. In the end his plan was so simple it was amazing terrorists like the IRA had not tried to carry it out. He would create a trap which was so secure nobody would escape. To help the carnage he would organise the release of a deadly gas. He calculated he could kill or seriously wound perhaps four hundred people. He needed seven brothers to complete the task. They were now ready. There had been an eighth, but he had talked in a Highgate pub and died screaming as the pliers tore out the nails of his toes before he was shot in the head. His body now lay beneath some concrete.

Rashid, responding to the Planner's instructions, was spending many hours travelling the route leading to the target area. There was no security in place. The British obsession with punctuality meant that he was able to plan almost to the minute the time of entry. The bombs were being made in South London. The gas proved more of a problem and would not come in for another month.

The Planner was pleased with the reports he was receiving from his brother. He pulled out his prayer mat and committed himself to the service of Allah.

"Watch Rashid," a husky voice had said.

\* \* \*

He was nervous and he wasn't sure why.

They met as agreed at six o'clock on the south side of Oxford Street by the Tube station exit. He led her south past The London Palladium and into Kingly Street. Her off-white dress was partly obscured by a pale-green jacket. They arrived at Shampers Wine Bar. Had she read the website it would have told her that she should *Ask about our dessert specials: yesterday we served a rich pear and almond tart with a glass of fragrant Black Muscat from California.*

They found a secluded table towards the back of the bar area having decided to remain upstairs rather than go down to the forty seats dining area below. He immediately ordered a bottle of Chablis Daniel Dampt 2011 and a bottle of sparkling mineral water.

21

Jessica was impressed. They were quickly served and neither said anything. The waiter handed them menus and they avoided eye contact by studying the choices. For her it was marinated unsalted anchovies followed by a grilled aubergine salad with roasted peppers and Buffalo Mozzarella. He selected the Shampers charcuterie platter followed by grilled lamb fillet with Arrocina beans and spinach.

They then both read a promotional leaflet left on the table suggesting they might come in a week's time to a jazz evening when they could hear the Greg David Quartet. Their starters arrived. Their glasses were topped up.

"How was banking today?" Matthew asked.

"Targets."

"Excuse me?"

"Banking is all about targets, Matthew. You were a target. I have to earn so much in interest every week or else I'm reprimanded." She hesitated. "No, don't worry. I did you a good deal. I charged you around 6 percent." She laughed. "If you hadn't been so good looking it would have been nearer 8."

She drank some more Chablis and looked puzzled.

"Did you read the paperwork I gave you?"

"You were saving me £800 a year. Why would I look at the paperwork?"

"Ah ha. You're cash flow managing aren't you? Most people are. Bet you're spending too much."

"My bloody ex-wife is."

"You should stay single like me," said Jessica.

He wondered about changing the subject. She made him feel uncertain because he felt she was like a coiled spring.

"Why are you here?" she asked.

"Do you think we'll meet again?" he replied.

She looked intently at him. He hadn't answered her question.

"I think I could get to like you," she said.

"What marks are you awarding me?"

"Marks?"

"Yes, Jessica." He stopped as their plates were cleared away. They both drank some more wine and he indicated to the waiter that they'd like a second bottle.

"I get the feeling," he continued, "that you're judging me."

She resorted to the sparkling water while she considered his latest comment.

"I suppose it's my job. I have to assess customers all the time."

"And how much interest you can charge them."

"That doesn't apply to me, Matthew. I never fail to meet my targets."

He leaned over and, using his paper serviette, wiped a small amount of anchovy from the corner of her mouth.

"Usually by this juncture I've been told how attractive I am," she said.

"Why do they say that to you, Jessica?"

"Probably because I'm gorgeous."

"More likely because they're hoping you'll go to bed with them."

She smiled. It was the first occasion on which she had offered him her real facial seduction. Her whole personality lit up as she radiated her inner warmth.

"Don't you want to go to bed with me?" she chuckled.

"Not after you've eaten anchovies," said Mob.

The main courses arrived and soon they were absorbed by the results of some superb cooking.

"How was your day?" she asked.

"Profitable. The brokers sold a good line of stock."

"What does that mean?"

Matthew explained that as a market broker his team of dealers sold investments to their client base. That day they had been offered shares in a new wind farm business. They managed to sell them to six clients making a commission of nearly £20,000. They had bought the shares in at ten pence each and sold them on to their clients at eleven pence.

"I think I've got that," she said.

"The markets are still tough, Jessie, but things are slowly picking up."

She leant over the table and brushed his hair to the side of his head.

23

"I like it when you call me Jessie. I know what I said but, with you, it feels nice."

"Jessie," he repeated. "And me? You have the options of Matthew, Matt or Mob."

"Choices, choices," she mused as she pushed her plate away from her. "Matthew is cultured, gentle but old-fashioned, Matt is shortened making you sound like a radio presenter and Mob is different. I don't know anybody else called Mob." She smiled her smile again and it made her face light up. "I could of course call you 'lover'."

"I prefer Mob."

"What does your wife call you?"

"Ex-wife. Matthew."

"Hmm. I guessed she would."

"Are you courageous enough to select a dessert?" he laughed.

"I'd like a piece of stilton and a glass of Riesling please, Mob."

Thirty minutes later they left Shampers. Matthew gave a generous gratuity which reflected his growing excitement about his companion.

"Where do you live?" he asked.

"Fulham," she replied.

"I'm in Covent Garden. I'm going to walk."

He hailed a taxi and gave the cabbie £30. He told the driver to take care of her.

She placed her hands on his shoulders.

"You're different, Mob. Lovely evening."

She kissed him fleetingly on his cheek, boarded the taxi and was driven away.

As he walked down Oxford Street towards Tottenham Court Road he felt the pulse on his mobile throb. He read the text message.

*Thirty pds. It's only about twenty to my flat.*

He replied immediately.

*Can you put a price on your safety Jessie?*

She did not reply for the next three days.

* * *

24

The Great Train Robbers gathered at a smallholding near to Brill, a sprawling Buckinghamshire village on the edge of the Chiltern Hills. At around thirty minutes after midnight on Thursday 8 August 1963 two Land Rovers and an Austin lorry left Leatherslade Farm and, in convoy, drove east around Aylesbury and on to Leighton Buzzard. An hour after leaving they reached bridge number 127 and parked by the pond. They were to load one hundred and twenty mailbags, in total weighing two and a half tons. They left Bridego Bridge at 3.30 p.m. As they travelled on the return journey they listened to their radios that were tuned to the police frequencies.

They passed through Brill and completed the two and a half miles to the farm arriving back at 4.30 p.m. Several of the men started counting the money almost immediately after the unloading had been completed.

There was over two and a half million pounds in five pound, one pound and ten shilling notes. They disregarded about £20,000 in Scottish and Irish currencies. There were sixteen train robbers who each received around £143,000. The police were later to retrieve about £360,000.

* * *

She sent a text to him later in the week.

*I'm free Saturday. Are you doing anything? J.*

*I am now* he texted back five minutes later having cleared his diary for the day.

They met at Paddington Station at 8.00 a.m. and caught the train to Bristol. They proceeded to spend the day doing what many visitors undertook which included seeing the Clifton Suspension Bridge, the fast-flowing River Severn and the harbour where there was a range of yachts of various sizes.

She was casually dressed at Matthew's request, wearing a light blue track-suit and she looked as refreshed on the journey back as she had done ten hours earlier. She enjoyed travelling first class and readily accepted his suggestion that they should share a bottle of white wine on the return trip. They had talked all through the day but mainly about the scenery, the history, the artefacts and the river estuary. The rocking of the train induced a trance-like hypnosis on the two of them. There had been no physical contact. He opened doors for her and always invited her to go through first. There was no furtive arm on the shoulder. He didn't want to scare her off.

They found themselves laughing together. For some reason he offered to tell her a silly joke.

"I like jokes," she said. "But I'll only listen if it's seriously stupid."

"It's definitively daft," said Mob.

"The build up's good, Mob," she laughed. She pretended to blow a trumpet to announce the commencement of his joke. They didn't realise that several other passengers were waiting with baited breath.

"Steve Davis goes to the doctor."

"Who's Steve Davis?"

"The snooker player. Many times world champion."

"Oh, ok. Steve Davis, the world champion snooker player goes to the doctor."

"No, he's not world champion now. He's past his prime."

"So why not select the current world champion?"

"He didn't go to the doctor. Steve Davis did."

"Why?"

"That's the point of the joke. He was not feeling well."

"What was wrong with him?" Jessie drank some more wine. She was enjoying Mob's discomfort and she was watching him getting hot under the collar.

"That's what puzzled the doctor. He couldn't find anything wrong with him."

"Rotten joke."

"No Jessie. The doctor thought it might be his diet."

"Why, was he a vegan?"

"The doctor asked him what he'd eaten for breakfast."

"Muesli and brown toast."

"Steve Davis said that he did not eat much breakfast. He'd had two reds and a brown."

"Pardon? That would make him ill." She put on a furrowed frown.

"No Jessie. It's part of the joke. Steve Davis eats snooker balls."

"No wonder he's ill."

"No. It's make believe. You have to laugh at the fact that he's eating billiard balls."

"You said snooker balls."

"Same thing. The doctor asks him what he had for lunch."

"I just can't imagine," she said.

"Steve Davis tells him he had spent most of the morning practising so he'd had a light meal: three reds, two pinks, a blue and a brown."

"Did he have sauce on the brown ball?"

"What are you doing tomorrow, Jessie?"

"Recovering from today, why?"

"Because at this rate of progress I'll need the whole of Sunday to finish telling my joke." The other passengers looked disappointed. They could not work out the punch line.

"My lips are sealed," she promised as she pretended to zip up her mouth.

"The doctor asks Steve Davis what he'll have for his evening meal. He replies that it will be his big feast of the day: seven reds, six blues, two browns, two yellows and a black."

Jessie remained speechless.

"There's your problem Steve," says the doctor. "You're not getting enough greens."

Three other travellers tried hard not to reveal their merriment at the punch line.

Jessie remained impassive. She then rose from her seat and came round to sit with Mob. She put her arms around him and kissed him.

"I hope you make love better than you tell jokes," she whispered as she collapsed with laughter.

* * *

Matthew had booked his National Speed Awareness Course for the following Friday. It cost him £95. It was run by AA Drive-Tech in association with the Thames Valley Police. He had been rather casual in his reading of the papers and so he arrived at the Milton Keynes location without the required identity. He eventually found some papers in his brief case which satisfied the organiser. Apparently offenders would sometimes send somebody else in their place. With good reason because, as Mob discovered, it was going to last four hours. He was picking up Olivia at 6.00 p.m. and taking her to the cinema.

It started badly. In the introduction, the speaker Philip, a former police officer, said that he assumed that of the twenty people present, twenty were there to avoid the three penalty points on their licences. He then said that anybody who thought it avoided the hike in car insurance premiums was wrong because failure to disclose the taking of the course to an insurance company could invalidate the cover. Matthew inwardly groaned.

His attention was then diverted by the last man who had joined the group of seven women and twelve men. The latecomer jumped up and pointed a finger across the room.

"What the fuck are you doing here?"

He was asking the question of his wife who could also have made the same inquiry. It became apparent that they had both been caught for speeding and had booked online for the course without telling their partner.

"You need to take this bloody thing," she said. "You're always telling other drivers what to do."

"So why are you here, Jenny?"

"I was unlucky."

Philip suggested that each person turned and spoke to the one next to them. Matthew discovered that Freddie was completely innocent. The road sign was hidden and he was only going 34 mph in a 30 mph limit. He dismissed the fact he already had nine points saying it was because he was black.

The speaker then said that the police held the record of the course for seven years. He added that it was their belief that attending the course lessened the individual's chance of being in an accident by 25 percent.

"Ok folk," announced Philip moving towards his white-board, "let's kick off by deciding what your main pet hates are when driving?"

"People using mobile phones," offered a lady on the front row. There was a smattering of applause.

"Tailgating," shouted a man at the back. This led to a discussion about the conundrum that if one drives within the speed limits other drivers came up behind much more aggressively.

"Sorry folk. It's wrong to break the law, whatever the circumstances," said Philip.

"Cars in the middle lane," suggested Jenny at which point her husband exploded.

"You cause more problems with your habit of hogging the…"

"How would you know? You're always in the outside lane driving like a lunatic."

"Four-by-four bloody women drivers collecting their kids from school." This suggestion produced enthusiastic support except from the two attendees who had arrived in the described vehicles.

"Are you denying me my right to protect my child?" asked one.

"Horses and their riders. I hate them," said a voice from the back row. "They rarely wear fluorescent clothing so you can see them."

"What's wrong with us riding our horses? It's our right," retorted a rather large gentleman wearing a tweed jacket and fairisle pullover.

Mob said to himself, 'this guy will never last four hours with us lot.'

Philip tapped the table.

"You've all missed the most obvious one."

Twenty people looked around at each other.

"Speed cameras," he suggested.

He turned over a sheet of paper on his board on which he had prepared a question.

*How long does it take to stop when travelling at 30 mph: 50/65/75 feet?*

29

About half the group guessed correctly at 75 feet. The next question and its answer did cause some surprise. Travelling at 60 mph requires a 240-feet stopping distance. Mob began to get interested in the proceedings.

Philip then showed that travelling at 32 mph (as against 30 mph) requires an extra 11 feet to stop. The same point was applied to travelling at 35 mph.

"Would anyone like to go upstairs and jump out of the window?" joked Philip.

"Are we allowed to volunteer somebody?" asked Jenny's husband.

"If you leap out of the room upstairs you'll hit the ground at the same impact speed as driving at 35 mph."

After an hour Mob was beginning to enjoy the course. The ex-copper Philip was good. He told of clearing up after road accidents.

"What do you think the worst bit is?" he asked.

There were varying suggestions including dead bodies, blood, controlling traffic, the smell of petrol and others.

Philip knocked his fist on the door of the room.

"Telling somebody their loved one is dead."

As they neared the two hour juncture Philip suddenly asked the question:

"Why are you here folk?"

Nobody managed to offer the answer he was seeking.

"So I can tell you about possible consequences. You were all speeding, a number of you on several occasions. You need to understand what might happen."

He said it was time for a break for refreshments, and so that the attendees could check their mobile phones. Mob was wondering whether to skip the next two hours.

Philip seemed to be looking directly at him when he advised them that failure to complete the course would mean a court appearance and a one thousand pound fine.

Matthew was encouraged by an enthusiastic text from Olivia saying how much she was looking forward to seeing him.

The next hour and twenty minutes dragged on. They were shown a video of the consequences of speeding, and there was an interactive session. They were to try to guess the percentage relationships between collisions and those killed on urban and rural roads and motorways. Mob pressed his remote control key-pad and found he was wrong on over half the questions.

The most instructive section was when Philip used still photographs showing a village street where a boy of thirteen had been knocked down and killed by a driver who had a clean driving licence. He had been distracted by a van backing out of a driveway. He was doing thirty-five miles per hour in a thirty speed restriction area. He was charged with careless driving and given a suspended sentence. The room became much quieter after this exercise. Some wondered why the driver had not been charged with manslaughter or death by dangerous driving.

Philip then asked for suggestions on how they could improve as drivers. Jenny suggested that the roads would be safer if her husband travelled by bus.

**"COAST,"** announced Philip. "**C**oncentrate, **O**bserve, **A**nticipate, **S**pace (between cars) and **T**ime (allow sufficient and anticipate delays)."

"Coast," he repeated. "I can do no more for you. Good luck folk."

Matthew walked thoughtfully to his car. He checked his mobile calls and as none were urgent put his phone away. He turned on his ignition, put the engine into gear, and prepared to exit the car park on to the busy A422 to the west of Milton Keynes. He thought about 'A' and anticipated that there was sufficient space for him to turn right into the traffic stream. He was right. He judged it correctly and had he reached the road ahead he would have fitted in well. Unfortunately the vehicle in front was driven by Jenny. She appeared to be using her mobile phone to tell her friend about the irresponsible behaviour of her husband in not telling her he'd been caught for speeding. While doing so she remained stationary. However, suddenly, her car started rolling backwards as she had apparently taken her foot off the brake. Mob's left-hand headlight disintegrated as her rear bumper hit it.

# Chapter Three

The Great Train Robbers were never happy at Leatherslade Farm. Despite their disbelief at counting out over two and a half million pounds a number of them wanted to be back in London with their families around them. They continued to monitor the Buckinghamshire police radio frequencies. They modified the Austin lorry by putting in a false floor under which they intended concealing some of the stolen money. The small-holding was cramped and although they had adequate provisions the tensions began to mount.

The news broadcasts began to worry the felons as the scale of their crime became clear to the British public. They started to re-spray their vehicles in case they had been seen during their journeys to and from the farm. They decided to evacuate Leatherslade Farm. Several were collected by relatives. Others bought cars and vans locally. They went to great efforts to eradicate all traces of their stay at the small-holding. They tried to burn some mail sacks but had to douse the flames due to the black smoke as a result of the wax waterproofing.

It was not until Tuesday 13 August 1963, five days after the robbery took place, that the police discovered the deserted Leatherslade Farm. They found an Austin lorry and two Land Rovers, tins of food, mail sacks, burned items, sleeping bags and dirty clothes. This evidence proved to be a key factor in providing the forensic material which would later convict a number of the thieves.

\* \* \*

Matthew gazed around the conference room and wondered if he should be doing business with Mark Patterson-Brown. He looked at the immaculately-dressed corporate financier who, as always, had Caroline Pennington of the law firm Christie Watson, by his side. Probably the Governor of the Bank of England, in his office less than two hundred yards away, was the only person in the Square Mile who did not know they were sleeping together and had been for at least three years. Caroline adored the ensuite showers adjacent to the bedrooms in the Threadneedles Hotel. She came from a lower middle class family in Norwich and, as she stood under the steaming hot water which cascaded down from the ceiling of the glass cubicle and felt her feet on the tiled floor, she decided that corporate finance law and Mark Patterson-Brown worked for her.

"Let me introduce my colleagues," said Matthew. He explained that he had with him his head of brokerage, the compliance officer and his analyst. A young girl at the end of the table remained unidentified.

Outside in Threadneedle Street, traffic flowed freely and business in the Royal Exchange cafe was brisk. The British economy was at the tail-end of a recession but there were still deals to be done, dreams to be chased and the endless search for money.

"Matthew, thank you," responded their guest. He looked around the table and smiled at the woman to his left.

"Caroline Pennington you know. My clients are, from left to right, Amanda Adams-Smythe, Richard Rochards, Osama Al-Kabal and Martine Madden." He paused for effect. The sun was pouring through the first floor glass windows. "I'll ask Amanda to explain their proposition."

The head of brokerage at Silverside Brokers, Craig MacDonald, immediately took a dislike to the speaker who explained that she was managing director of Six Weeks in Summer Production Limited. She said that she was also the producer. Matthew made a mental note to ask again for her track record in the industry.

"We're going to make a film called…" she laughed gently, and the Scotsman's antipathy doubled, 'Six Weeks in Summer'." She pushed her fair hair off her forehead. "It's a romantic thriller set in London, France and the Middle East. "It's a love story involving a London-based political public relations executive and an Iraqi businessman."

"Mob. I'm tellin' y'u. No more films. I'll no offer 'em to our clients." Craig banged his fist on the table.

"Mr MacDonald," interrupted Mark, "I sympathise completely. We at Maidstone New Issues thought long and hard before taking on this assignment."

"Which is?" asked the head of brokerage.

"Which is to raise £3 million to add to the £3 million that Mr Al-Kabal and his Middle Eastern backers have deposited in London. Isn't that so, Caroline?"

"Absolutely, gentlemen." She smiled around the table. "We should be receiving confirmation of the deposit of the funds in the next few days. I've spoken to the bank in Abu Dhabi."

"So you want us to raise the balance of £3 million?" said Matthew.

"Might I comment?" Richard Rochards was around fifty years of age and told everybody that he was the director of the film. "I'll let Martine, who's the casting director, tell you about the film. First, Mr MacDonald, we both know that there's been a lot of problems with the British film industry."

"Scam after scam after scam. I'll no…"

"There have been a variety of tax-based schemes where creative tax accountants have used generous tax breaks to produce incredible returns. There are two points to understand. Firstly the tax authorities have virtually closed down all the clever stuff, there are several cases going through the courts at the moment but take it from me, there are now only two tax incentives for film investors. We'll tell you about those later."

"What concerns Craig," interrupted Debra White, the compliance officer, "is that our clients have lost money and we're understandably nervous about offering these types of investments. You will appreciate it's a rather regulated world out there."

"What about those investors who backed 'Slum Dog Millionaire'? asked Caroline.

"Regrettably none of ours," replied Craig.

35

"Can I please make two important points?" said Mark. "Forget the days of tax-based cinema. It's now about the film and the investment proposal. We'll talk about 'Six Weeks in Summer' in a moment but Craig, Debra, would your clients like a return of 87.5 percent?"

"Scottish independence is more likely."

"Craig. I've set out the investment analysis on this piece of paper."

Caroline distributed two sheets to each person sitting around the conference table. Matthew had asked for further supplies of drinks which were now being served.

"But no emphasis on the EIS advantages. What the hell... ."

"Craig. This is not about tax incentives. The Enterprise Investment Scheme can work and our shares qualify. Not all investors will be able to use the tax breaks and so we're taking a different approach. Let me take you through it."

Over the next few minutes the boss of Maidstone New Issues, in a clear and authoritative manner, laid out the basis of the calculation showing that a return of 87.5 percent was possible.

"Let me summarise the calculations for you all. A client puts in half a million pounds. When the film is made, and the revenues are received, that investor is the first person to be repaid. So he'll..."

"Or she," said Debra.

"Will be returned their money plus 15 percent uplift. In other words they'll get back £575,000. But that's just the start."

'Should have been a market trader selling second-hand crockery,' thought the analyst.

"They will have already received a pro rata rebate of the tax credit which will be £66,667."

"Com' ag'in, Mon?"

"Craig. When a British film is made, about three months after it is completed the Revenue repay 20 percent of the costs. It's an incentive to the industry to make British films. There are thirty-two boxes on the application form to the Revenue and we have to tick at least seventeen to get the money. We already have twenty-two in the bag. So we'll receive about £800,000 whether or not the film's a success. That money will be refunded to our

36

investors. So, £500,000 as a pro rata rebate out of six million comes to £66,667."

Debra nodded. She'd already completed the calculation.

"So Craig your client gets £575,000 plus £66,667. Now the really good news. He…"

"Or she…"

"They get 50 percent of the profits, pro rata."

"It's Christmas Day already," said the analyst.

Matthew looked across the table and raised an admonishing finger.

"Let's say the film grosses £20 million. The distributor takes 30 percent so that nets to £14 million. Investors receive back their £6 million plus their 15 percent uplift which makes £6,900,000. This leaves £7,100,000 for distribution. 50 percent is £3,550,000. £500,000 pro rata of £6 million comes to £295,833."

All heads turned towards the analyst.

"Correct," she said.

"So, he or she receives back £500,000 plus £75,000, which is the 15 percent uplift, plus £66,667, which is the share of the tax credit, plus £295,833, their portion of the profits, all of which comes to £437,500 which is a return of 87.5 percent."

"Correct," repeated the analyst.

"Interesting," said Matthew.

"So convince me that your film will gross £20,000,000," challenged the analyst.

"I can't."

The people gathered around the table in the conference room of Silverside Brokers now knew that Martine was the casting director for 'Six Weeks in Summer'. She was in her late twenties, blonde and, in her own way, attractive. She was wearing a thick-striped business suit which, on the wrong woman, might appear bizarre but, in her case, it was dynamic.

"What I will do is show you a mood board." She paused before pressing the key on her computer. "It's all about casting. The story brings the script which attracts the producer who selects the director. I then cast the film. I assess the budget and break down the key roles. Often agents will insist that not only should they discuss it with their client but a condition will be imposed that we accept perhaps another actor also represented by the same person."

The blinds were closed and over the next twenty minutes the screen on the side wall was lit up by a slide-show backed by a Rachmaninov concerto. Debra was replaying 'Brief Encounter' in her mind but this was his third piece. It fitted the torrid love story of a woman, desperate for the man of her dreams, meeting a London-based media executive with whom she falls in love. His firm wins a prestigious contract for promoting a French-owned oil company operating out of Iraq. He goes out to work for three weeks preparing the ecological evidence to convince the doubters of the firm's good intentions when he is lured over the border into Iran. He is brutally tortured and it is several weeks before British officials are allowed to see him. She goes out to Tehran and despairs of the hapless efforts to secure his release. He's charged with spying. She meets a disaffected Iranian businessman with considerable funds deposited in London. He is worried that, if the tension between the two countries intensifies, he might find that his assets are frozen. He helps organise an escape but there is a betrayal. The party flee to the border as shots are being fired. They are finally free. As the sun sinks over the desert they stand together vowing never again to be parted.

The final slide seemed to leap off the wall as the couple are silhouetted against the background holding hands. The music reaches its climax and the screen goes blank. As the sunlight floods back into the room several eyes are being wiped.

"The film is costing £5,400,000 to make plus £600,000 to cover marketing and distribution costs. Here's a slide showing the top ten similar British films made in 2012. Six of these have already gone into profit."

She paused at this point to allow her audience to read the information.

"Your next question is about casting. Here are photographs of the two leading actors and the individual I want to play the Iranian businessman. We also have this person who has agreed to be the British official in Tehran." There were gasps around the table.

The young girl at the end of the table continued to say nothing. Inwardly she was having convulsions about the choice of the leading man. Matthew could not take his eyes off the female actor. She was shown wearing a bikini and standing in a shower.

Another photograph, another outburst of exclamations.

"Matthew. We'll take £2 million of the shares," announced Craig conveniently forgetting that he needed the permission of his investment committee.

The analyst nodded, Debra lifted her hand, and the girl at the end of the table continued to remain silent.

Matthew returned to his office, closed the door, sat down and googled Richard Rochards. The documentation had contained a full history of his career and his recent successes with 'The Girl from Heaven' and 'Mayfair Ball'. The first was a love story set in Cornwall starring two unknown actors. It was moderately successful and was now being shown on DVD and the TV channels. The second was an attempt to copy 'The Great Gatsby'. The timing was ideal as the British economy was being battered by the recession and take-home pay for those in employment, was, in real terms, falling. The social aspirations of the Jazz Age captured by F. Scott Fitzgerald's 1925 American best seller had already translated to the cinema. In 2013 Baz Luhrmann directed a remake with Leonardo DiCaprio as Jay Gatsby although it was Carey Mulligan as Daisy Buchanan who secured the headlines. 'Mayfair Ball' had been released in June and was already attracting attention as the publicists suggested that it might figure in the coming awards season.

Matthew returned to his screen and after a few minutes secured the information he was seeking: 'The Great Gatsby' had cost $105 million and box office takings were already past $330 million. 'Mayfair Ball' had a budget of £3 million and takings, so far, were £1.5 million.

Matthew could not understand why Richard Rochards had said so little, showed no body language, and seemed indifferent. After all, he was the director of 'Six Weeks in Summer'.

* * *

The call came in the middle of the night. It was the duty officer at Islington Police Station.

"Ma'am. Sorry. Two children. Our officers are attending." He gave her an address.

Detective Chief Inspector Sarah Rudd was dressed and out of her front door in less than fifteen minutes. She reached a back street house near to the Tube station guided by the flashing blue lights. A policeman rushed up to her.

"We were called by the neighbours Ma'am. They reported screaming. We're in there but the couple say nothing has happened. There's a doctor on their way. There are two children in an upstairs bedroom. We think the boy is about eleven and the girl is eight. We have two officers with them."

DCI Rudd walked towards the property. The hallway was tidy and smelt of disinfectant. She knew never to anticipate events but she went straight for the man. She passed a colleague inside the front door and walked into a lounge area. There were two adults sitting on the sofa. They were looking at a blank screen on the wall-hung television screen. She waved her warrant card at them.

"I'm Detective Chief Inspector Rudd. We have been called by your neighbours who have reported screaming coming from this house. Please tell me your names."

"You've no bleedin' right to come in here," said the man.

"Your name please."

"Alexander Binder. I'm called Alexi."

She looked at the woman.

"Are the children yours?" she asked.

"Yes. Zach is twelve and Marie is eight. I'm their mother. Their fathers have long gone."

"Fathers?" asked DCI Rudd.

"They have different fathers but both the bastards have disappeared. Alexi looks after me."

"Your name please."

"Elizabeth Angela Williams. I'm called Beth."

PC Michelle Everest came and stood beside her boss.

"Doctor's here. She's upstairs."

"You are going to sit here. I'm going to look round your house. Do you agree that I should do that?"

The couple remained silent. DCI Rudd told PC Everest to stay in the lounge. She nodded at the officer in the hallway and climbed the stairs. There were three bedrooms and she noted that the first belonged to the mother and her partner. The door to the small room at the back was closed. An officer indicated that the doctor was inside with the girl. In the room on the right she found Zach who was playing with an iPad. She noted a new computer on the table and a television set in the corner. There were several boxes of biscuits and bottles of fizzy drinks.

"Hello Zach," she said.

"Go away," he replied.

"I'm told there's been screaming in this house tonight. Was that you Zach?"

"Bollocks. We've both been quiet."

"Ma'am. The doctor wants to speak to you," said the officer.

DCI Rudd and the medical adviser went into the front room and closed the door.

"We've not met. I'm Sarah Rudd."

"Hey. You're the one who won the medal. It's fab to meet you."

"You're… ?"

"Dr Reed. I'm the on-duty doctor. The boy is fine. I've not examined him because there is no reason to do so. He's showing no sign of stress or trauma and there are no obvious injuries. The girl is more of a worry. She's saying she's fine but she did agree that I could check her over. There is some sweating. There is no indication of any sexual injury although her anus is a little red. That in itself is not enough."

"Is the girl scared?"

"Not obviously so, but she's possibly holding something back."

"Do we take her into care?"

"That's your decision. I would certainly keep a watch on her. Are you planning to visit her school?"

"We have other things to do first. Thank you doctor."

DCI Rudd returned to the lounge where the couple continued to sit on the sofa. She noted that they had not switched on the television. She asked PC Everest to move to the rear of

41

the room. She called in the other officer and told him to stand in the doorway.

"It will save us all a lot of time if you tell me who screamed earlier this evening."

"Must have been on the television," said Alexi. "We have it loud. My hearing's not good. I served in Afghanistan and was near a bomb. My ear drum's burst."

"Do you get on well with your neighbours Beth?"

"Next door. She's ok but she works all the time. Trying to bring up two kids on her own. Other side. She's a bitch. Always asking questions."

"Have you any children of your own Alexi?" asked DCI Rudd.

"Why don't you piss off and leave us alone. Nobody screamed. Got it?"

"Yes. I agree. All seems fine here."

PC Everest looked across the room to her male companion and shook her head.

"Sorry to bother you. Oh. Just before we go I'd like to know the weather forecast."

She snatched the remote control from off the table and pointed it at the TV.

"No!" shouted Alexi. He tried to grab the equipment from out of her hand but the screen was flickering into life. Suddenly all the occupants of the room were watching a fuzzy picture of a young girl who was tied to a bed with her legs spread. Two men were about to commit inhuman acts on her.

"You fucking bitch," screamed Alexi who had now produced a long, army style knife from under the chair. He hesitated for a few moments too long before trying to attack DCI Rudd. The X26 Tazer was fired by PC Everest. Two dart-like electrodes, which were held connected to the gun by conductive wires, hit the man in the chest. He suffered immediate neuromuscular incapacitation. He was apprehended by the male officer who was quickly joined by his colleague from up the stairs.

Zach and Marie were taken away for hospital checks and then into care. Beth then started talking and would not stop. It had been all Alexi's idea to spice up their sex life. The children were encouraged to simulate sexual acts in front of their mother. When Alexi was pleased with them they received generous gifts.

The screaming occurred earlier in the evening because Zach had been told to put his organ into Marie from the rear.

DCI Rudd and PC Everest looked on in amazement as Beth suggested that she thought her children enjoyed their games.

As the house was secured Sarah Rudd asked Michelle if she wanted counselling.

"Thank you Ma'am but I'm alright."

"Good shot," smiled Sarah.

"Call me PC Bruce Willis Everest," chuckled the young officer.

As Sarah left the building she breathed a sigh of relief that her colleague was still able to find some humour. It was one way to deal with human depravity.

She wandered back to her car and decided to go home. Her personal mobile phone rang. She answered it immediately. She always thought about Nick and the children.

"Watch Rashid," said a husky voice.

\* \* \*

"We'll have to use contraception, Mob."

He sighed in frustration. The late night traffic in Covent Garden was flowing freely despite the ongoing road-works. The noise barely penetrated the top floor penthouse suite. The air-conditioning was silent. Jessica lay on the sofa with her legs straddled over the one end. She was sipping another glass of champagne. They had enjoyed the theatre. They both knew that the inevitable row was about to take place. They had not yet consummated their relationship.

"I hate the things. It's not sex."

"Nor is oral sex but that does not seem to diminish your enthusiasm."

He was pacing around his apartment wearing boxers.

"Because you won't have intercourse."

"I want it as much as you do Mob. I'm just not prepared to take the pill. You know I want a baby but not with you. If I take the pill it will affect my fertility in the future. So, my randy little friend, put this rubber on your dick and make love to me."

The CD player was on repeat. For the fifth time that evening Adele sang her Oscar-winning song from the James Bond movie 'Skyfall'.

"She co-wrote that, Mob," said Jessica.

"I'd like to co-host something with you, Jessica. It's called sexual intercourse. It's where two people, who adore each other, demonstrate their affection."

Jessica leapt athletically to her feet, went over to Matthew and put her arms around him.

"Agreed. We love one another and we both want full sex. I don't want your baby, Mob and I will not take a prescription. We have to use a rubber. They're marvellous these days. You won't know it's on. Come on, Mob. I'm very turned on tonight."

"Let's try it without," said Matthew. "If you get pregnant you can always…"

She pulled away from him.

"Always what, Mob?"

He gulped some champagne and threw the glass down on the chair.

"Come on, Jessica. I'm hurting."

"Always what, Mob?" There was a look in her eyes which should have warned Matthew to be careful.

"There are ways of dealing with these things."

"What ways?"

He pushed his manhood back inside his underwear.

"Surgery."

"Are you suggesting an abortion, Mob?"

"It's a remote chance. You know that."

"Looking at what's just reappeared down there I think I'm on my way to having triplets. Tell me, Mob. Please. You are not suggesting I have an abortion?"

"I don't know what I am saying, Jessie. I just want sex with you."

"Using a rubber."

44

"No rubber, Jessie."

"Then it can't matter much to you."

"It reminds me of my ex-wife, Jessie. At the end of our marriage she started insisting I use a rubber. I didn't know it was because she was sleeping with John Sneddon. I still shake when I remember what she put me through."

She took him back into her arms and they snuggled down together on the sofa.

"Why didn't you say?" she asked.

"I've been separated for seven years now, Jessie. Most of the girls I've been with couldn't care less. I've never used contraception again."

A quizzical look flashed across her face but she decided that the issue they also had to discuss could wait for another time. She kissed him gently.

"I can't bear the thought of you making love to me, Mob and thinking of your ex-wife."

"With your body, Jessie I can assure you there's only one thing I will be focused on."

"You won't wear a rubber?"

"I can't, Jessie. I just can't."

"And what if I can find a solution?"

Mob's eyes lit up and he smiled his smile.

"Now?"

Jessica put her arms on his shoulders.

"Give me a little more time."

# Chapter Four

The English Electric Class 40 diesel locomotive and its five coaches left Glasgow at 6.50 p.m. on the evening of 7 August 1963. Four more coaches were added at Carstairs and three more at Carlisle. At around 12.15 a.m. the next day the train reached Crewe where Jack Mills joined as the replacement driver and David Whitby as fireman.

At just after 3.00 a.m. the convoy, which was travelling on the 'up' fast line, was stopped by a red light at Sears Crossing just south of Leighton Buzzard. The driver was attacked and coshed by one of the robbers. Their replacement operator could not move the train and so Jack Mills moved it up the line to Bridego Bridge. He was handcuffed to his fireman, put in a van and later rescued. He was taken to the Royal Buckinghamshire Hospital in Aylesbury.

It is not known which of the Great Train Robbers attacked the driver. It is also suspected that his main trauma occurred when he fell in the cabin of the engine and hit his face on a metal obtrusion.

Jack Mills was born on 1 September 1905 and was therefore fifty-seven years old when he suffered his injuries. He returned to light duties in May 1964. In November 1965 until December 1966 he was ill with shingles. He finally retired in December 1967. He died in February 1970 of leukaemia with complications due to bronchial pneumonia. He received £250 compensation for his injuries sustained during the robbery and the *Daily Mail* launched an appeal on his behalf which reached £34,000. He died in comfortable surroundings in Crewe.

To the British public he was the victim of a violent attack by vicious criminals. His damaged face and his shattered appearance played a major part in creating the folklore surrounding The Great Train Robbery.

* * *

Detective Chief Inspector Sarah Rudd knew that she was falling into the trap to which so many professional groups are vulnerable. It was similar to some doctors who prescribe statins for themselves so that they can eat a fattier diet, to accountants who know how to reduce their tax liabilities, to lawyers who manage to avoid speeding penalties and to Council officials who take every possible job benefit, such as sick days, which their system delivers.

In Sarah Rudd's case the occupational conundrum was that she had an amazing instinct for knowing when a person was lying, and was usually proved right. There was a difference between strategically not telling the truth ('do you like my new hair-style, Darling?') and uttering words which not only were nowhere near honest, but which were spoken to deliberately mislead the listener.

She was sure that her husband Nick was lying. She was adding to the general signs (loss of libido, not shaving, eating more quickly, avoiding eye contact) her conviction that her husband was troubled: she knew all was not well.

She was now on Plan C. The first had been to ask him if there was a problem. She knew that you ask once and if there is no response you move on to Plan B. That involved a withdrawal of sexual contact. In the end she was forced to try to interest him only to find that he went and slept in the spare room. Again, don't ask.

Plan C was more subtle. Her request that they go walking in the Chiltern Hills was readily agreed. His parents arrived to provide a secure home base although both their children were happily at school.

They caught the train from Euston to Berkhamsted and took a taxi to the edge of the farmlands through which the paths threaded. It took time for him to relax as he was expecting an interrogation. Sarah knew better.

"'Watch Rashid.' That's what the voice said?"

"Yes, Nick. A husky voice." She knew she was breaking the rules and she should not be talking to Nick about police matters. But Plan C would only succeed if there was an element of surprise.

"But surely your anti-terrorism officers are responsible for this?"

"They're fully supportive but they depend, to some extent, on our local knowledge. Islington is generally a peaceful community but we have our share of racial groupings. We keep the peace fairly well but, under the surface, we suspect that a minority of fundamentalist Muslims are fermenting jihadism."

"The Arab Spring?" suggested Nick as they climbed over a stile. The May sunshine was warming their backs.

"That's a term used by the newspapers." She stopped and turned towards her husband. "Do you know what *Ash-sha'b yurid isqat an-nizam* means, Nick?" She laughed. "Of course you don't." She ruffled his hair. "It translates roughly into *The people want to bring down the regime.*"

She took off her back-pack and undid the buckles. She took out a flask of coffee and poured them each a cup. She then removed from her side pocket a small bottle of whisky and poured a generous measure into their drinks.

"All over the Middle East there is revolution. This new wave started in December 2010 in Tunisia when the people overthrew President Ben Ali. This was the start of The Arab Spring and we know that Algeria, Iraq, Jordan, Kuwait, Sudan and Libya have been, and are, affected. Sometimes the revolutionaries win. As in Syria, the Government may well fight back and get the headlines. In this case President Bashar Assad is dividing world opinion." She wiped her face with her handkerchief. "The revolt in 2011 in Khuzestan was bad because of its proximity to Iran but it was not reported very much."

She stretched her legs and drank some coffee.

"The situation my colleagues are watching is the recent activities of the Muslim Brotherhood in Egypt. The current leader of al-Qaeda, Ayman al-Zawahiri, comes from Cairo."

They had both finished drinking their coffee and the addition of the malt whisky was already relaxing them. Sarah decided to pounce with the culmination of Plan C. There were two possible outcomes. Nick would tell all or he would storm off.

She stood up and looked down at him.

"I think you need to tell me the truth Nick. You have another woman."

DCI Rudd was certain that her husband was not playing away. There were no signs of that. But Plan C was dependent upon the target being put on the defensive. It was the oldest trick in the book. The strategy also involved a slight flattering of the other person. Her accusation implied a suggestion that her husband was attractive to other women.

Nick Rudd stood up and emptied his cup over the fence and into the fields behind them. There were about seven young bullocks less than fifty yards away but the barbed wire was enough protection for the walkers. He hurried away. Sarah was waiting to see if he looked back at any stage. That was the sign she needed. She found herself pleading inside.

He reached nearly eighty yards towards the north when he suddenly stopped and turned around. When Sarah reached him he was disturbed. He turned his head away in an attempt to conceal his embarrassment. Plan C required her to continue to give him space and time.

They walked back towards their packs. The bullocks had reached the fencing and were sniffing the air.

"Please sit down, Sarah," said Nick.

One of the animals let out a loud snorting sound.

She did as she was told. Nick stood over her.

"I had no choice, Sarah. I had to say 'no'." He was now pacing around but always coming back to his wife.

She remained still and silent. She knew that how she handled the next few minutes would determine the outcome of their conversation.

"It was the job I had always dreamed of, Sarah. Headmaster of a public school in Devon. The status, the achievements, the salary, the boost to my pension, the lifestyle. You should have seen the house in the grounds. The playing fields made Lords cricket ground look second rate.

"What could have caused you to say 'yes', Nick?"

He laughed. "Still adhering to Plan C Sarah? You must never forget that I remember everything you tell me. Two years ago. When you managed to get the man, who was beating his wife, to confess. How did it go? Plan A, direct question, Plan B, you kept him waiting for hours in the cell and Plan C, you played to his belief about his attractiveness to women and he told you everything because he thought you were on his side."

DCI Rudd grimaced. All she could recall was the judge who gave him a suspended sentence and the visit to the wife in hospital who'd been beaten to a pulp.

"Gloves off, Nick?" she asked.

"I was never going to accept the job. But, since you ask, so much revolves around you, Sarah. It was nice to find myself in the spotlight."

She recoiled at his words. At times she simply did not know whether she was Mrs Sarah Florence (her mother's name) Rudd, mother of Marcus and Susie, or Detective Chief Inspector Rudd of the Metropolitan police. She had her office phone with her at all times and it was switched on throughout the night. She thought like a law enforcement officer. For most of the time it seemed enough for Nick but they were reaching a stage where he was asking for more attention.

"I've always wanted to live in Devon. I think the school you're talking about is in Frome," she said.

"That's in Somerset and you're lying through your teeth."

Two of the bullocks seem to be shaking their heads in agreement with this accusation. Three others were sniffing out the roots at the base of the fence.

"So why did you not discuss it with me, Nick?"

"You were lying in a hospital bed with your chest shattered by a bullet. But that's not the real reason. They gave me all the time I wanted. They really put pressure on me to join them."

"I would have backed you, Nick."

"The kids are happy, my parents adore them, I love my job and I'm married to an amazing woman." He took her into his arms. "No day with you, Sarah is ever the same. It's the most fantastic experience any man could have."

They kissed and hugged each other.

"Can you remember what Plan D is, Nick?" she asked with a chuckle. She was quietly undoing the buttons of her blouse.

"Plan D," he sighed. "Don't tell me. I cook dinner."

"Plan D involves experimentation. Does the feel of grass on a woman's back increase the sexual experience?" He had not noticed that she had been checking that they were isolated in the fields.

Her clothing was now open as she lay back only to discover a brown coloured bullock, with a piece missing from its ear, looking down at her from over the fence. Its nostrils were dribbling.

"This gives a new meaning to group sex," she said to herself.

* * *

It had been a rotten week for both of them. Jessica had found that she'd been given increased targets as the bank was panicking into searching out new sources of earnings. Matthew had taken a line of stock involving a Home Counties house builder only for the economy to pitch nearer to a double dip recession. Markets had fallen and his brokers were left to sell the shares at a discount to the price they had paid to buy them. Mob hated making losses and the tongue lashing delivered to his staff dented a number of weekends as the threat of job losses hung vocally in the air.

They discussed a possible visit to the theatre but finally decided just to walk and talk. They left Covent Garden and strolled towards Holborn. They found themselves wandering around Grey's Inn and they soon became lost in their conversation together.

Jessica wanted to understand better why Matthew's marriage had ended in divorce. She accepted that Anne had started an affair with a local solicitor but she was puzzled as to the reason for this.

"Mob. You're rather dishy, you're fun, you love your work and you're successful. What more did she want?"

He explained that when they first moved south she was earning more than him and it was a constant cause of friction.

"Anne thought that her money was her own and that I should pay all the bills."

They crossed over and decided to walk south towards the river Thames.

"The turning point, however, was the birth of Olivia. Although she was planned and, of course, we loved her from the first minute of her birth, I'm not sure that Anne really wanted children. She refused to breast-feed our daughter saying that it made her nipples rather sore. Her parents had emigrated to Australia and rarely came back to this country. When she worked in London she seemed to have some good friends but back in Leighton Buzzard she felt isolated. I was working longer hours. It was an accident waiting to happen."

They found a pub and Matthew bought them both drinks, which they had in the lounge.

"And you, Matt. Another woman perhaps?"

He remained silent.

"I need to know, Mob. I need to understand you better."

He finished off his pint and returned to the bar to buy another round. He came back looking serious.

"It was not the woman that was the problem. Her name was Anna and she was Irish. It started with a casual drink and the rest you know. It was what she was. She was fun and bright. We talked about work and she made me think about things differently. She made me look at myself."

He put his hands on Jessica's shoulders and squeezed her.

"Jessie. It was all so uncomplicated. Anna was Anna. She was a very complete woman. I once told her that I loved her and she just laughed at me. We were in bed together at the time. We spent a lot of time there."

"Are you still in touch with her?"

"Anna knew how to make love. One night, even by her standards, it was rather special. When we were finished she took me in her arms and asked me if I had enjoyed myself. I knew something was wrong." He drank some more beer. "I told her it was the best ever and she told me it was my last time. The love of her life had walked back into her affections. She left her job and I believe they went to Paris together. I never saw her again."

"So how do I compare with Anna?" she asked.

"When we sleep together I'll let you know. You don't compare Jessie. Anna came into my world when I was struggling with my job and my wife. She knew how to help me."

"So tell me who Matthew Orlando Buckingham is tonight."

"Your round," he said.

Jessica wanted to walk. They turned east and after ten minutes were looking up at St. Paul's Cathedral. The lights were on. There was a reverence about the building.

The news about Anna seemed to stop Jessica in her tracks. She knew that it was because she was beginning to feel that Matthew belonged to her and now another woman was in the way. She had long dismissed his ex-wife as requiring any attention. Jessica was treating Matthew as her property. There was the vexed issue of sex but she was well on the way to solving that conflict. She was dreading the time when Matthew asked her about children. The time clock was ticking and she wanted a baby. She felt increasingly close to Matthew. She just couldn't put the two together.

She also knew that it would not be long before they started having unprotected sex together. She had found her solution and would soon be ready for him. She decided that now was the time to raise the question. She anticipated, correctly, his reaction.

They found a bench in the courtyard and sat down.

"Mob. Since leaving your wife…"

"She chucked me out Jessie to accommodate her new man."

"Yes. Since you and your ex-wife separated, how many women have you slept with?"

The question appealed to Mob's male egotism and he began mentally to tick off the list. When he reached nine he stopped.

"Perhaps eleven," he said.

"Eleven!" gasped a shocked Jessica.

"It might be twelve," suggested Matthew who was enjoying the conversation.

"Full sex with twelve women?" she continued.

"And the rest, Jessica. There was a member of the gym who gave a new meaning to the treadmill."

"Yes, of course she did, lucky girl." She sighed.

"And how often did you use a contraceptive Matthew?"

He stood up and raised his arms to his waist.

"Please, Jessie, not again. We've been all through that. I thought that you were making… er… arrangements?"

"Unprotected sex with twelve women? I can't believe it."

"They didn't complain," boasted Mob.

"I bet they didn't," she gave him a weak smile. "How well did you know these women?"

"There was Filomina from our accountants. I gave her a lesson in auditing, I can tell you." He thought that he was impressing her.

"Stop there, Matthew. The truth is you have little or no idea who these women were."

"Hang on Mother Teresa. I was separated, thrown out by my wife, I was free, in London. I've done nothing wrong."

"You're also incredibly good looking, wealthy – although we both know you're not as prosperous as you pretend to be, but the girls were not to know that – libidinous, that's randy in your case, and a chaser. They didn't stand a chance did they, Mob?" She stood up.

"Put it that way, Jessica," he beamed. "No. It's a record of success."

"It might seem like that to you, Mob but it's also the behaviour of a selfish, self-centred, suicidal lunatic."

"Why don't you say what you really think, Jessica," snapped Matthew as he stormed off towards Fleet Street.

She caught up and pulled him back towards her.

"You just don't get it do you, Mob? You've been sticking your manhood into any women you could find. You knew nothing about them."

"So fucking what? I'm proving that I'll wait for the right woman. That's YOU Jessica, you stupid, lovely woman."

"Which is why you're going to see a doctor and have a blood test."

A couple passing near to them gave some thought as to whether they should intervene in what seemed to be a serious row. The man looked at Matthew and hurried on.

"A test for what?" shouted Mob.

"Use your fucking brain, Matthew," she yelled.

She turned and hailed a taxi.

"I'm going home. I'll phone you sometime."

And she was gone.

* * *

The reason the atmosphere in the boardroom at Silverside Brokers in the City of London was tense, was because each of the individuals present had different agendas. As Chief Executive, Matthew Buckingham had overall responsibility. He wanted to make profits and pay himself mouth-watering bonuses. His shareholders would readily agree to that if their dividends were increased. This was only possible because Matthew, even in a period of economic recession, had managed to attract a significant investment from a Chinese Fund. It was, of course, crazy to take the incoming funds and pay them out as bonuses for the shareholders but that's the way the City does these things.

He was also in charge of staff matters where his ability to lead by example and hard work gained him significant respect and support. They were all affected by compliance matters.

The financial services sector was in the grip of a draconian regime of punitive rule-making led by the Financial Conduct Authority. The FCA, as it was known, had created an atmosphere of vilification and fear. They trumpeted their successful prosecution of wrongdoers. The problem was they nearly always caught nonentities. The real villains were staying out of sight in their Mediterranean villas waiting for the good times to return.

Debra White sighed.

"We have to complete 'know your customer' procedures before I can allow the brokers to sell the stock," she said.

"We do understand who they are," interrupted Craig MacDonald.

"Well you're changing your tune, Craig. One minute you'll have nothing to do with film finance and now you can't wait to sell the shares to our customers."

"Mr Buckingham, I'm worried."

All eyes turned towards Ashtella Khan. This was the first time she had spoken. She reported to the compliance officer, Debra White. Her role was to ensure that the brokers sold the shares correctly. The system worked as follows:

Silverside Brokers made its profits by buying shares in at one price and selling them on to their clients at a higher amount. The resulting profit would be divided between the company and the brokers. Craig MacDonald had agreed to buy in twenty million shares in Six Weeks in Summer Production Limited at ten pence per share. This generated £2 million for the company as part of the £6 million which they needed to make the film.

Working with him Craig had eighteen brokers who spent all day on the telephone. They would try to sell the shares at prices up to 12 pence. If successful this would result in profits of up to £400,000.

Before this happened the compliance officer, as advised by the analyst, had to approve the transaction deeming it a fit and suitable investment proposition for their clients. A 'script' would be agreed setting out what the brokers could say about the attractions of the shares.

Ashtella Khan wore headphones all day long and sat with the brokers. She had the ability to listen in to any conversation she selected. Her role was to ensure that the brokers were sticking to the agreed script.

If, for example: "This is a high risk investment and we cannot guarantee the success of the film" became "This is a fantastic chance to double your money; it's the next 'Four Weddings and a Funeral'", the transaction would immediately be aborted, the funds refunded to the client and the broker suspended.

"Mr Buckingham," she pleaded, "I'll never monitor the calls. What if a broker says 'We think Kate Winslet is on board'? The next thirty minutes will be spent with the broker and the client discussing film stars."

"I no like what y'u are saying young lady," exclaimed Craig.

"Your brokers will say anything to get a sale Craig," said Debra. "Ashtella is making a good point. I'm nervous about this deal. There is also another issue to discuss. Do we really know who we're dealing with?"

"What does that mean?" asked Matthew.

"We've tried to find out all we can about the people involved in this film. Amanda Adams-Smythe has a limited track record. She has never been the main director of any film."

"She won a nomination at…"

"They all win awards. The industry promotes itself. What worries me more is Osama Al-Kabal. Caroline Pennington promised to send his details, including his passport. We also asked for confirmation that the £3 million from the Middle Eastern backers has been received. She is proving difficult to contact."

"Get real people. I'll no tell y'u all ag'in. There's a fuckin' recession out there. Four hundred thousand p'unds in commission. Come on. Let me start sellin' it."

Matthew looked at Craig and sighed.

"Not good progress ladies and gentlemen. Far too many loose ends. We'll meet here again in forty-eight hours. Get your act together folks please."

Craig's look suggested that a terrifying Scottish weapon might be appearing in the back of Debra White who was following Matthew back to his office. He sensed that she was behind him.

"Come on in Debra," he said and he closed the door as she reached the chair in front of his desk.

"I feel as though…"

"Yes, Debra. I know exactly how you feel," said Matthew. "It's a difficult balance between…"

"No it's not. The rules are quite clear. We can't operate without our financial permissions from the regulator and those depend upon me doing my job properly."

"What do you want, Debra?"

"I want to know that I have your full backing at all times."

"You know that you already have that."

As she left the room she turned. "Do I, Matthew? Can I rely on that statement you have just made?"

As he descended the stairs to leave the building he decided to walk back to Covent Garden. He hated the hypocrisy of his position. If he kept to the rules Silverside Brokers would be bankrupt within six months. His task was to work out how far he could stretch the tolerances of practical business activity without letting Debra know.

# Chapter Five

The trial of the Great Train Robbers began on Monday 20 January 1964 at the Buckinghamshire Assize Court, Aylesbury. The presiding official was Mr Justice Edmund Davies who was to sit for nearly sixty days of hearings. There were around two thousand three hundred written statements.

He began by saying:

"Let us with good heart embark on our respective tasks."

There were, initially, seventeen accused men and three women. Seven were 'put down' to be heard at a later date, one pleaded guilty, twelve were tried, one was discharged and one was tried later, for technical reasons. On Thursday 26 March 1964, after the judge had summed up for over thirty-two hours and the jury had deliberated for around sixty-five hours, nine were found guilty and one not guilty.

The sentences of up to thirty years in prison handed down by Mr Justice Edmund Davies, and later supported by the Appeal Court, caused amazement and then, from some quarters including the national newspapers, disapproving comment. This contributed to the future personalisation of several of the robbers by the media.

Several of the felons were still at large but Detective Chief Superintendent Tommy Butler was never to give up chasing them around the globe.

\* \* \*

The envelope was hand written and marked 'Personal'.

Jessica took it into the lounge along with her other post and placed it on a table. She switched on her CD player and heard some ballet music drift across the room. She went into the kitchen and made herself a cup of herbal tea. She returned, sat down in her favourite chair, and used a small knife to slit open the envelope. She knew it was from Matthew.

It was now ten days since they had last spoken. She had cried herself to sleep on the first night and regretted the manner in which she had approached the subject of a blood test. She had repeatedly gone over their conversation and tried to work out how else she could have raised the subject.

She knew that she had made him appear like a naughty schoolboy masturbating behind the changing rooms. She had belittled him. He was a healthy, good-looking man who liked sex. The twelve women were all probably good-lookers. Perhaps she was a bit jealous.

She imagined what he had written.

*My dearest Jessica.*

*I'll probably never love a woman as much as I adore you.*

*It does not matter if it was seven, ten, twelve or two hundred women. For me there will only ever be one person who has reached inside me in the way you have.*

*Jessica, my beloved, do you know what you really mean to me?*

*Get this. It's not sex – surprise! It's because, Jessie, you, like no other human being in this world, can make me a better person. You seem to know how to dig deep and bring out the best in me.*

*But I can't live with your standards and your demands.*

*You're right Jessie. I'm just randy.*

*Take care of yourself.*

*Matthew Orlando Buckingham aka Mob.*

She wiped a tear away from her eye and took out the single piece of paper.

She stared at the copy letter she was holding. There was no attachment. There was no compliments slip. It was from a Harley Street doctor and addressed to Matthew.

She rushed to her computer and switched it on. She googled the name of the practice and read its website. 'Only the best for Matthew,' she laughed to herself.

The opening paragraph explained the request from his patient for a full blood test to establish that there were no sexual infections.

The doctor then went on to confirm that the opportunity should be taken for a much greater scope to the tests and Mr Buckingham had agreed to that.

There followed a summary of his findings:

The sexual issue was dismissed immediately as every test was clear. However there were concerns about his liver enzymes which might indicate an early sign of alcohol abuse.

Jessica re-read the copy letter and placed it back on the table. She reached over and lifted the receiver from the phone. She pressed the buttons of a number she knew rather well.

\* \* \*

"She's a protective little bitch."

Matthew nodded in agreement although his male testosterone would occasionally imagine her in the shower with Mark Patterson-Brown at Threadneedles Hotel.

"She is making me go through her on every single detail." Debra White clenched her fist as she gave expression to her frustration.

'You were in my office a few nights ago complaining about a lack of commitment to detail,' thought Matthew to himself.

Caroline Pennington, corporate lawyer with Christie Watson, who was based in Lincoln's Inn Field, near to Chancery Lane Tube station, was making life difficult for Silverside Brokers. She knew that it was in her client's best interests for Craig to place £2 million in shares in Six Weeks in Summer Production Limited. It therefore made little sense for her to delay unnecessarily in providing the required information.

"Summarise the position please Debra," asked Matthew.

"The company is fine. We have most of the information from Companies House. It's formed and they have applied to Her Majesty's Revenue and Customs that the shares to be issued qualify for Enterprise Investment Scheme tax reliefs. That's almost certain anyway because it's a virtual automatic agreement provided you have given the Revenue the correct information."

"So what's the problem?" asked Craig.

"It's the directors that we're having the problem with and Caroline is being decidedly unhelpful. There are supposed to be four of them. Amanda Adams-Smythe is the film producer and obviously the driving force. We have her passport and utility bill and, of course, there's a lot about her on Google."

"Sounds good to me," said Matthew.

"She is the only director as yet registered with Companies House. That leaves Richard Rochards, Osama Al-Kabal and Martine Madden. Martine is casting director and so we have been able to check her out. But, despite repeated requests, Caroline has not sent copies of her passport and utility bill. On Richard Rochards, the director, again no documentation from Caroline but we have been able to generate a considerable amount of information about him."

"More frustration than anything else," observed Matthew.

"Perhaps," acknowledged Debra, "but when it comes to Osama Al-Kabal, we have nothing. Importantly we have no evidence that his £3 million have been paid into the bank account."

Matthew held his hand up as the office manager brought in fresh supplies of tea and coffee. She collected the used cups and left the room.

"We have to be careful that we're not seeing 'reds under the beds' too quickly. Caroline may herself be having difficulty in getting the information. She's an arrogant bitch and she'd never tell us if she was being held up."

"There's another problem."

All heads turned towards Ashtella Khan.

"I can't get a copy of the film script. There must be one because you can't raise funds without it. I've asked Amanda and Richard and they keep saying that it will be emailed to me. It's not come."

"Matthew. Have you spoken to Mark Patterson-Brown?" asked Debra.

Matthew laughed.

"He's always been elusive has Mark. He spends a lot of his time down at Goodwood. He owns about five racehorses. He delegates everything to Caroline. I called him this morning on his personal mobile and drew a blank."

"When are we buying in the shares?" asked Craig.

"Our lawyers have prepared the placing letter and sent it to Caroline. She's yet to respond."

"I canna sell the bloody things if we no have 'em." He groaned. "There's £400,000 in commission waiting to be earned and you fairies are faffing around."

"It's the selling side that worries me."

Ashtella was looking down at her papers.

"We have to agree the investor story that the brokers can tell to our clients. I then have to monitor that they are keeping to the script."

Matthew looked intensely at her.

"Ashtella. The British film industry is buoyant at the moment. It's a known fact that in recession cinema takings increase. It's because people are more careful with their money. They see a cinema ticket as giving them value. We know the director, the producer and the casting director. I think once you've read the script you'll feel more comfortable. Our analyst has verified their profit projections. If the film takes, let's say, £20 million there will be good profits to share out. Add to that the tax breaks and I think our clients are getting a good deal. Of course the brokers must spell out the risks but Craig will ensure that we only approach experienced and high net worth individuals." He paused. "When you think about it, we run a filter system. We start with a deal and try to iron out any flaws. As I say, providing the brokers spell out all the risks to our clients this is a good deal."

"Which will make us a lot of money," added Craig MacDonald.

Debra sighed and applauded her boss.

"Great speech Matthew. There's just one flaw in your summation."

"Och. Do tell us," snapped Craig.

"I don't think we really understand what the risks are."

* * *

Sarah and Nick were enjoying their three-day break and warm sunshine on the Grand Union Canal. They had left the children with his parents (at their choice because of school holiday activities) and collected their friend's boat from its mooring at Kings

Langley. They had sailed through the Chiltern Hills and passed beyond Slapton Fields in the late afternoon of their second day and moored beside the tow path at Lock 28. This was dominated by The Grove Lock English Inn and its preservation of the original lock keeper's cottage. They enjoyed their evening meal. Nick wanted to walk the canal path but Sarah was again reading her book. They would be leaving their barge the next afternoon, north of Leighton Buzzard, and returning to London by train.

Early the following morning Sarah announced that they were going for a walk. Nick protested that they were having a canal break.

"All your own fault, Nick," she said. "You chose to buy me this book."

He groaned. Sarah never read crime literature preferring on her holidays to absorb herself in biographies or historical novels. A colleague had told her to read Kate Mosse but that remained on the 'to-do' list. He had discovered the title he had purchased for Sarah from one of his senior pupils who was rather interested in current affairs.

"Sir," asked the future Cambridge honours graduate. "What historical event took place on 8 August 1963?"

"Bastard," thought Nick. "Must get this."

The next ten minutes were spent with the headmaster trying to remember when John Kennedy was shot, the Korean War, who was on the throne, when Prince Charles was born, when England won the world cup and, as he became more desperate, when we joined the European Union."

"You really don't know very much, do you, Sir? I'll give you three clues. Ok?"

"I don't really need them," pleaded Nick, "but I have a class to teach. Quickly, clue one then."

"Phil Collins."

"Phil Collins? He was about twelve years old in 1963."

"I'm impressed. Do you want your second clue, Sir?"

"I'm getting there Beachcroft-Norbury. But I must start teaching. Number two please."

"A Groovy Kind of Love."

"That's a Phil Collins hit. Made in the 1980s."

"Number three, Sir?"

"No. Definitely not. Let me think. It was a success but I think it was on an album."

The bell rang and Nick looked at his watch.

"Would you like the name of the… ?"

"Buster. That was it. Buster Edwards. Hang on. It was from the film. It was about…"

"What was it about, Sir?"

"It was about crime… er… Brink's-Mat gold. No, that was later… Got it! The Great Train Robbery."

"Well done, Sir. The Great Train Robbery. 8 August 1963."

"Where did it take place, Sir?"

"Beachcroft-Norbury. Would you like a hundred lines for being late for class?"

They laughed together and shook hands. His pupil was impressed. The first three members of staff he had tried all failed to get anywhere near the answer.

"Just a moment," chided the Headmaster. "Where do you get all this knowledge from?"

"There are several books out on the robbery and I saw a review in the paper and decided to read it. The Library ordered it for me. It was particularly interesting. We are so used to modern police methods. It took the local bobby on his bike hours to discover a train had been robbed. He then had to find a phone box to tell his sergeant." He laughed and walked towards the classroom.

Nick had googled the topic and called in at his local book shop to buy a copy of *The Great Train Robbery: Crime of the Century: The Definitive Account*, by Nick Russell-Pavier and Stewart Richards. He had wrapped it up and given it to Sarah as a present about two weeks ago. He had then forgotten about it until he noticed that she was avidly reading it when she was supposed to be helping him negotiate the locks.

The Sunday morning calm was punctuated by birdsong. Sarah was wearing shorts and a fleece top. She locked the boat and grabbed her husband's hand.

"I've not had my breakfast," he moaned.

"Later. Come on, Nick. This is exciting. It was only yesterday that I realised we are here."

"It's reassuring to know that the policing of our nation is in such safe hands. What do you mean, 'we are here'?"

"Fifteen minutes. That's all."

She almost ran down the drive leading out of The Grove Lock and pulled Nick along with her. They turned left onto a road which led from the south side of Leighton Buzzard towards Cheddington and on to Hemel Hempstead. They strode quickly for ten minutes. Sarah was continually peering towards her right.

She stopped, let a car pass them, and then she crossed the road and slowed down. Ahead of her was a country lane. She went on, almost unable to contain her interest.

"That's it, Nick."

He could see a rather dirty, sad-looking brick-built crossing with wires and what he realised were rail tracks.

She held his hand and squeezed.

"It's Bridego Bridge Nick. It's where The Great Train Robbery took place." She ran on again. "This is where they parked their vans and scrambled up the embankment. They coshed the driver and handcuffed him to the fireman. They had to crawl back down here afterwards."

Nick realised that Sarah was relishing the atmosphere. She was sniffing the events of nearly fifty years ago. She was Detective Chief Superintendent Tommy Butler, Head of the Flying Squad, relentlessly pursuing the fugitives around the world.

The sun was rising in the east and the warmth of the day enabled Sarah to loosen the buttons on her jacket. She breathed in deeply.

"I can hear them, Nick, loading the postal packages and running off to Leatherslade Farm. They were nasty men. They deserved what they got." She turned back and faced him. "Hardly any of the robbers really gained from their success and yet it remains one of the most successful thefts of all time."

"Yet they were all caught."

"Well perhaps not the Irishman who they said masterminded the event. But Nick…," she started walking away and back towards the canal, "it was all so different. The police were a law unto themselves. They did what they wanted. There were no budget cuts. The chapters on the trial are fascinating. The judge was in total command. No human rights to worry about."

"Could it ever happen again, Sarah?"

"It changed attitudes towards security. The train was unguarded. The robbers simply stopped it and pinched two and a half million pounds from it."

"Was it difficult to stop the train, Sarah?"

"It was a comedy show, Nick. They halted it further up the line at Sears Crossing and then discovered that their driver couldn't work the engine. That's why Jack Mills became so involved. He drove it up to here."

They stopped as the Manchester to Euston Virgin train came hurtling through on the fast line. They instinctively ducked as the bridge shook with the vibrations.

"Fancy trying to stop a train up there today, Nick." She laughed.

Nick grabbed his wife around her waist.

"At last. We've found something even beyond the skills of Detective Chief Inspector Rudd."

They walked away to have their breakfast back on their boat by the canal side. They would need to go through four more locks before leaving the barge and returning home to their children.

Sarah stopped and looked back at Bridego Bridge.

"Nick. If I had to stop the train, I would," she said.

He looked at his wife.

"Yes," he said under his breath, "I think you probably would."

* * *

"Mob. Would you like to hear a joke?"

He looked up from the sofa and yawned. They had both experienced a long day at work and the sound of the evening traffic in Covent Garden was beginning to diminish. Jessica was wearing a shirt and white panties.

"You don't tell jokes, Jessie," he answered.

She came and sat down by him.

"There was this lecturer talking to a class of adult students who were undertaking a social awareness course. The theme of the night's talk was sexual relationships between couples. Professor Alan Darling was warming to his theme: 'Some couples have sex every night. Most twice a week. Tell you what. Let's do our own survey. Hands up if you have sex every night?'"

Mob put his hand on Jessica's upper thigh and she removed it.

"A few people admitted to that," she continued. "'Ok. Hands up if you have relations twice a week?' asked the lecturer. A forest of arms were raised. 'Ha. Yes. Right. Who has sex, say, once a month?' Two hands were raised. Professor Darling tried not to smirk. 'Is there anyone who only has sex once a year?'"

Mob's hand made another attempt to caress the joke teller. This time it was allowed to stay where it had reached.

Jessica carried on.

"This man at the back jumped up and down. 'Me. Yes. Me.'

Professor Darling was amazed. 'You only have sex once a year?'

'Yes. Yes Sir.'

'So why are you so happy?'

'Tonight's the night.'"

Matthew laughed out loud and wondered if he dare move his hand a little further up. He then noticed that Jessica was looking rather seriously at him.

"Mob," she said. "Tonight's the night."

She stood up and pulled him to his feet. They went into the bedroom, undressed and disappeared underneath the bed-clothes. Matthew was later to wonder whether any single event in his life could match the first occasion in which he and Jessica came together.

It was only when he was holding her in his arms that he noticed the plaster on her arm. He rubbed his fingers over it.

"You injured, Jessie?" he asked.

She laughed out loud.

"It's why you are so happy, Mob. It's a contraceptive patch. My doctor thinks that it's the best method for us to use due to your refusal to use normal methods."

"A piece of sticking plaster, Jessie!"

"It's not so different to a nicotine patch, Mob. It releases hormones into the body via the skin. As you know I absolutely refuse to use anything internal and I'm not willing to take the pill. This is the best option. They last a week. I use them three times and then have a week off. Timing is important but you can leave that to us girls."

"Are they fool-proof Jessie?"

"Where sex is concerned nothing is certain, Matthew. But my doctor says that it has one of the best reliability records."

She put her hand down between his legs.

"And, Mob, you must admit, it's rather uncomplicated. It means I can concentrate on giving you… Mob… please don't do that… Mob… yes… ."

\* \* \*

The Planner stepped off his prayer mat and resumed his place at a desk. He took out his Quran and reminded himself of the teachings of Muhammad. He was a Hafiz; he had spent his early years memorising all 6,236 verses of the Holy Book.

The room shook as the Northern Line Tube train left Angel to travel to Kings Cross. He completed his four times a day ritual and decided, yet again, to go through the summary of his attack. He knew that it would result in the death of around four hundred people. As far as he could be certain nearly all of them would be white English. There might be the odd Muslim but Allah's needs must be served and the Brotherhood needed to reinvigorate al-Qaeda's strategy to stretch the Arab Spring further west.

The timings were the easiest part of the planning down to the last minute. It could be possible for an outside factor to interfere but his research showed a remarkable 98 percent reliability. The bombs were tried and tested. The sample gas container had now arrived and they had tried it out on a transgressing brother who died in agony in under a minute.

What worried the Planner was that it was such a simple concept. Six of the seven terrorists were certain to get away and there was every chance that they would be back in Islington before the police got to grips with the events. Five of them would be out of the country by the next morning. The brother who would release the gas was due to die. The Planner had concerns about him and he would be tested in the next week to confirm his commitment. He needed to know he was a true Shahid; a Muslim martyr preparing to enter Allah's paradise.

There were ample funds available as his bank account was replenished on a regular basis. The Planner was set to punish Little Satan.

He decided to go over the plot, step by step, until it was time to pray again.

# Chapter Six

Among the Great Train Robbers Charlie Wilson was the hard man. He was a good-looking South Londoner known and liked for his wisecracks. He was part of a gang which in 1962 stole the wages from the offices of the State Airline BOAC, collecting part of the sixty-two thousand pound haul.

He was one of the main assault team that stopped the train and then carried the mailbags to Leatherslade Farm. He was arrested on 23 August 1963 and later sentenced to twenty-five years imprisonment for conspiracy to rob and concurrently thirty years for robbery. He was held at Winston Green prison near to Birmingham in the maximum security block where he spent most of his time in his cell.

In 1964 he was taken by three gunmen out of the prison, and at the end of 1964 crossed the Channel. He may have planned this himself or was taken for his money. He ended up a little way outside Montreal in Canada, via Mexico City, where he was joined by his wife and two daughters. On Thursday 25 January 1968 he was re-arrested by Tommy Butler who was accompanied by fifty Royal Canadian Mounted Police.

He was returned to HMP Parkhurst on the Isle of Wight where he was held in 'The Cage', a newly-built high security wing. He was released in 1978. In 1990 he was assassinated by a gunman hired by a drugs ring while relaxing by his swimming pool in Marbella on the Costa del Sol.

\* \* \*

During the first week of June it was Jessica's thirty-eighth birthday.

She and Matthew both took the Friday as holiday and set out early to drive south to Lymington. They crossed the Solent and booked into their room at the West Bay Club just outside Yarmouth. After dinner they planned their Saturday together.

"Six o'clock we make mad, passionate love," proposed Matthew.

"50 percent of the Isle of Wight is designated an area of natural beauty, Mob," read Jessica from the guide book placed in their lounge area.

"Seven o'clock I'll take you into the shower and soap the whole of your body."

Jessica carried on turning the pages. "There are thirty miles of seashore which is called Heritage Coast."

"At seven-thirty I'll dry you and carry you back into the bedroom whereupon I'll show you perhaps the largest..."

"There are five hundred miles of pathways and two hundred miles of cycle tracks."

"Once you have recovered from my revelation I'll make your body tingle with..."

"Woodpeckers, owls and dragonflies. That's what it says here. If we hire bikes we can go into the marshlands and see them."

Jessica looked up from her reading.

"Mob. Why was Anna so special?"

He looked at her and frowned.

"That was some time ago, Jessie."

"Of the twelve women you have slept with since leaving home, how many can you remember?"

"All of them." Mob was struggling because the actual total was probably seven."

"Tell me about them."

"Er... why are you asking these questions?"

"Who were they, Mob?"

"Ingrid, who I met in a bar. That lasted six months. The accountant, then several more."

"So why when we discussed it did you remember Anna?"

He stood up and walked over to the open window. The evening offered a cloudless sky and there was clearly a wonderful night and day ahead.

"She was in charge. She loved discussing life: the arts, religion, politics. She never intruded. She was sensational in bed."

"Just like me," suggested Jessica.

Matthew poured them both a drink from the fridge and sat down at the table. He looked tired and had heavy eyes. The demands of running a brokerage firm in continuing recessional times were taking their toll. He was also thinking about Olivia. She had been withdrawn during their time together last Sunday. She had said the right things, she had enjoyed the cinema and all was well at school. She was not, however, Olivia as he knew his daughter.

"Just like me," repeated Jessica.

"You are wonderful in all directions, Jessie," he said.

"Except we have a problem, don't we, Mob?"

"I don't. Therefore you must be the one with the challenge."

She stood up and strolled over towards him. She sat down and held on tightly to her glass.

"I want a child, Mob. I'm now thirty-eight years old. The clock is ticking. I've nowhere to go in the bank and I'm bored with dishing out loans. I'm happy to bring up the child on my own."

"You're not going to get pregnant if you continue to use those patches, Jessie."

She looked at him and placed her hand over his.

"I don't want your child, Mob."

"Why not?"

"Because we need time to develop our relationship. It's going well and I love you to bits. But you have an ex-wife, there is Olivia to think about and you have a heavy workload. If we have a child it complicates matters because I'll also get a partner which is not what I planned."

He went quiet. He could see her point of view. He wanted them to carry on as they were. She stayed at the flat regularly and they were having fun.

"Let's give it six months, Jessie. That leaves you plenty of time to find a sperm donor if we decide to break up."

Jessie groaned inside. She did not want to end her time with Mob. He was what she had always wanted. His first marriage had broken down after their daughter was born. She was worried that Mob would change if she had his child. She put her glass down and moved round to him. It was time to go to bed. She was already looking forward to the early morning passion awaiting her only a few hours ahead.

Tomorrow they would cycle into the marshlands and she'd ask the owls what they thought she should do. Then she remembered that they were nocturnal. She'd see what the woodpeckers thought, after all, dragonflies don't talk.

* * *

"Watch Rashid."

"Yes, Sir. That's all the voice said."

"You've had two calls."

"Three. There was another two days ago."

"On your personal mobile"

"Yes."

Detective Superintendent Khan sat back behind his desk and drank some more decaffeinated coffee. He trusted DCI Rudd. But on this occasion he was not sure what she was thinking.

"Thought of changing your mobile?"

"Can't see the point."

"No. Why you, Sarah?"

"Because my name's been everywhere. I don't think it's personal. Anybody can get a mobile number."

"What do you think?"

"We traced the caller each time. They're using a fresh phone on every occasion. We have no way of knowing who it is. The message is so short I've virtually nothing to go on. Male. Perhaps thirtyish. No attempt to disguise the voice so almost certainly not known to me. The words are significant. He knows that 'watch Rashid' seems meaningless. So he's trying to say something else."

"And you get no chance to ask him a question?"

"He kills the line immediately."

"Rashid is meaningless?"

"I'm not so sure. It's a common Arabic name and the speaker realises it conveys nothing to us." She stopped and sipped some water. "There's another way of looking at this, Sir."

D/Supt Khan relaxed. This was the whole point of their

meeting. He wanted to understand what one of his best officers really thought.

"I think it's a community message. We know that the majority of people living in Islington relish a peaceful life. They want it their way with their culture. The fanatics are few and we've not really ever identified serious problems. I think the caller knows that there is a possibility that a future event could destabilise things here."

"How does that work, Sarah?"

"Simple. There's going to be an incident. A killing. A bomb. A Tube train is to be blown up. Whatever. The person making the call knows that whoever is involved will be traced. That suggests a suicide mission. He's certain the individual will be found to live here. What will happen? The heavies, the press, public opinion will all combine to destabilise the way of life in Islington. The blame game will take over. Years of your hard work, Sir, could be destroyed in days."

DCI Rudd was not to know that Detective Superintendent Khan was appearing in front of a promotions board in the next two weeks.

"I want all available officers put on to this immediately. Find the caller DCI Rudd. That's an order."

"Absolutely the wrong thing to do, Sir."

"Oh?"

"If we send our force into the community asking about something we know nothing about it will scare the fanatics away."

"Isn't that what we want?"

"No. We must catch them."

"And how do we do that?"

"I think we begin by thanking her Majesty the Queen."

Majid Khan was beginning to lose the thread of their conversation.

"Has she time to help us?"

DCI Rudd laughed.

"She gave me that bloody medal. I'm a hero in the locality. I get stopped almost every day. I hate it. But now I can put it to good use. I'm going to go into the heart of Islington. I'll be there twenty-four hours a day."

"And you'll identify the criminals."

"Unlikely." She stood up and moved towards the door. As she started opening it she turned back and said, "They'll find me, Sir. Someone out there is trying to tell me something."

"DCI Rudd," said D/Supt Khan. "You are not to put yourself in any danger."

"Me, Sir? I'd run a mile first. Biggest coward on the force."

The senior officer groaned inwardly. He was not to know that less than half a mile to the north, in a disused shop, the Planner was finishing his prayers.

\* \* \*

He praised Allah and turned to his seven companions. He threatened, as always, that no names were to be used. He pointed a finger and instructed that he should be taken through the timetable. They all spoke in English which was not surprising because four of the group were converts.

"We can rely on the timings," said a terrorist. "We have checked the schedule over the last two weeks. The time of entry is always within two minutes."

"What time?"

"Six twenty-eight."

"When do you detonate the first explosive?"

"Six twenty-eight. We do not want to give any reason for there to be an abort."

"That seals the exit."

"The brickwork is old. It will crumble. The top will cave in but we think more slowly."

"We do not think. We know."

"We found a disused cave in Yorkshire. We tried it out. We are certain we have it right."

"How long is it?"

"One thousand and fifty-five yards."

"It hits the blockage."

"It slows and there will be a blast of air. It will stop after eight hundred yards."

"When do you blow the entry?"

"Immediately it enters."

"That seals it," continued the Planner.

"Yes. Mo…"

"No names," chided the Planner.

"My brother will be in the middle of the combination. He will be carrying two cylinders of the gas. He will throw them out each side. The blasts will cause heat waves and we expect everybody to be dead within seven to fifteen minutes."

"How big are the containers?"

"Here is one."

The Planner nodded his agreement.

"When does the proper gas arrive?"

"There is still an issue with the final mixture. We are combining sodium fluoride with dimethyl methylphosphonate, phosphorous, alcohol, carbon, hydrogen and oxygen. That's the basic structure to make sarin but we're not happy that it kills quickly enough. Our brothers are adding something else but will not tell us. We'll need to test it."

"But it will bring death within seven to ten minutes?" asked the Planner.

"It paralyses the muscles around the lungs. They will be gasping for air. We will not fail."

"You will die if…"

"I am going to Lebanon. I want to try it out on some people. I need to be certain it kills quickly enough."

"How are you getting the gas out of the country?"

"It's already there."

"We must pray. We will talk again tomorrow. You will repeat everything you have said today. There must be no mistakes. No names. No contact. You will each tell me exactly what your role is and how you are preparing to serve Allah."

As they left the shop at set intervals Saleem looked up the road. He watched Rashid striding quickly back to his business.

The bastard, as he called him, was due to suffer. They all thought he was their hero. The follower who would release the gas and die himself, would be hailed as a martyr. But Saleem did not believe him. He dare not denounce him. It would be he who would end up beneath the concrete minus his finger nails.

His evidence was not strong enough. But he knew that Rashid had a reason to live. It was one of the best of incentives to keep on living.

When Rashid was not praying to Allah he was fucking Saleem's fifteen year old sister.

\* \* \*

The water was streaming over their two bodies.

Caroline had lost count of the number of times that she and Mark Patterson-Brown had finished their copulating by hurrying into the cubicle, closing the glass door, turning on the shower and waiting for the water to get hotter. They then squeezed the creams and shampoos out of the tubes and lathered each other. Mark was skilful and made her wait for quite a time until he began to massage her private areas. She found it unbelievably sensual and within thirty minutes she would perform an act on him which gave her an equally libidinous satisfaction. They would always dry each other, put on their bath robes and return to the lounge. Mark usually selected a jazz composition and Caroline will have pre-selected a white wine which she'd have chilling in the fridge. They were both weight conscious and so avoided the nibbles.

For over two years they had left the social chat alone. Mark lived on the south coast with his wife of twenty-four years and his two daughters. He visited his geriatric mother every Sunday. His special love was his horses, which were stabled at Goodwood. Caroline had other friends and occasionally slept with them. She was mainly focused on her work. It was more difficult for a woman to become a partner in a corporate law firm but she had done just that. To everybody's disbelief she had secured it on merit. The earnings from Maidstone New Issues certainly helped but Caroline had three other clients who regularly provided business for her firm.

She and Mark were rather fond of each other. They enjoyed their dinners together during the week before he returned home on Thursday evening. They were serious in their love of the theatre and adventurous in their choice of plays. Their relationship was going nowhere because there was nowhere for it to go. This suited both of them.

"Mark," said Caroline.

He looked up. He was trying to read the writing on the CD cover so he could understand Miles Davis's moods better.

"Uh?"

"Amanda Adams-Smythe, Richard Rochards, Osama Al-Kabal, Martine Madden: which one is the fraudster?"

"What! We're making half a million from the deal. Stop wrecking it. Your job, Caroline Pennington, is to make sure that my deals complete."

"My role, Mr Mark Patterson-Brown, is to keep you out of prison."

"We vet the client, we write a document and structure the share issue. We then get the brokers to sell the shares, deduct our commission and we transfer the balance to the client's bank account. We all live happily ever after and I buy you one dozen red roses."

"Until the financial regulator knocks on your door because those poor investors who purchased the shares have lost their money."

"Nothing to do with me. We always spell out the risks."

Caroline stood up and let her robe fall open. His groan of desire filled the room. She pushed him back down in his chair.

"The regulator expects us to complete due diligence." She poured each of them fresh amounts of wine.

"But, Caroline, you do that. That's why you are paid so much. You always manage to produce complete files showing that we have met all our responsibilities."

"Not always, Mark. There is no such thing as a 100 percent certainty. We'd never finish anything if we checked all the detail. You and I have completed thirteen deals now. We know how each other works. You are honest. You're also greedy but I can control that. You never question me. You will remember when I pulled the Amazon Mines deal.

Two years ago they had their one and only row and went to bed separately. Caroline had refused to complete a transaction and refused to say why. Mark went ballistic. The clients threatened to sue. The problem was that Caroline would only say that it was her instinct. She could not give a reason. Three weeks later the firm was raided by the Serious Fraud Office. Mark received a phone call from the regulator congratulating him on his compliance process and for working to the correct standards. That night Caroline thought she might be propelled into the heavens such was his passion.

In a pub near to New Scotland Yard a senior crime detective was looking at the text message he had received earlier that evening. It was from Caroline, postponing their date but promising a night to remember in two days' time as her thanks for his information.

"Please, Caroline. Don't do the instinct bit this time. It's a great share offer. It's going to be a terrific film when it is finished."

They were beginning to dress ready for dinner in Threadneedles Hotel. They both had early starts in the morning.

"They don't trust each other," added Caroline. "Debra White at Silverside Brokers is giving me a difficult time because I'm not supplying all the information she needs. She became quite pushy today so I had to put her down."

"I know," said Mark. "I had a call from Matthew."

They turned off the lights, left their room and reached the lift which would take them down to the ground floor. They entered the dining-room and secured their usual table in the corner.

Mark looked over the top of his menu. He always made the same choices.

"So who is the guilty party, Caroline?"

She was deciding on a Caesar Salad and the Vegetarian Risotto.

"You must understand financial regulation, Mark. The system which has been introduced by the Bank of England is so prescriptive that it actually encourages the fraudster."

The waiter took their order and returned shortly afterwards with a bottle of Riesling.

"You've just ruined the Governor's evening," laughed Mark.

"I'm sure your name-sake knows the truth. What we have now is a check-list mentality. No transaction can be completed until, and unless, hundreds of boxes are ticked. What do the crooks do? Frankly it's their lawyers who actually do it but let's skip that bit. They simply understand the process and make sure they meet the criteria."

She returned her starter explaining to the waiter that she did not want smoked chicken with her salad.

"When I first started in corporate law we relied heavily on the old boy's network. Take Six Weeks in Summer Production. I'm having difficulty finding out about Osama Al-Kabal. In the past I would have made some phone calls to other firms and perhaps the markets. I would obtain 'off the record' references. Regulation always works better when we, the practitioners, are involved. Sadly, Mark, it has all changed and not for the better."

"It usually happens in a recession, Caroline."

They stopped as her salad was re-served. She asked for some still water.

"I've seen it before."

"I can live with that, Mark. The problem is that even if the four of them tick all the boxes I'm certain one of them is not kosher. My problem is that I daren't ask around. We're not allowed to do that anymore." She laughed. "I received a call about you the other day. I refused to comment."

"Who was it asking?"

"Ha ha. Not telling."

Their main courses were now on the table and the pianist was beginning her recital of, inevitably, Lloyd Webber music.

"Why only one?"

"Pardon me?"

"Why one? Why not Al-Kabal and perhaps Martine Madden?"

"Trust me, Mark. Just one of them is off beam."

She drank some wine.

"The problem I have is that I don't know which one of them. In fact I haven't the foggiest idea."

# Chapter Seven

Ronnie Biggs was thirty-four years of age at the time of The Great Train Robbery. He was born in Lambeth and was one of London's petty criminals who was in and out of prison. In 1963 he asked Bruce Reynolds, a future leader of the criminal gang, if he could borrow £500. He was to become embroiled in the stopping of the mail train. He was arrested on 4 September 1963 and found guilty of conspiracy to rob (25 years) and robbery (30 years).

On 8 July 1965 he escaped from Wandsworth prison by scaling a wall using a rope ladder and dropping on to a waiting furniture van. He fled to Brussels and then, joined by his wife and sons, to Paris where he changed his identity using plastic surgery. In 1966 he reached Australia but was forever on the run. In 1970 he reached Brazil.

The *Daily Express* found him in 1974 but he avoided extradition because his girlfriend, Raimunda de Castro, a nightclub dancer, was pregnant. In 1981 he was kidnapped by a group of British ex-servicemen but managed to escape and return to Brazil.

The United Kingdom and Brazil eventually signed an extradition treaty and on 7 May 2001 Ronnie Biggs returned to prison in Britain to complete his sentence. He continually petitioned for early release on grounds of ill-health but it was not until 30 July 2009 that he regained his freedom. He continued to be dogged by illness.

When he fled from Australia he left his wife Charmain and their two sons behind. In 2012, after the publishing of his biography *Odd Man Out: The Last Straw* he co-operated in a TV series about his wife: the programme was called 'Mrs Biggs.'

* * *

Matthew was getting rather confused by the rules. It was a Sunday in late June and he and Jessica were on their way to meet her mother. He had reached a point where he had stopped asking her to accompany him on a visit to Ledburn offering the opportunity to get to know Olivia. Jessica said she had no intention of crossing Anne's path.

They had been travelling for over an hour and a half and took the turning off the M40 motorway towards Stratford-upon-Avon. They reached the home of the Bard and made a detour around the back streets. Mob was quite surprised when the road broadened out and Jessica turned into the driveway of an expansive Edwardian detached property.

Her mother appeared at the front door. She was a shambles. Her clothing was predominately brown in colour and seemed to comprise a thick skirt and a scarf which was wrapped around a dirty cream blouse. Her auburn hair was uncombed. She had slippers on. It was nearly twelve noon and the temperature was over twenty degrees centigrade.

"Jessica. On time as always."

She turned and went inside. Three cats rushed away in different directions. Mob wondered if there were bats in the loft.

They went into the front room and Mrs Lambert returned with a tray of tea which she intended to serve in chipped china cups. There were pictures all around the walls each with a Shakespearean theme. 'Double, double toil and trouble; fire burn, and cauldron bubble,' Mob mused to himself.

"So you're Matthew," said the mother. "Tell me about yourself. I hope that you're Protestant and vote Conservative."

"Mother!" gasped Jessica.

"Shush, girl. Mr Buckingham has come a long way to see me. I want to know all about him. Do you know Shakespeare young man?"

"Neither a borrower nor a lender be; For loan oft loses both itself and friend, And borrowing dulls the edge…"

"Splendid. Hamlet. My favourite."

"But I came here to learn about you, Mrs Lambert," flattered Matthew.

86

"Me. Bah. One daughter long gone. Shit of a husband who spends his time shagging young girls in Portugal. Lots of money which my father bequeathed me. You can have that, Jessica, although some will go to the cats' home. Nothing more to say really. What's this Mob name all about?"

"His initials are Matthew Orlando Buckingham, Mother."

"Shush Jessica. I asked Mr Buckingham."

"Same reply, Mrs Lambert. My initials make 'Mob'."

"I love it. You will always be 'Mob' from now on."

"What do you think about David Cameron's chances of winning the 2015 election?"

"Mob, what a fascinating question. I love the Fixed Term Parliaments Act 2011 which means a Government has five years in office. It cuts out all the crisis debating, not that Mr Miliband would understand what a crisis is. David Cameron is brilliant. He's from a wonderful family and his wife Samantha is so well connected. They are rich. He went to Eton. He ticks all the boxes. He's chucking out the immigrants and getting rid of Scotland. He's the finest Prime Minister since Anthony Eden."

"The Health Service, Mummy?"

"My experience is wonderful. I've just had the fingers of my left hand straightened. The surgeon was so kind."

"You went privately, Mummy."

"Doesn't everybody, Darling? When are you having a baby? Mob – get on with it. It's time Jessica produced something. I'll be too old to cuddle it at this rate."

"How old are you?" asked Matthew.

She looked at her visitor with a degree of surprise and then laughed out loud. I'll give you the month and the year and you have three seconds to tell me. February 1926."

"Christ. You're eighty-seven," exclaimed Matthew. "You were forty-five when you had Jessica."

"The bastard had left me. He called home one weekend and I weakened."

Jessica stood up and left the room.

"She's never forgiven me Mob. She says she was not wanted. It's not true. I would not have relations with any other man and so after Henry left me I was celibate until he came home that one weekend."

Matthew stood up and moved towards the door.

"I do love her, Mob. Please tell her."

She stopped and pulled him back.

"Will you come again?"

"Yes," he said and he kissed her on her cheek.

He reached the car and quickly sped out of the drive. He drove back into Stratford-upon-Avon and parked near to the river. They found a place by several oak trees on the water's edge. He gazed over the water and looked at the Royal Shakespeare Theatre. Jessica remained subdued.

"Lovely woman," he said.

Jessica stood up and walked away. Mob caught her up but she shook him off her. He ran over to a vendor and bought them each an ice cream. As he handed her the creamy cone with a chocolate flake sticking out of the top of it she laughed.

"You know a way to a woman's affections."

They walked on and she began to unload.

"See it from my point of view, Matthew. A mother…" she stopped because the ice cream was now dribbling down her front. Mob took out his handkerchief and wiped it clean. "A mother in her eighties and seriously mad, a father chasing girls round Portugal, three failed relationships and I'm running out of time."

Matthew sensed that they had reached an important moment.

"Anything interesting happening at the moment?" he asked.

They turned round and began to walk back to the trees.

She kissed him.

"Darling Mob. You have so much to put up with me."

"The sex is good."

"I want a baby, Mob. I wanted someone to share my life with and to take an interest in me. Perhaps I might have had two children. There's still plenty of time. The doctor says I'm in great shape. Now I just want a baby."

"But you don't want my baby?"

Jessica stopped. She put her hands on his shoulders.

"You have a daughter and an ex-wife. You're immature. You are successful but we both know that you are heavily in debt and there's a recession taking place. Businesses such as Silverside Brokers are experiencing tough trading conditions. You don't usually do long-term relationships. What was the name of the girl who you fell out with over French art?"

"But we're secure, Jessie. I've met your Mum."

"And you charmed her. We've been together, Matthew, for five minutes."

They stopped again and Matthew faced her.

"Shoot, Jessie. What's really wrong?"

She used her left hand to wipe her eye. Several swans landed on the water and started to fight for territorial ownership.

"I'm scared, Mob."

"Of who, me?"

She kissed him again.

"I'm scared of the time clock. It's ticking far too quickly."

\* \* \*

The first suspicion Sarah had was when she went to pay the newspaper account at her local shop. She thought it was about six weeks outstanding and she had £30 in her purse.

Mr Shah tore the yellow weekly tickets out of his deliveries manual and asked for £26.40. He then added to that the cost of a packet of bourbon biscuits. Sarah remained overweight but adored the creamy taste with her coffee.

She pulled out her purse and gasped. There were two five-pound notes and a few coins. She checked her other pockets. Where was the twenty pound note that had been there last night?

Mr Shah was polite and said that she was solving too many crimes to remember all her household chores. Sarah laughed and promised to call in later in the day. As she walked back to her car her police instincts started to kick in. She had been in denial and she knew that. There was the strange phone call several nights ago when a voice, which raised her hackles, rang off immediately she said that Marcus was out at school cricket practice. There was the missing clock. It was an antique given to her by her mother. They kept it in the spare room because neither she nor Nick liked it. But she noticed several days ago that it had disappeared. There were the mood swings. They had rowed over nothing during the previous weekend but that in itself was unusual, because she was more usually the peace-keeper between him and his father.

That evening, after another demanding day at work, she asked Nick if they could go for a drink. He raised his eyebrows because usually Sarah wanted to go to bed to catch up on her missing sleep.

"Is it about your new pair of handcuffs?" he asked in antici-pation of a romantic culmination to their night out. But he knew what was coming. Because he was driving he ordered a coke with no ice and a double vodka and tonic for Sarah.

She went straight into the matter at hand and detailed, almost like a pleading to a judge, the evidence she had accumulated. He noticed she was drinking quickly. He put his hand on hers.

"Stop there, Sarah. There is some good news."

"Tell me the bad news first, Nick?"

"He's taking drugs. He's stealing money and household goods to pay for them."

"And what's the good news?"

"He's on low dosages and they're soft. He's in no danger."

"What the hell are you talking about, Nick? He's committing a crime and it's a police matter."

"How many people have you and your fellow officers arrested for taking this drug Sarah?"

She held up her glass and Nick went away to re-order their drinks. He put a double vodka into hers. He placed the glasses on the table and checked around to ensure that they could not be overheard.

"That's not the point, Nick. Our son is a criminal."

"So you've already convicted him have you, Sarah?"

"Damn it, Nick. Don't you see the position this puts me in?"

"'m within seconds of getting cross, Sarah. You will be fool-ish if you try my tolerance much further. At this moment in

90

time you are off-duty and you are a mother whose son needs your help."

"A police officer is always on duty, Nick." She took another large gulp of her vodka.

"Crap."

They went into a period of silence, each lost in their own thoughts.

"How long have you known, Nick?"

"It's a common problem at school. We have a standard procedure."

"Which is what?"

"Every case is different. Our first action is to make sure that all members of staff know so that we can work together. We then assess the home situation and occasionally I'll call in the parents. Usually we talk to the pupil."

"Then what?"

"On two occasions we have called in the police."

"Just two."

"We have a high rate of success. We usually manage to get the individual to stop. We've also provided loans to pay off the suppliers. They get themselves into debt."

"So are you expecting a result with our son, Nick?" The atmosphere was turning unpleasant.

"I'm not dealing with it, Sarah."

"So you don't even care."

"It's my son, Sarah. I've handed him over to my deputy. He has my full authority to act as necessary."

"Will he go to the police?"

They paused as a youngster asked to take the spare chair.

"If he thinks that's the right course of action he will."

"And what about me, Nick? I'm his mother."

"You're a police officer."

"I'm his mother, Nick."

"That's not what you said a few minutes ago."

"What did I say?"

"You said that you're always on duty. Do you want me to play back the tape?"

Sarah stared at her husband. Her face began to redden.

"Oh God, Nick, what have I become? My own son and I'm acting as a police officer."

He stood up and they went back to their car.

"He wants to talk to you, Sarah."

They reached their road and Nick turned slowly into the drive.

"What do I say to him, Nick?"

"You could try listening."

As they went through the front door there was a light on in the front room. She could hear the sound of One Direction. She took off her coat and went to the bathroom. She returned quickly. Nick had not moved. She went towards the door and stopped. She took out of her pocket her two mobile phones and handed them over to him. She opened the door and went in.

\* \* \*

Matthew put his hands on his head and thought of Jessica's mother.

What was it that Brutus said in Julius Caesar?

*There is a tide in the affairs of men,*

*Which, taken at the flood, leads on to fortune.*

The first Monday of the last week of June had been a disaster for Silverside Brokers.

They had worked over the weekend together. Debra had finally given permission for the shares of 'Six Weeks in Summer' to be sold. Craig had persuaded Matthew to buy the whole thirty million shares on offer because he was concerned that other competitors might try to get in on the act once the market place became aware of the deal. Matthew had spent three hours with the bank, securing increased facilities for the additional overdraft funds, including giving a second mortgage on his flat.

Debra was ill at ease. Caroline Pennington had turned on the charm and given her a personal promise that all the necessary documentation would be delivered by courier on Monday morning. It remained outstanding and Caroline was unavailable for the day. Her mobile phone was turned off and Mark Patterson-Brown was horse racing in France.

Ashtella Khan was in a rage.

It was agreed that the broker's script would be limited to the following statements:

*This is a high risk investment and you could lose all your money.*

*It is a British film costing £5.4 million together with £600,000 for marketing costs, a total of £6 million. Of this £3 million have been raised.*

*The company will receive a UK Government tax credit thought to be worth £800,000.*

*These are the names of the producer, director and casting director: we suggest you research them yourself.*

*I can send you a summary of the story. It is a romantic thriller and available on Amazon. There are seven reviews in.*

*I do not want a decision now. I will phone you this afternoon when you've had the opportunity to consider it carefully.*

*I am now going to read you a series of risk warnings. Please listen to them carefully. I will then email them to you.*

Craig had, under pressure, agreed that the selling would be done by his five most experienced brokers. By eleven o'clock mayhem had broken out. Silverside Brokers had not sold a single share. More worryingly, there seemed to be no investor interest.

Matthew convened a meeting in the Board Room at one o'clock. Craig complained about the quality of the sandwiches which had been bought in. He insisted that he and his senior dealer be allowed to have a drink from a bottle of red wine.

Ashtella shouted at him.

"You've broken every single thing Mr Buckingham agreed. You've now got over ten brokers selling the shares. They are all flouting the agreed script. Just listen to this from Jacob Riley.

*"Fantastic opportunity. I've nearly placed all the shares I've been given but I've held back two hundred thousand for you. Risk? It's the next 'Slumdog Millionaire'."*

"You must have misheard him, Lassie," said Craig.

"Craig?" asked Matthew. "Why are we unable to sell the stock?"

The senior dealer spoke first.

"It's early days, Mob. The producer is not well known. Despite what Ashtella is saying we are only contacting our very wealthy clients and they inevitably do their own research. One of mine was back in an hour saying he could not satisfy himself on the director."

"To add to that, Mob," continued Craig, "the film industry has been hit by the scandals of these tax schemes. You may remember it was the first thing I said."

"You also ended up in raptures about the deal," said Debra, "and made my life a misery until I agreed to let you sell the shares."

"Debbie…"

"Don't call me Debbie. It's Debra."

"Debra. You make a good point." Craig turned to Matthew. "We'll carry on this afternoon but I think we're going to have to put on investor presentations and allow our clients to meet the people involved. That Amanda will go down well."

By the end of the day they had sold one hundred thousand shares and Ashtella was challenging that transaction.

Matthew sat alone in his office and wondered about cancelling his evening with Jessica. She often chose to stay at her place on a Monday and complete her washing. But the weekend was dominated by her seemingly wanting to get closer to him. They had discussed the film deal and she had told Matthew he was gambling.

He thought again of her mother.

*On such a full sea are we now afloat,*
*And we must take the current when it serves,*
*Or lose our ventures.*

He kicked the table.

"Sod Brutus," he shouted. "Fuck! They must sell those shares tomorrow."

It was at this moment in time that he thought about a way to offset the risk his firm was taking. He was proposing to meet with one of the few women who could intimidate him. He made a phone call and an hour later he was sitting in the lounge of the Chancery Court Hotel in Holborn sipping champagne.

"Sam," he began. "Can I say how gorgeous you are looking…"

"No, Matthew, you can't. You only charm females for two reasons. What mess are you in this time?"

Sam Fullerton was the chief executive and major shareholder in one of the City's most successful stockbroking firms. She had a moneyman behind her but it was generally accepted that it was her flair, hard work and financial ability that had put the business where it was today, despite the recession.

"Sam, I want to offer you an opportunity to make real money."

"Zambezi Mines you sold to us at twelve pence and they are now four."

"We couldn't have known that the roof of the mine would cave in under the flood waters, Sam."

"It's in the middle of the monsoon area. Of course the area would flood."

"You've had three successes from me. Florin Fashions is up over 90 percent."

"Granted. What have you got for me?"

Matthew explained the film proposition and offered her twenty million shares at nine pence. He would sell the other ten million shares at twelve pence to cover his losses.

"That's a good price, Matthew."

"Good, I'll send the…"

She sipped her wine.

"You'll send nothing. I'm not buying them."

"Why. It's a real opportunity to make profit."

She sighed as though she was dealing with a naughty school-boy.

"Craig has already been on to us. Your presentation is good."

"You'll buy ten million shares?" he pleaded.

"I'll purchase nothing." She looked at him seriously. "Matthew. You need to get a grip of your compliance procedures. We have knowledge that one of the directors is, shall we say, questionable."

"What does that mean, Sam?"

"It tells you that my firm will have nothing to do with your Six Weeks in Summer company." She left soon after leaving Matthew to ponder on their conversation. He reasoned to himself that her cash flow might be tight and she was just making excuses. On the other hand she just might have some intelligence that he would dearly love to know.

# Chapter Eight

No Great Train Robber better disabuses the media's glorification of the event than James (Jimmie) White. He was born on 21 February 1920 and was therefore the oldest member of the gang. He was athletic, energetic, competent and reflected his military background by sporting a neatly trimmed moustache. He was invalided out of the army due to stomach complaints in 1944. He subsequently felt betrayed by his country because his pension was cut and then stopped altogether. He became a café owner near to Smithfield Market in London and a small-time crook.

It was Jimmie White who was the quartermaster for the robbery and obtained the three vehicles used to transport the mailbags from Bridego Bridge to Leatherslade Farm. He fled from there to London and then purchased a caravan at Clovelly Site near Dorking. He continually changed locations and found that the criminal world was extracting significant amounts of money to protect him. Leaving his partner and daughter in the south, he went first to Mansfield and then purchased Crown Edge Farm in Glossop. In July 1965 he moved again to Littlestone-on-Sea on the Kent Coast.

In April 1966 he sold his story to *Stern* magazine in Germany. This led, on 21 April 1966, to his arrest by Detective Sergeant Jack Slipper to whom he said, "I'm glad it's all over." He was taken to London where Tommy Butler transported him to Aylesbury for his official arrest. He was tried on 16 June 1966, pleaded guilty to robbery, and went to prison for eighteen years. He was released in April 1975, went to live in Sussex and was never heard of again.

* * *

Three weeks had passed since Jessica made the decision to introduce Matthew to her mother. Much to his surprise Mrs Lambert had started to text him. He adopted the routine of not replying immediately but he never failed to send a thoughtful, and sometimes, amusing response with the occasional Shakespearean reference.

At this moment in time he knew that she had sent him a reply to his last message. It had contained a play on words spoken by Hamlet referring to 'hoist with his own petar.' As a canon was now blowing up in his face he did not have time to read her words.

Jessica had been quiet and sullen ever since they had booked in at the Blakeney Manor Hotel. They had agreed two nights earlier that they needed to talk. The next morning she had made a phone call advising her bank that she was unwell. This was a first for her as she had never before phoned in sick unless she really was ill and she felt a pang of guilt as she spoke to one of her colleagues. She insisted that Matthew told his office that he'd be away for two days and she had then driven him up the A11 to the north Norfolk coast. She also locked his mobile phone in her bag, allowing him just one stop to check his calls. She didn't want the ping of the phone interrupting them every time an email came in.

The hotel was ideal and Jessica admitted they were fortunate to find a room in late July. Matthew loved the pebbled courtyards, the spacious bar and lounge areas and the bedroom with a view over the marshes. Once they had unpacked, Matthew put his arms round Jessica and gave her a huge hug.

"Thank you for this," he said waving his arms round the room, "it's perfect."

He grabbed her wrist and pulled her over to the bed where they flopped on to it. He gave her a long lingering kiss and made slow passionate love to her. Later on they wandered into the lounge and, as Jessica had seen something she fancied on the snack menu, they decided to eat in the bar where it was less formal.

They went for a short walk down to the harbour and then strolled slowly back to their room and watched late night television until they found themselves drifting off to sleep. Morning came with the sound of the dawn chorus. They again made love before going over to the restaurant where they ate a full English breakfast.

It was a lovely warm sunny day and they decided to go for a walk. They changed into their shorts and tops and walked down to the harbour where they read that there was a sea trip due to depart shortly to view the seals. They managed to board the 9.30 a.m. boat. As the twelve-seater *Lily-Too* ploughed its way out to Blakeney Point a voice talked about the common and grey seals. The pups swam around the boat watched by their attentive parents. Their guide pointed out the oyster catchers and the ringed plover. For an hour Matthew and Jessica were able to forget their tensions.

In the early afternoon they found themselves alone in the middle of the fens.

"Why are we here, Jessie?" asked Matthew.

"We agreed that we need to talk."

"That's not what I asked," he snapped. "It's not the bloody answer to my question as far as I'm concerned."

They climbed over a stile and he managed to trap his finger in the iron bracket. Jessica ignored his cry of anguish.

"You know exactly what I'm asking, Jessie." He paused as a couple with an excited Labrador puppy passed them. "Why are we here in Blakeney Point? You just happened to choose it, did you?"

She turned and faced him. She was not smiling. At that moment he thought how beautiful she seemed even when angry.

"I was here just over a year ago with Ian. He organised a surprise weekend for us. He's an associate editor on one of the broadsheets and it was difficult for him to get time off. We had an amazing time until the last evening. It was always the same with him."

They carried on walking and were distracted by several birds playing at the water's edge. Neither of them had any idea what species they were but their attention was briefly diverted. Jessica took out the suntan lotion and rubbed some into Matthew's face and upper body. He rather enjoyed it when she applied it to the back of his legs. He returned the gesture and she allowed him to give special attention to her chest despite the fact the solar rays were unlikely to penetrate her white t-shirt.

"So what did Ian do that upset you?" asked Matthew with a hint of sarcasm.

"He didn't do anything specific. There was a girl in the bar in the evening. She couldn't have been more than twenty-two or three. She was quite pretty and she had all the right equipment. He could not take his eyes off her and she played up to him. She was sitting on a high bar stool and she managed to show a lot of herself every time he went to get drinks. I was never sure but I think he met her outside later in the evening."

She wiped the corner of her eye.

"Ian was everything I ever wanted, Mob. We were just great together. But I never fully trusted him. He couldn't stop flirting with other women."

"What's wrong with that? The day I stop undressing the ladies in my mind's eye is the time you should start worrying."

Jessica laughed and sat down in the grass. She applied some additional cream to her legs and handed Mob a bottle of water.

"You're just randy, Mob. What worried me about Ian was that there was something sinister about his attitude. We split up almost immediately after an incident in the Ritz. I heard later there was a problem at work and it was only because he was so highly rated by his bosses that there was a cover-up and a girl was paid off."

"So you made the right decision?"

"Yes. No doubts there. But I missed him for a long time."

"You said that in the past tense, Jessie."

She was looking at the rows of off-shore wind turbines which were generating electricity and helping to save the planet.

She stood up and walked a few paces away from him. She turned and faced her man.

"I have begun to realise that you're beginning to get under my skin, Mob."

"But you don't want my baby." It was week four and she was not wearing a patch.

100

"Sex is fine thanks."

"And you won't come and meet Olivia."

"It's too soon, Mob."

"So why are we here Jessie?"

"Because I think I am falling in love with you and I'm pretty sure you have strong feelings for me."

Matthew stood up and moved towards her. He kissed her.

"That's a rather serious thing to say, Jessie."

She kissed him back and, to his surprise, put her hand down his shorts.

"Make love to me, Mob. Now. Please. There's no-one for miles."

They moved over twenty yards into an area covered with long grass and several bushes. He removed her two items of clothing in seconds. She wriggled as she removed a stone from under her and then she lay back and held her arms up towards him. He quickly joined her. Seventeen minutes later she gave a groan of total pleasure. She later realised that she never again thought of Ian.

That evening Matthew chuckled as he sent a longer than usual text to her mother. He had worked out where the quote came from. He searched around until he had a signal. He pressed the send button.

*Ans. The M of V. U r marvellous. In fact can one desire too much of a good thing?*

He guessed that she'd know immediately that the words came from 'As You Like It.'

Mrs Lambert was not to realise that at that moment in time Mob liked her daughter very much indeed.

Matthew Orlando Buckingham was falling headlong in love with a dark-haired and beautiful woman called Jessica.

And she was in deep over him.

\* \* \*

It had been decided to stop the sale of shares in 'Six Weeks in Summer'. The tensions were mounting at Silverside Brokers as the brokers, at the end of the following week, had sold around three hundred thousand to five different clients. Ashtella Khan was challenging two of the transactions and she and Debra White were spending their time listening to the tapes of the phone calls.

There was an individual called Harry Redstone. He was one of the most popular members of Craig MacDonald's team. He was good looking, played football to near professional level and was generous in the pub, particularly if the girls were around. That was his problem. Harry had married young and now had three children and a lovely wife. He was up to his eyes in debt. His ability to pay his monthly mortgage depended upon his commission earnings. Each night when he arrived home, although this was also an issue as he was getting later and later, Petrona Redstone would search his face for signs. The rows were getting worse and the credit cards were reaching their limits.

"Debbie, you need to hear the whole of this call," said Ashtella. "It took place at around two-fifty this afternoon. The client is a retired dentist who we have classified as an experienced investor. He has a portfolio of around half a million pounds with us. He has traded seven times this year. He is about 8 percent up."

"He sounds right for 'Six Weeks in Summer', Ashtella."

"Debbie. Hear this. Please." She pressed the start button on the tape. The opening sentences had not recorded well but it was soon clear that Harry was talking about the shares.

Harry: "Congratulations on your stock selections, Mr Wallis. You are one of my most successful clients."

Mr Wallis: "At my level of gains, Harry, you can't have many. Do you know what's the rate of inflation?"

There is the sound of laughter between them.

"Seriously, Mr Wallis. I've got the deal for you that will propel you to the top of the list."

Debra turned pale with anger and Ashtella gripped the side of the table.

Mr Wallis: "You said that about, what did you call it, the fracking exploitation business. Blowing up rocks to find oil. I paid five pence a share and they're now four. I know you're not very good with numbers, Harry, but that's 20 percent down. If I'd been as gung ho with my patients' teeth I'd have been banned. How are your children by the way?"

Harry: "Thanks for asking, Mr Wallis. Pettie is fine but my youngest needs an operation. She's got a twisted intestine. Eight weeks waiting on the NHS and I can't afford it privately."

Debra was now standing up and banging her hand on the side of her chair.

"It gets worse, Debbie," said Ashtella.

Mr Wallis: "Surely Harry that's an emergency. The doctors won't let a young child suffer?"

Harry: "That's what I said to the doctor. She said it might cure itself naturally and it was a simple operation. Mr Wallis, you should hear my daughter screaming at night."

Mr Wallis: "Can I help you, Harry?"

"I simply don't believe this," said Debra.

"It gets worse, Debbie," repeated Ashtella.

Harry: "Thanks. I'll sort it out. I never let my family down. Can I tell you about these shares please, Mr Wallis?"

Mr Wallis: "You've chosen the right day, Harry. I've had a tax rebate from the Revenue. It's already in the bank."

Debra and Ashtella looked at each other. The next three minutes were taken up with Harry explaining the investment proposal. Every word he spoke was exactly in line with the agreed script.

Mr Wallis: "You're bloody good, you are, Harry. I'll give you that. You could sell Ed Miliband to me, you could."

Harry: "I'm not that good, Mr Wallis! When did you say you met David Cameron?"

The next few minutes were taken up with Mr Wallis recounting his years as chairman of the local Conservative Association. He explained why party membership was falling. Harry was just about to say that the union links were hurting his local Labour recruiting campaign when he managed to stop himself.

Harry: "The Conservatives are lucky to have members like you, Mr Wallis."

Mr Wallis: "Nonsense. But thank you, Harry. I have put in years of service and quite a lot of money. We must stop this Farage bloke."

Harry: "Mr Wallis, I'm emailing you a list of risk warnings. You must read them."

Mr Wallis: "You do that every time, Harry. I hope I'm not taking up too much of your time. You must have other people to talk to about these shares."

Harry: "I do, Mr Wallis. There's a lot of demand for them."

Debra hit the panic buttons.

Harry: "But you are my most important client, Mr Wallis and I want your shares soaring in value. How much did the Revenue send you?"

"You can't do that you stupid bastard," yelled Debra.

Mr Wallis: "I'm glad you asked me that, Harry. I argued the case with my accountant on the sale of a property. I said we had overpaid the tax in the previous year. It was in my name and I transferred it into joint names to get all my wife's allowances. He had said 'No, it's tax evasion' and I said 'Yes, it's tax avoidance.' I was right. We asked the Revenue for a review and we won. We received a rebate of £98,666."

Harry: "Congratulations, Mr Wallis. You should sack your accountant."

Mr Wallis: "I have, Harry. Tell me. How much commission do you make if I buy £50,000 worth of these film shares?"

Harry: "That's a lot of money, Mr Wallis. I was thinking perhaps ten or twenty thousand."

Debra and Ashtella looked at each other and nodded.

Mr Wallis: "How much commission do you make on £50,000, Harry?"

Harry: "If you pay 12 pence each for the shares?"

Mr Wallis: "That's possible. What did you pay? Ten pence? So you're making £8,000 and I guess you'll get 50 percent so you'll make £4,000."

Harry: "That doesn't matter to me, Mr Wallis. All I want…"

Mr Wallis: "Harry. Stop it. How much is your daughter's operation costing?"

Harry: "We're waiting for the NHS, Mr Wallis."

Mr Wallis: "How much, Harry?"

Harry: "£7,400."

Debra looked down. "You've just lost your job, Harry," she said in a quiet voice.

Mr Wallis: "I'll spend £80,000, Harry. Send me the contract."

Harry: "But the risk warnings, Mr Wallis."

Mr Wallis: "I like the story. I've been googling the director. He's good. It's enterprise investment scheme and my wife and I are selling another property. I'll get full loss relief if it fails. And I get inheritance tax relief and my children can't wait to hear my will. But there is a condition, Harry."

Harry: "I don't do conditions, Mr Wallis."

Mr Wallis. "You get that intestine untwisted tomorrow. And change your doctor. It's a very serious condition." He paused. "I hope that you're listening to me. I'm waiting for your document, Harry."

At six o'clock that evening Harry Redstone was fighting for his life.

"Craig. Mr Buckingham. I did nothing wrong. I stuck to the script. He asked me about my family. We build relationships with our clients. The only half truth I told was about the Conservative party."

"It were a grit sale laddie. Well dun."

Debra exploded.

"It broke every rule in the book, Mr Buckingham. You never bring in personal matters. If the regulator listens to that tape they will discipline me."

"Harry," said Matthew. "Tell me about your daughter. I don't get it. Surely a twisted intestine is an emergency. That's certainly what Mr Wallis thought."

"It's hopeless, Mr Buckingham. Pettie spends half her life trying to get appointments. When we get there we never see the same doctor. We've had three different diagnoses. They interpret the hospital report in different ways."

"Did you say anything to Mr Wallis that was not true?"

"I wasn't at the last appointment because I was trying to sell these shares. I think Pettie might have exaggerated a bit. Things are a bit rough at home. But Estelle needs an operation and there is a two month wait. Pettie phoned the local clinic. They'll do it within three days for £7,400."

"You can't do this," shouted Debra.

"Shut up," ordered Matthew. "Craig. You are Harry's boss. Do you think that Mr Wallis was influenced by what Harry told him about the operation?"

"Not a chance, Mob. He's an experienced investor. He obviously likes Harry and if you listen, particularly you, Miss Sherlock Holmes White, you'll hear Mr Wallis talking about himself. He's lonely. Many of them are. They love talking to Harry. This was a fair trade."

"It's a breach of regulations," said Debra. "Isn't it, Ashtella?"

"Harry. Go home and book the operation."

Harry looked at Mob in total amazement. Debra looked daggers.

"Harry. I am transferring £7,400 from my personal bank funds to your account tonight: text me the details. Craig. You will telephone Mr Wallis tomorrow to thank him for his purchase. I want it limited to £25,000. You will also tell him that Harry will be able to save his commission as his family have found the money. I want it on file that Mr Wallis knows his commission is not needed to pay for Estelle's operation."

As they left the building Craig asked Harry if he fancied a pint. But Harry was already heading for the Tube train and home.

Later that night Matthew told Jessica the whole story. As they rolled over in bed Jessica squeezed him as tightly as she could.

"Matthew. You are truly a wonderful man."

Matthew's hand was travelling upwards.

"Just one thing, Mob," said Jessie. "You haven't got £7,000. You haven't even got 7,000 pennies."

Matthew's hand reached its destination.

"Do you know a friendly bank manager, Jessie?" he asked as she moaned with pleasure.

\* \* \*

DCI Rudd was spending hours, often late into the evening, making herself visible on the streets of Islington. She chatted to the shopkeepers and emphasised how the peace of the community so helped their businesses and, even better, their daily lives. She turned a blind eye to minor offences and watched the white vans bring in contraband. She spoke severely to the minor drug pushers but made no arrests. She cleaned up the drunks, bought the hungry kids snack meals, showed her medal when asked and always had time to tell the story of her rescue of the Duchess of Cambridge in The Mall. She speculated with the women as to the gender of the royal baby.

On one occasion she had been delayed by a mother who was trying to get her child to hospital. The ambulance was not appearing and it was clear that the spots on the face of the baby were worrying. Sarah, breaking the rules, called in a police car and dispatched the mother and child to the hospital. The later diagnosis was an allergy but that did not matter. The community saw what she did.

She now found herself passing a less-than-reputable public house. Two late night drinkers came out and started molesting her. She was well able to cope with these situations but began to realise that this was a little more serious. She went for her taser gun and found that her arms were pinned to her side. She then felt a blow to the side of her head.

There was a shout and suddenly a group of around five black men and women came from nowhere. The two assailants were removed from the scene and taken down a nearby passageway.

"Don't hurt them," Sarah instructed but her plea for leniency went unheard. In the early hours of the next morning two damaged youths attended A&E requiring help with their broken bones.

The first serious breakthrough in her search for information came in the back of an all-night convenience shop in a side street of Islington. An anonymous call had been made to her mobile phone.

DCI Rudd had been told to arrive at nine thirty-five in the evening and in plain clothes. She knew the owners well and they both nodded as she went alone into the back. They called her back and asked her to leave her phone with them. She felt herself being patted down.

In the stockroom there was a man. He was making sure that his face was concealed. He smelt of eastern odours. He seemed nervous.

"I need to know your name."

There was no reply.

"I'm leaving now," she said.

"Saleem."

"That's not enough. Saleem what?"

There was a noise behind her and she realised that the door had been closed. She now regretted not following standard procedure and telling her office where she was going. But her instinct took over and she had decided to follow the injunction to go alone.

"Saleem what?"

"They aim to kill four hundred people."

"Who do?"

"In a few weeks."

"Where?"

"You'll not stop them."

"Saleem. Please tell me what you want. You are putting yourself in great danger."

He stood up from the box he was sitting on and exposed his face.

"You are the police person who won the medal. I'm told I can trust you."

"Saleem. Please tell me what you know."

"I need a promise."

"No."

"You can't tell anyone."

"You know I have to."

"We know everything that goes on in the station office."

"No you don't."

"There are two of them. One takes money. One is scared."

"Name me the one receiving bribes."

Saleem did just that and DCI Rudd then knew he was for

real. He had given her a name she had been watching herself. 'That makes things rather tricky,' she said to herself.

"I can't make the promise you need Saleem," she continued.

"In that case you will be buried under the concrete."

"I'll take that risk. Four hundred people. That must be a building. What are you planning to blow up, Saleem?"

"No. That's a risk. This is better planned. We are certain to kill that number."

"Saleem. You are fantasising. Nobody can do that."

"We did it. 9/11 Detective Chief Inspector Rudd. We can do anything."

"So it's in America."

"Our brothers over there fail every time. We will show them."

"London."

"No."

"Saleem. Please tell me what you want to tell me. Why are you here?"

"He's fucking my sister."

"Who is?"

"Rashid."

"And you'll tell me about the plot just because of that?"

Saleem shouted out in a foreign language. He banged on the door and was gone.

"Damn," said DCI Rudd. She put her head in her hands and shook.

"You've let your son and your family down and now you've blown finding out about a terrorist threat."

She slammed her hand against her side.

"You'd better give that bloody medal back you pathetic woman," she said to herself.

# Chapter Nine

The 1988 British comedy-drama film 'Buster' featured Phil Collins as a loveable rogue.

Buster Edwards, one of the Great Train Robbers, was five foot six inches tall, tended to be overweight and was a boxer who carried his violent nature before him. He was born on 27 January 1931 in Lambeth. When not running his drinking club he was a petty criminal. He was involved in the BOAC wages snatch in 1962.

After taking part in the robbery he fled to Mexico. He exhausted his funds and became homesick. He returned to England and was arrested on 19 September 1966. He was sentenced to fifteen years imprisonment for conspiracy to rob and twelve years for robbery. He spent nine years in his cell and was released in 1975.

He then ran a flower stall outside Waterloo Station. He died on 28 November 1994. He had committed suicide by hanging himself from a steel girder inside a lock-up garage in Lambeth. He had been drinking very heavily. At the time of his death he was being investigated by the police as part of a large-scale fraud inquiry. His wife June and their daughter Nicky survived him.

The film 'Buster' included the song 'Two Hearts' which had the following lyrics:

*Two hearts, believing in just one mind*
*Beating together till the end of time*
*You know we're two hearts believing in just one mind*
*Together forever till the end of time.*

\* \* \*

The decision which Jessica made on a Saturday in August was to have devastating consequences for her relationship with Matthew. She had not been too perturbed by his oft repeated suggestion that she should meet his daughter. She had resisted even though she realised that it mattered to him. Eventually she agreed. Perhaps the summer sunshine affected her and the thought of a proposed picnic on Dunstable Downs seemed irresistible. They left after a late breakfast and arrived at Ledburn just after eleven-thirty. She had seen photographs of the solicitor's smallholding but the driveway to the front door was impressive. She knew that the girl waving from the animal sanctuary was Olivia.

Even before they had parked the car Anne came hurtling out of the front door holding Thomas in her arms.

"Matthew," she shouted. "John's been taken ill at the golf club. Please stay here until I get back."

As Jessica exited the passenger side Anne rushed round and thrust the baby into her arms.

"Olivia knows what to do," she said. She jumped into her car and drove rapidly down the drive and turned left. She joined the ring road and, to avoid the town traffic, she travelled north. She reached the A4146 to Milton Keynes but turned right down the Stoke Road towards the golf club.

Jessica looked at the howling baby in her arms and realised that he needed a change of nappy. Olivia was now with her father and waved a hand at her. They went inside the house and into the kitchen: it looked as if a bomb had hit it.

"Can you change Thomas please Olivia?" she asked.

The shake of the head was firm and so Jessica suggested the two of them start clearing up the mess.

"Olivia. Please can you do the washing-up while your father collects the dishes. Matthew, open the door and the windows. This place needs some fresh air."

He was holding a glass to his nose and frowning. Olivia was sitting at the table with her head in her hands. She moved closer to her father. Slowly they began to move the unwashed plates into the sink. The waste bin needed emptying. Matthew slipped on some grease and banged his knee. Olivia watched him.

"Time for a coffee," he announced but he could not find the kettle. Eventually it was located under a black bin liner. He looked up to see that Jessica had returned to the kitchen with a grave expression on her face.

"Olivia. I want you to go to your room. Shut the door and stay there until your father comes to get you. Will you agree to that?"

She nodded her head and climbed the stairs to the first floor. They heard the door shut.

Jessica located the telephone on the wall of the kitchen and made a call. Matthew stared open-mouthed as he listened to her side of the call.

"Ambulance and police. It's very urgent. A young child. I'm at The Laurels, Ledburn. My name is Jessica Lambert. No, the parents are not here. Are you on your way?"

She put the phone on the side table. She told Matthew to follow her. She opened the front door as wide as she could and then went up the stairs. They entered a room and looked down into the cot where Thomas was screaming. He had no clothes on. There was a savage red mark on his upper left arm. There were bruises on his ribs.

Matthew yelled out several expletives.

"No, Mob. Don't pick him up. I can't be sure what the injuries are. Leave him be. Go and wait for the police."

The paramedic arrived first followed almost immediately by a police car. Within minutes the ambulance arrived. The senior police officer took charge and ordered Jessica and Matthew into the kitchen. Matthew asked that he be allowed to collect Olivia. The police refused and waited until a second vehicle arrived. A public protection officer rushed upstairs and disappeared into Olivia's bedroom.

Thomas was taken away in the ambulance and, as soon as the vehicle exited the driveway, Olivia appeared in the hallway led by the police officer.

"Just show me where please, Olivia," she asked.

The frightened girl went into a cupboard and rummaged in the back. She reappeared with two full bottles of vodka. During the next ten minutes which involved visits to the garage, the

113

den and the animal sanctuary a total of eleven full bottles and several empty ones were collected.

Matthew looked at his daughter.

"Why didn't you tell me?" he pleaded.

The officer said that they were taking Olivia away and placing her in care. Matthew said that he was her father and he wished to exercise his rights.

"At this moment in time, Mr Buckingham, you have no rights at all."

He and Jessica were taken to Dunstable Police Station. New officers appeared and announced their names and ranks. They asked for full statements which were taken down in separate rooms. Six hours later Matthew found himself in a new interview room with Detective Constable Barnes.

"That's a rather impressive woman you have with you, Mr Buckingham. She's waiting for you in the reception area. You'll be free to go shortly."

DC Barnes explained that Mr Sneddon's 'heart attack' was, in fact, a severe case of gastric wind. Thomas was dehydrated and had been assaulted: the injuries were recent and probably inflicted within the last twenty-four hours. Both the parents had been arrested and were being held overnight. He realised that Olivia was Matthew's daughter but she was being cared for in a special home and would be examined the next day by the child care consultant."

"Why?" asked Matthew. "How could any human being do that to a young child?"

DC Barnes decided not to educate the troubled man on the state of British society. He had, earlier that day, arrested a father for crimes which even he found hard to stomach.

"It's early days, Mr Buckingham. We'll get to the bottom of things but drink and marriage problems seem to be present in this case." He then went on to explain what Olivia had been telling them. Matthew stood open mouthed at what he heard.

"But that can't be right. I would have known."

"It doesn't work that way," explained DC Barnes. "Those closest are often the last to understand."

They spoke for a few more minutes and then Matthew left

the office and went down the stairs to the reception. Jessica stood up and wrapped her arms around him.

As they walked to the car Jessica turned to Matthew.

"Gastric juices like hell. Fucking soaked in vodka and then attacks his son. Bastard."

Jessica stood by the wall. She was trembling with anger.

"Mob," she cried. "I'll never, ever, forget those marks on his body. They were vivid, Mob."

Matthew stopped as they reached his vehicle.

"Thomas will forget them, Jessie. Young children have great powers of recovery." He sighed. "You keep telling me I'm the greatest lover in the world, Jessie. You watch me now. I'll give that little boy more love than anyone has ever had before."

She looked at her partner. There were so many questions to be asked and answered. She knew that when Matthew Orlando Buckingham was focused anything was possible.

"Vodka," she said. "Ask the Russians. The most dangerous drink in the world."

They drove away from Dunstable and quickly reached Ledburn. As the car slowed in the driveway of John Sneddon's home Matthew turned and faced her.

"You're right about the vodka, Jessie. There's just one problem."

"You make excuses for him Matthew and we're finished. I'll get the train back to London. Did you see his arm, Mob? It was broken."

"Probably just bruising, Jessie, but there is something you need to know."

He looked at her rather intensely.

"The vodka had been drunk by my ex-wife."

\* \* \*

The row between Nick and Sarah Rudd exploded on the Saturday afternoon when their two children were at either birthday parties or sporting events. Unusually Nick had opened a second lunchtime bottle of wine having already put the car away in the garage.

They were in the garden finishing off their barbecue which featured burnt sausages and undercooked steak. Sarah was scruffy and had turned off her phones.

The touch paper was a glass of water which she managed to knock over and down onto his legs.

"Nice to know that the security of Britain is in the hands of dithering, ageing police officers."

Sarah pondered on the word 'ageing'. She had been to see her doctor who'd said that she was a few months into her menopause. He'd explained how quite naturally her ovaries had stopped working. He'd checked her over and decided to refer her for an examination of her chest area.

"You're forty-four years old Mrs Rudd. Overall you are in good health but we both know that you have taken several brutal beatings in your career. I'm not satisfied that your bone structure in your upper body is fully recovered. The bullet you took in The Mall hit you at a fearful velocity."

Sarah would have liked to ask him about the grey hairs which were appearing and how best to conceal them.

"There is also another small problem which I noticed when I examined you. I'll give you a prescription and the rash should clear within ten days. Please come back if it persists." Her doctor's words faded as she returned to the sound of Nick's voice.

"He's stopped, Sarah."

"I was scared to ask."

"You were very good with him. You were his mother. He's not taken any more substances as far as we know."

Sarah looked at her husband.

"Do we have a problem, Nick?"

He poured himself a glass of Merlot: the supermarket's special offer of the week.

"No. You do."

He paused and quickly drank nearly half the glass.

"If it helps I like women with grey hair."

She was open mouthed.

"Sarah. I work with a lot of women. You're going through the change, aren't you?"

She told him of her appointment with the doctor. For some reason Nick focused on the chest injuries. He wanted to know when her appointment came through. He would go with her to the hospital. He would be asking the specialist for a full report.

The next twenty minutes were spent with each of them lost in their individual thoughts and occasional small talk. Nick made a flask of fresh orange juice and poured them both full glasses.

"You'll tell me in the end, Sarah," he said.

She looked at him. She'd been inside the house to check her phones. Their daughter had texted Nick to ask for an extension which was agreed. This then became a sleepover which Nick also approved: he knew the parents well. Sarah wondered why her daughter had not asked for her permission.

"Nick," she said. "I think I've blown my career."

He felt a massive sense of relief. It was not about them. He stayed silent.

"You might not want to hear what I'm going to tell you. It could put you in personal danger."

He stood up and took her hand. They walked to the bottom of their garden and watched the river traffic four hundred yards away. There were planes heading for Heathrow but very little birdsong.

They sat down in the long grass and she began to tell him the whole story. He let her talk without any interruption. Finally she completed her story.

"Saleem. Do you know who he is?"

"I've been back to the shop several times. They're scared and I suspect that they're being intimidated."

"And Rashid?"

"He's local but I need help to find him."

"You must talk to D/Supt Khan."

"He'll suspend me. I committed a serious breach of the rules by going alone into the meeting with Saleem."

"Why did you do that, Sarah?"

She stood up and brushed down her clothing. She then sat down again.

"Gut feeling, Nick," she said. "We're always getting threats and every one has to be investigated."

"So why break the rules? I don't understand."

"Because…" She hesitated. "Because my whole being tells me this is for real. I think they're planning to kill four hundred innocent people."

She again hesitated.

"Nick. There's another issue. What Saleem said to me. There have been rumours in the station that there's an officer on the make. The whispers are that it's at a senior level. It's rare but it can happen. A number of police officers spend their lives in financial difficulty. If it's known that Saleem is talking to me the terrorists will be told and he will die."

"You have to find him."

"Or her. Not on my own, Nick."

"But you're in danger, Sarah."

"I have Her Majesty the Queen to protect me, Nick," she laughed.

"Pardon?"

"The medal, Nick. I'm a hero. Even the bad guys know that if anything happens to me the force will wipe them out. I'm a 'trophy' officer."

"We need a plan."

"Will you help me, Nick?"

"How?"

"I'll tell you the whole story from the start. You'll write it all down and we'll put together every piece of information that we have."

"What happens then?"

"How many glasses of wine did you drink with your lunch?"

He pondered her question.

"Six, five, seven. Does it matter?"

"Every little detail matters. Somewhere there is a clue and you're going to help me find it, Nick."

* * *

118

Seated in the back row of the traders based at Silverside Brokers was a young woman called Sabina Morina. Her mother still lived in Southern Italy. Sabina had come to the United Kingdom seven years ago and graduated at the London School of Economics. Her mother had chosen her name because it meant 'blonde or fair-haired'. The world of finance dazzled her and after two periods at different corporate brokerages she was finding her feet with Craig MacDonald who she adored.

Sabina was attractive with a 'buona giornata' vivacity and a 'buona serata' seductive style. She also had a set of rules: it was always 'buonanotte': no involvement at work (there was a man in Muswell Hill who attended to that matter), no alcohol in trading hours, total honesty at all times and she worked long hours. She read every research note she could find.

She had not been included in the original programme of approved dealers for the selling of shares in 'Six Weeks in Summer'. She had watched, listened, grimaced and researched. One evening she took Craig out and ensured that he consumed considerable amounts of malt whisky. The next day she was added to the list.

Seventy-two hours later she was in the offices of a private fund which specialised in higher risk investments. It was run by two cousins known in the City as the 'Pretty Pair'. The elder one, Jonathan Pretty, was the front man and his younger colleague was the son of his aunt. Roger Pretty was the brains.

Jonathan was a libidinous individual who assessed people and who had built up a seriously successful track record for sound judgements. His exploits with women were well known in the Square Mile. Roger had an honours degree from Cambridge University and was pragmatically astute with his investments. His 'return on capital employed' (the City mantra meaning 'how much dosh have you made, buddy?') was 'top ten' territory. He used his substantial bonuses to collect paintings by modern artists. He was rather successful at that, as well. Work hard, play hard: the City doctrine.

Sabina turned it on for them. It was August and very warm. She wore a knee-length tight-fitting, mainly white dress which was tinged with green to protect her modesty. It still left little to the imagination. She had on sandals and not much else. She had been to the salon the evening before and had her nails manicured and also a pedicure showing off her brightly-coloured toe-nails. She wore her almost white hair long. The perfume had been selected for her by a male friend back in Italy. He would send her bottles through the post every so often.

She deliberately made excuses that she could only see them after six o'clock. She wanted the Pretty Pair to be into their second bottle of wine. She sipped her glass of water. She had been up nearly all night planning her presentation. She made no gestures whatsoever. She simply sat in front of them, just once shaking her hair. Roger decided that he did not know where to look and Jonathan's concentration was on the beautiful young woman in front of him.

"Right," Sabina announced. "Let's cut out the crap."

Jonathan was mentally undressing her and Roger was trying to read the briefing notes she had presented to them.

"We don't want to talk about tax reliefs, do we? Put your hand up if you agree."

Two hands went up in the air and Jonathan imagined his hand going up somewhere else.

"Good. We don't want to spend hours with me telling you what a fantastic opportunity this is. What a great film it's going to be. The details of the producer, the director, the casting director, the actors, the scriptwriter and so on. Put your hand up if you agree?"

Roger carried on reading the notes, not daring to look at their visitor. Jonathan was trying to wipe the sweat from his forehead without her noticing. Two hands zoomed upwards.

Sabina decided to omit the next question as the fund managers were now both in a state of hypnosis. It was already time to strike.

"So why are we here?" she asked. "The answer comprises one word."

Both Jonathan and Roger thought of differing options.

"Profit, gentlemen. That is why I'm here."

She decided not to let them rest.

"Roger, I'll talk to you. Jonathan is wondering whether he stands any chance of a night out with me. The answer is about 20 percent. Roger, do you agree we should talk about profit?"

Jonathan was feeling encouraged. A one in five chance now, whereas for the previous year she had rejected all his suggestions and advances.

"Roger. I asked you a question."

He looked at her with a growing fondness.

"Sabina. Please tell me about profit."

"That, Roger, is the correct statement. Please may I have a glass of wine?"

Jonathan decided that this upped the odds perhaps to two in five. He never noticed that she never touched the alcohol during the next hour spent in their offices.

"Roger. The film generates £20 million of revenues. You'll have done your research. You'll have looked at 'Slum Dog Millionaire' and similar movies. It's probably an under-estimation but I want us to be cautious."

"You'll not get £20 million without American cinema, Sabina."

"Brilliant point, Roger. Here's a letter from their sales agent giving an estimate of a possible order from the US distributor. Happy?"

He read the correspondence while Jonathan noticed that she had the most luxurious nipples.

"We'll agree £20 million takings, Sabina."

"No we won't, Roger. That's my minimum. Read this."

She had prepared an analysis of the top UK produced films in 2012. Five had exceeded £20 million in revenues.

"Five out of the twelve you've selected. I find that persuasive."

"Let's concentrate on… Jonathan, what's the most important word in this room at the moment?" Sabina then stood up, shook her hair, and sat down again. It was a blatant attempt to get his attention and it worked.

"Profit, Jonathan. Not intercourse. Please concentrate on profit. Roger, what percentage will the distributors take?"

"Thirty."

"Correct. Now I want you guys to put in all the money as a loan."

"£3 million."

"£6 million."

"But," said Jonathan, "your documentation is for £3 million."

Sabina drank some water.

"Guys, listen to me. I don't want the Middle Eastern money. Don't like him. The budget is £5.4 million but I want £600,000 for marketing expenditure. You're going to invest £6 million."

Jonathan sensed a chance to dominate her and smiled.

"Got you, you sexy thing," he thought to himself.

"Aren't we forgetting something, Sabina?" he sneered.

'If you'd stopped thinking about your prick and started concentrating, Jonathan, you'd stop falling into my traps,' she thought to herself.

"What might I have omitted, Jonathan? I bow to your greater knowledge."

"The UK tax credit. The government will pay them about £800,000 when the film is completed, regardless of whether it is ever shown."

He was elated. He'd beaten her for once. The odds were now soaring. Perhaps three in five.

"The tax credit will be, according to the accountants, £788,900. Please read this letter." Sabina handed over a piece of paper.

It was from the producer confirming that if an investor puts in £6 million the UK tax credit would be paid to that investor as a bonus.

"Fuck me," exclaimed Jonathan.

'That's your only hope,' thought Sabina to herself. She decided to up the tempo. She pulled out her chair, hitched her dress up a little and then crossed and uncrossed her legs. She lingered just long enough for Jonathan to see a flash of femininity.

"Roger. Profit. There's much more to talk about."

"Is there, Sabina?"

"Follow me through. The film takes £20 million. Less £6 million in distribution costs. That leaves £14 million. The loan, plus a 15 percent uplift, is repaid. That's £6,900,000. That leaves £7,100,000. 50 percent goes to those sharing the profits: producer, director, actors, author and so on. That leaves £3,550,000, which goes to you. That's a return of 87 percent."

The Pretty Pair were now soaked in sweat. Jonathan had become enchanted by her thighs and was imagining her rear. Roger was calculating the actual return on their investment: it was getting better and better.

The meeting ended because Sabina was due in Muswell Hill by nine o'clock. As Jonathan showed her through security and hailed her a taxi he turned and looked at her.

"One in five chance?" he asked.

"Not even that, Jonathan. Sorry."

He watched her being driven away and reached for his mobile. There was always Cathy and she was due to get an almighty surprise later on in the evening.

Four days later Craig MacDonald was found squeezing the life out of Sabina who was hugging him back for all she was worth. The Pretty Pair had spent the whole of the previous day locked in a room with the four directors of Six Weeks in Summer Production Limited. Early that morning they had emailed a confirmation of their loan of £6 million. There were eleven conditions and the executive team at Silverside Brokers had spent the day with Caroline Pennington and the client working out the details. By early evening it was all agreed. The shares were returned to the company who agreed to pay a commission to Silverside Brokers of £400,000 plus a 5 percent profit share in the film.

Matthew emailed his bank cancelling the next day's appointment.

As Sabina walked towards the Tube station she received a text message.

*Hoping for one in five chance? U r sensational. Jx*

She stopped and sat down on a wall. Muswell Hill man was fading. He drank too much and he had a wife. He had said that he would tell her that he was leaving her. But they never do.

*I'm free tomorrow night. U cool. Sx*

Matthew sat at his desk and emailed his confirmation that he was free for dinner and agreed the time and place. The invitation in itself was unusual because his hosts preferred to spend their time elsewhere. He wondered about the legality of the Pretty Pair's loan. The documentation used was the responsibility of the directors of the company. His regulator would not see it that way and, most certainly, nor would Debra. He was still mulling over his conversation with Sam Fullerton.

Matthew had other worries. He had faced obstructions to his suggestion that Jessica should attend the meeting in Aylesbury about Olivia. He had fought hard especially as his partner was so keen to be part of the inquest into his daughter's future. Thomas was recovering but would remain in emergency care before being placed with a long-term foster family.

The commission from the Pretty loan had certainly eased the cash flow pressures and, as is so often the case, Silverside Brokers had picked up another lucrative transaction almost immediately.

"It's like the London buses," Mob thought to himself. "You wait ages for one and then three come together."

He pondered further. Was he in control of events? What was written in the stars?

He decided to text Jessica's mother:

*My fate cries out*
*And makes each petty artery in this body…*
*Complete and source? Mob x*

Almost by return came her response:

*As hardy as the Nemean lion's nerve.*
*Hamlet. Love Mrs L x*

# Chapter Ten

The last of the Great Train Robbers to be captured was Bruce Reynolds. After leaving Leatherslade Farm he flew in a private jet to Ostend and then caught a scheduled flight to Mexico. With his money running out he returned, via Canada, to France and then back to England.

On 8 November 1968 in Torquay, Devon, Detective Chief Superintendent Tommy Butler finally caught the supposed leader of the gang. In reply to his greeting Reynolds said, "C'est la vie." He pleaded guilty to conspiracy to rob (twenty-five years) and robbery (twenty-five years). He was released from prison in 1978. He died on 28 February 2013 aged eighty-one, penniless and living alone.

Reynolds, who was nicknamed 'Napoleon', was a complex character. Essentially he was a criminal. He was a fantasist who probably lied daily to himself. He had expensive tastes and dreamed of the good life. He wore handmade shoes and dined in London's top restaurants. He quoted literature and his *Autobiography of a Thief* was critically acclaimed. He was considered to be the inspiration for Michael Caine's 1965 depiction of fictional spy Harry Palmer in the film 'The Ipcress File'.

Neither he nor any member of the gang has satisfactorily explained one of the conundrums concerning The Great Train Robbery. Why, when the theft itself was so meticulously planned and executed, was their escape so mishandled? Why flee to Leatherslade Farm from where most of the forensic evidence was gathered to convict the accused? Why not simply drive back to their lairs in South London?

If Bruce Reynolds was the leader of the gang he failed completely to plan the getaway so subjecting a life of future misery on many of the Great Train Robbers.

* * *

Within the City's Square Mile the new Governor of the Bank of England, Mark Carney, was promising to keep interest rates low until the country's unemployment fell to below 7 percent.

A few hundred yards away, in the 1776 dining room to the rear of One Lombard, Mark Patterson-Brown was trying to ensure that Matthew's costs were as high as possible. He was being ably assisted by Caroline Pennington who had stopped anticipating the hot waters streaming over her body in the shower of Threadneedles Hotel.

They had selected the Degustation Menu which allowed Philippe, the chef, to demonstrate his culinary skills with the serving of six smaller courses. The objective was, according to the menu, to provide the guests with 'a careful appreciation tasting of various foods'.

Caroline was joining in with gusto. She had selected artichoke, followed by Mazara del Vallo red prawn carpaccio, black truffle risotto, caramalised black cod and mint-crusted fillet of lamb. There was a sixth dish somewhere but the wine was now being served so she decided to wait for a surprise.

Pierre, their host, poured a white Burgundy into their glasses. She sipped the Pouilly Fuisse, Les Crays, Domaine des Vieilles 2010 and sank back into her chair. She thought that Matthew was dishy.

Matthew raised his glass and they shared a celebratory moment. The day before, the funds had arrived in Caroline's client account from the Pretty Pair fund and filming would be starting early the following week.

"Your Sabina Morina sounds quite a girl, Mob," laughed Mark. Caroline froze.

"She's pulled off the big one this time, Mark. She thought outside the box."

"She's not that good," hissed Caroline. "I had to work through all their conditions."

The two men decided to let the solicitor sulk.

The small talk continued through the various courses. Both Mark and Matthew agreed that the economy seemed to be picking up, and the London financial markets were showing signs of life. Caroline quickly brought this to a halt.

126

"Mob, come on. I'm hearing things. Who is Julie?"

Matthew drank some sparkling water and looked at his stunning guest. He had, sometime in the past, asked her out, but he was tipped off that she slept only with Mark Patterson-Brown. This was not true but it deterred him. She had never let Mob forget that she had put him down with a thump. She was a woman who had it, who knew how to use it and who relished rejecting potential suitors. She gave him a 'we know, don't we, that you can't have me' look.

"Julie is the girl in Starbucks who serves me my morning coffee," said Matthew. "I think you are referring to Jessica who is my partner."

Mark roared with laughter. He was now drinking the red wine: a Rhone Valley Chateauneuf du Pape Le Sunard 2007.

"Another in the long line," said Caroline.

"The first in a short queue of one, Caroline," retorted Matthew. "She's rather special."

"So you've got her into bed."

Matthew looked at her.

"Frankly, Caroline, I can't keep her out of bed. But we have so many interests between us, we so enjoy each other's company and we never stop talking about life, that being with Jessie is a privilege. She is very successful in her career but always has time to help me unburden myself about work." He stopped and wiped his mouth with his napkin. "One thing you clearly have to learn, Caroline, is that deeper relationships go beyond physical contact."

'Bugger. She'll be petulant all evening now,' thought Mark to himself.

'Time to spoil your evening Mr Goodiebags,' thought Caroline.

"Thanks for the lecture, Matthew. I'm going to read 'The DUMMIES Guide to Men' before we next meet. But…" she paused, "there is something we feel we should tell you."

Matthew tensed. He was on his guard immediately.

"Nothing to worry about, Matthew. You won't need, what's-her-name, Jackie, to wipe your perspiring brow, but we've lost Amanda Adams-Smythe."

Matthew angered immediately.

"Please explain 'lost'?"

"She went to Paris a week ago to meet a potential actor and his agent. She was due back three days ago. She hasn't been seen since."

"You've spoken to the agent?"

"They had their meeting and all seemed well. They were due to meet in the evening for dinner but she never showed. They assumed she'd lost interest in their client." She paused. "Her phone is switched off, she's not replying to texts and she's not tweeting."

"Have you been to the police?"

"Why? She can do what she wants. She's probably met somebody."

"So why are you so worried?" asked Matthew.

"She's due to get married on Saturday," replied Caroline.

"Did you know about this before you accepted the Pretty Fund's money?" asked Matthew.

"No," said Mark.

"Yes," said Caroline.

"But you have the funds in your client account, Caroline?" Matthew's rhetoric echoed around the building.

"No," she replied.

"Where are the proceeds?"

"I sent them straight off to the company. We received cleared funds from the Pretty's account."

"And have all the conditions of the loan been satisfied?" he asked.

"Yes," said Mark.

"No," said Caroline.

* * *

Matthew and Jessica sat nervously in the Social Services Offices in Aylesbury where the interested parties were meeting to discuss Olivia's future.

"As the law stands, Ms Lambert, you should not be present at this meeting."

Head of Buckinghamshire Social Services, Dame Sheila Smythe-Lyons, had impressed them both with her no-nonsense approach.

"But these are difficult circumstances. I consider it is in Olivia's best interest that she should remain with us."

She smiled and asked those around the table if they agreed with her decision. The doctor nodded, the schoolteacher raised a hand, the three police officers stayed silent, the children's care officer smiled and Matthew put his hand on Jessica's left arm.

"In summary we are focusing on the future care and upbringing of Olivia Buckingham, later to be called Olivia Sneddon, and Thomas Paul Sneddon. Both children have a common mother, Anne Elizabeth Sneddon, previously Anne Elizabeth Buckingham. Olivia's father is Matthew Orlando Buckingham and, of late, her step-father has been John Sneddon. Thomas's parents are Anne and John Sneddon. You, Jessica Lambert, are the partner of Matthew Buckingham, the father of Olivia Sneddon. Does everybody agree with my opening summation?"

There were a few muttered whispers. The senior police officer said that she was happy with the accuracy of the statement.

"We now know that in the last six to nine months Anne Sneddon had been experiencing serious mental health difficulties."

"No," interrupted Dr Hamilton. "Mrs Sneddon was, to all appearances, in good health during her pregnancy and the birth of Thomas which took place without problems at Stoke Mandeville Hospital."

"So there was no evidence of excessive drinking of alcohol?" asked Dame Smythe-Lyons.

"None of the blood tests gave us cause for concern. Of course, with the benefit of hindsight, one or two of the blood counts might have been investigated but as the pregnancy was normal that did not happen."

"So when were you put on notice about a deterioration in Mrs Sneddon's condition?"

"She suffered almost immediate post-natal depression. It's obviously not unusual. I treated her with the usual medication for this illness. She did mention that there were problems with her husband but there was nothing else. I felt no need to follow

129

up apart from encouraging her to come to the surgery every two weeks. I did decide to call at the home which I did when Thomas was eight weeks old. I thought that the place was a mess but the baby was fine and appeared to be in good health, so I left. He was being brought to the surgery for his regular clinic checks."

"Did you see Olivia in that time?"

"No. Olivia hasn't seen a doctor since she had chicken-pox two years ago."

Dame Smythe-Lyons established that Olivia was happy at school and then turned to the senior police officer. Detective Inspector Rosie Adams coughed and then delivered a full and complete review of the case.

"Both parents are under arrest on suspicion of causing grievous bodily harm to Thomas Sneddon. There had been only one obvious assault on the child which had taken place that morning. He sustained bruising to his ribs and a bruised upper left arm which the doctors believe was caused by a strong person shaking the child. Both the parents are saying it was the other." She turned to Jessica.

"If I may say so, Ms Lambert, bearing in mind the circumstances in which you found yourself, you behaved with remarkable presence of mind. You did all the right things."

The Public Protection Officer continued with her statement.

"We now suspect that Mrs Anne Sneddon had started drinking heavily following the birth of Thomas. This is not uncommon. There are a growing number of middle-aged women who seek solace in the bottle. The latest figures we have show that in 2010 there were a hundred and ten thousand, one hundred and twenty-eight alcohol-related hospital admissions for women in England aged between thirty-five and fifty-four. There's a website based organisation called Soberistas and Mrs Sneddon had been in touch with them. Mr Sneddon obviously knew about the problem but failed to understand what his wife needed."

"Did Olivia understand what was going on?"

"Yes. Fortunately she's happy at school and she has her animals. She lives for the visits of her father. Before you beat yourself up Mr Buckingham she didn't say anything to you because she was scared you would stop seeing her."

"Thank you, DI Adams. It's clear that both the parents of Thomas Sneddon are unable to continue in that role. DI Adams, I think you have more to say."

"Yes, Chair. Anne Sneddon is an only child and her parents live in Australia. We have been in touch with the Perth authorities. They are both suffering ill-health and can offer no help. John Sneddon was adopted at birth. There are no relatives available."

"There's me, her biological father," interrupted Matthew.

"We'll come to that, Mr Buckingham." She turned to the children's care officer. "Madeleine, can I have your report please?"

"Ma'am. Olivia is a normal, bright child. She'll be ten years old in two weeks' time. We recommend that it is in her best interests to stay at her present school where she has many friends and, if possible, arrangements can be made so that she lives within the area."

"You, I believe, live and work in London, Mr Buckingham?"

Matthew coughed.

"I've been contacted by a representative of John Sneddon: his solicitor in fact. He met with my legal representatives three days ago. He's offered to transfer The Laurels into Thomas's name and for me to live there and take guardianship of him if I'll live in Ledburn and look after both children. They are siblings. He'll agree never to make contact with Olivia again."

Jessica turned open-mouthed and glared at Matthew.

"Are you mad, what's this about Thomas?" she hissed in his ear.

He turned to her and whispered, "I'd like to be responsible for him. He's Olivia's half-brother."

"But, Mr Buckingham, Thomas needs a mother."

"Yes, Chairman I know. I'm working on that."

* * *

131

Sarah Rudd yawned and announced that she was going to bed.

Nick was at the dining-room table writing copious notes which were the result of their detailed conversations about her contact and the potential terrorist threat.

"I'm almost through," he announced.

"Any clues?"

"Fascinating. I would never have believed that so much can be achieved by thinking through the detail. I'll be ready tomorrow evening to debrief with you." He winked at her.

"There was an interesting development at work today," she said. "We've been told to be extra vigilant."

"That happens all the time, Sarah. They are always giving out announcements at railway stations."

"Yes. It's just that the officer who told us is the one who I think might be the mole."

"I'll tell you one thing, Sarah."

"Tell me now, Miss Marple."

He laughed. "The solution to this will not come from inside Islington Police Station. My hunch is that your 'mole' as you call him…"

"Or her," interrupted Sarah.

"Or her, is being set up."

"Oh. So where do the answers lie, Nick?"

"Although we've talked over the years about murders in Regent's Park, kidnappings in Ealing and assassination attempts in The Mall, I've never before had to solve the crime myself."

"You've worked it out, Nick?" she exclaimed.

"No. But I've managed, I think, to find the key question."

"Which is, please, Nick."

"You'll have to wait. It's necessary to follow through the pathway to the vital unknown point."

"Point?"

"Question." He smiled. "As Mr Hercule Poirot said: 'It is the brain, the little grey cells on which we must rely'."

"And where are your little grey cells taking you, Nick?"

"To a question and a frightening conclusion, Sarah."

* * *

Nine days later Jessica arrived at Leighton Buzzard station to be met by Matthew. They drove immediately to The Laurels. She was amazed by the transformation which had resulted from a firm of house cleaners spending three days renovating the property. Olivia waved from the paddock and before long she and Jessica were sharing the private world of Rustic (the donkey), numerous rabbits, sheep and two chickens and a pond where the inhabitants rather sensibly stayed at the bottom.

At around two o'clock she happily prepared to be collected for a school friend's party in Linslade on the Buckingham side of the town. As she left, Matthew brought out a bottle of white wine and seafood salads for each of them. Jessica told him about her week at the bank and then asked him for a summary of the situation.

"John Sneddon has now admitted that it was he who injured Thomas and he'll go to prison. Anne has had a breakdown and will be in a psychiatric hospital for some time. Thomas is with foster parents and Olivia is fine, as you will have seen."

"Why did he do it, Mob?"

"They are saying that he blamed Thomas for his deteriorating relationship with Anne. He just flipped."

"And you, Mob?"

"One more week and then I return to work. Olivia will be collected by the neighbours for school and if I'm late back from London she'll stay with them until I collect her. It's what she wants."

"And Thomas?"

"I'm having discussions with the Social Services."

"Who say what, Mob?"

"As things stand he'll be staying with his foster parents."

"And can things change?"

"If I can find a mother for Thomas they'll watch what happens over the next few months and they might allow me to have him."

"Which is what you want?"

"He's Olivia's half-brother, Jessie."

"So how's the search for a mother going?"

"She's thinking about it."

"Is she? When will you know her decision?"

"When you make it, Jessica."

She paused and sipped her wine. She stood up and walked over to the paddock. She ruffled Rustic's head and then went back to Mob.

"Why are you here, Jessie?" he asked.

"I'm asking myself the same question."

"You did say when we first met that it was time for you to have a baby."

She looked at him in amazement.

"You've managed to find the father and an adopted daughter and son."

"But they're not mine," said Jessica rather quietly.

"If we have children 50 percent would be mine. So 100 percent of Olivia is half you."

It took her a little time to work out the logic of Mob's reasoning.

"I would be her step-mother. But with Thomas there is nothing. Anyway there's no knowing whether they'd let us have him."

"He's a one-year-old baby whose father is going to prison and whose mother will take months, if not years, to recover."

He stood up and moved behind her. He slid his hands down her sides and hugged her. He kissed the back of her neck. A plane coming in to land at Luton airport was possibly saving fuel by cutting the flight path corner and flying lower than the regulatory descent levels. The noise temporarily disturbed the peace of the afternoon.

"We're rock solid, Jessie. Even after just a few months we know it's right. This can be your home and your family. My business is prospering and 1 can look after us. With John letting us live in The Laurels we are rather well placed financially." I can rent my flat out in London.

He decided not to tell her about 'Six Weeks in Summer' and the missing director.

He came round to face her and kissed her again.

134

"We can, of course, have children of our own."

"It's all so easy for you, Mob. The pieces all fit together."

They decided to go for a walk after tidying up. When they arrived back Jessica had become more subdued. She collected her belongings together and explained to him that she was returning to London and would think things over. He ran her to the station and arrived back home just as Olivia was dropped off from her party.

She started to ask questions and was particularly interested in hearing all about Jessica. Matthew tried to avoid telling his daughter that her further commitment was unlikely. They heated up some soup together and chatted about the party. He had trouble concentrating as he was thinking of Jessica and the look on her face as she left him at the station.

Later that night his phone flashed showing that a text message was waiting to be read. It was from Jessica. His stomach turned over in dread: had he scared her off?

*Home safely. You've given me lots to think about. It'll take time to sort my thoughts out so leave it for me to contact you when I'm ready. J xx*

'Ouch' thought Matthew: no contact until she was ready. How was he going to get through the next few days or week? He had to be patient. At least she had not said 'no.'

* * *

Sarah was tossing and turning in bed. She was going over and over in her mind what her husband had said. Generally, professional police officers detest outsiders trying to solve crimes. Sarah knew that Nick was gifted and understated. For him to use exaggerated language was unknown.

"A frightening conclusion," is what he had said. He must be referring to the possible deaths of up to four hundred people.

Nothing DCI Sarah Rudd had faced before, even the incident in The Mall which was pure instinct, compared to this situation. Tomorrow she'd make decisions but only after she had heard his full presentation.

As she finally lost consciousness her brain was still digesting his words.

'Four hundred people,' she continued to think.

* * *

Olivia was still fast asleep when there was a light tapping at the front door.

Mob was sitting in the kitchen drinking freshly percolated coffee and thinking about the previous day's events. He had prepared a text message for sending to Jessica and then he had deleted it. She had to be given time to make up her own mind.

He thought he heard a noise and then he realised that it was coming from the driveway. He put his cup down, tightened his dressing gown cord and strode through the hall to the entrance. He opened the door and looked at Jessica. She was holding out a letter to him.

"Please read it," she said.

He took the sheet of paper out of the unsealed envelope. It was addressed to her manager at the bank and gave him three months' notice of her decision to resign her position.

She was now inside the house and they went together into the kitchen. He poured her some coffee.

"I thought that the trains don't run on a Sunday?" he said.

"A friend drove me up."

"You must have very good friends to be able to ask such a favour."

She was pleased that he was suspicious.

"A girl friend, Mob. We girls stick together, I've told you that before."

He poured some more coffee into her cup and handed her some toasted granary bread. He pushed the dish towards her. She took some time to spread the butter on her two slices. She lifted her eyes towards his expectant face.

"It won't work, Mob. It's not fair to Olivia. And there's Thomas to consider. It won't work."

"Why have you resigned your job, Jessie?" he asked.

"You can't uproot Olivia to London. She needs the stability of her home here."

He went out of the room and reappeared with a small glass of scotch. Jessica had never seen him drink alcohol before lunchtime before. He sipped the malt rather slowly.

"Jessie. Please, help me. You've come out of London to tell me that you have resigned your job and to inform me that it won't work. Could we have not done this over the telephone or by email?"

"I'm due a week's holiday, Mob. I've sent a second letter telling the manager I won't be back until a week tomorrow."

He ran the fingers of his left hand through his hair.

"You deserve a week's break, Jessie. Where are you going?"

"Visit the scene of The Great Train Robbery. It was all over the local newspaper."

Matthew looked at her in surprise. He drank a sip of the whisky and then some more coffee. He spluttered.

"A week in Leighton Buzzard. Where are you staying?"

"Here. If you'll have me."

Matthew began to get flustered. He was becoming ever more confused.

"Why do this to me, Jessie?"

"Do what?"

"It won't work. That's what you have been saying but now you are proposing to be here for a week."

"Longer than for a week, Mob. Try 'forever'."

She smiled the smile that he so adored.

"What won't work, Mob, is for you to try to raise Olivia and possibly Thomas and run your business in London. There's a straightforward solution. I'll run your home and help you bring up Olivia and Thomas if they'll let us have him. You can make us lots of money in the City."

"You're willing to help me bring up Olivia and Thomas?"

"Olivia is bringing herself up, Mob. She and I are destined to become friends although I suppose I'll be second to Rustic."

He laughed. "But we both know that Thomas is a bigger challenge, Jessie?"

"We first of all have to bring him home."

137

Matthew mulled over the word she had used: 'home'.

"Do you think they'll let us have him?"

"Yes, Mob. The only doubt is how quickly Anne recovers from her addiction to alcohol. She might want him herself."

"I'll fight her," he said.

Matthew paused and looked at his partner.

"But what about your own child, Jessie. The one you want so much?" He laughed. "The one you don't want me to father."

"How many bedrooms does this house have, Mob?" she asked.

# PART TWO

*I once knew a girl*
*who was very, very shy*
*She never ever seemed*
*to catch any boy's eye*
*She hit on a trick*
*that made all the boys stare*
*She'd leap up and down and*
*wave her knickers in the air.*

Written by Keith Hancock of the band
St Cecilia in 1971 but banned and not
performed live (on the BBC) until 1985.

# Chapter Eleven

"Watch Rashid."

The words hung in the air of the late August evening as Nick began his presentation to DCI Rudd. They had decided, as a family, to have several long weekends away rather than a summer holiday. As a result Marcus had now left for a week at school camp in France and Susie was having a sleepover with her best friend Natalie.

"You returned to work in the third week of March and at that time there were increasing racial tensions in Southern England. A group known as the 'Muslim Patrol' was carrying out revenge attacks for what it saw as breaches of Sharia law. You are saying that there were, at that time, no reports from within Islington Borough of any religious-based insurrections."

Sarah went to say something but Nick held up his hand to indicate that she should remain silent. She sipped her drink and then put her glass down on the garden table. The barbecue fire was dying down but it was still warm and pleasant. She poured her husband the remaining lager from the bottle which she put down by the side of her chair.

"On your first day back to work you received a call on your police mobile. You had no idea who Rashid was and the attempts to identify him came to nothing. Rashid is a common name in the Muslim world." He sipped his Australian brew and again held up his hand to signal to Sarah to remain quiet.

"The next incident came in the first week of May after you had arrested the war veteran for child abuse. You were walking back to your car when you took a call on your personal mobile. The message was the same. The caller could not be traced. You are placing little or no importance on the fact that both your phone numbers are known to this third party. You have told me that the voice was the same: we are dealing with one person.

You are also saying that it was a husky voice but there were no other significant features. It was a male who, at that point in time, had spoken four words." He paused and turned over the first page of his notes.

"In May, when we were walking in the Chiltern Hills, you told me about the Arab Spring in the Middle East and the increasing violence of the Muslim Brotherhood. You discussed matters with your specialist colleagues and you sensed some increasing tensions within your community but nothing more sinister." He continued talking with only a brief pause to open another bottle. He then reached for her bottle of wine but Sarah put her hand over the top of her glass to indicate that she had drunk all the alcohol she would allow herself.

"There was a third call in late May. You discussed the matter with Detective Superintendent Khan and suggested that the phone calls were a 'community message'. Those were the words you used. Your theory was that there would be a terrorist attack, a possible suicide bomber, and some members of the Muslim groups do not want their peace disturbed. You had his agreement that at this stage you should say nothing more to your colleagues. You would go into the inner streets of Islington and try to find out more."

They cleared the table and closed down the barbecue. They took a late evening call from Marcus and Sarah texted Susie only to receive a silly response which made her smile. Twenty minutes later they had settled down in their lounge. Sarah drew the curtains to shut the world away. She served them both cups of coffee.

"You sensed that your questions were quickly picked up by the terrorists and last month you broke the rules and went alone to a convenience store where you were known to the owners. The man searched you for weapons and then you went into the stockroom at the rear of the shop where you met Saleem, if that's his real name. You think it probably is which might be important. They are aiming to kill four hundred people and the attack is expected to be in a few weeks' time.

Saleem said he was speaking to you because you won the Queen's Gallantry Medal. He said there were two police officers

142

in Islington who are bent: one's getting money and the other is scared. He named the receiver of the cash but you can't tell me who it is."

Nick looked at his wife and realised that there was no way he could persuade her to name the officer. He continued with his summary.

"Saleem wanted you to help stop Rashid from abusing his sister. You inadvertently put him down and he fled. You've been back to the shop but they've closed ranks. The police officer, who you think is the insider, has told you all to be especially vigilant."

Nick put his papers down and asked Sarah if she thought that he had accurately summed up the sequence of events up to this point. She was secretly impressed and nodded.

"I have concluded, Sarah, that there are five key facts:

One: there is to be an attack against the British people and they expect to kill around four hundred people.

Two: it is being developed in Islington but will take place elsewhere.

Three: the terrorists are ruthless and they rule by fear and violence.

Four: the individuals you have come across are minor players. Rashid is assaulting Saleem's sister: he's therefore not a serious member of the group. You think that Saleem is worried about the consequences to the community, as are the shop owners, and yet he is part of the group. The officer taking money is probably being used as their source of information on police activities. If there is a second constable involved he or she is being bullied by the more senior officer.

Five…" Nick stopped and invited Sarah to comment.

"Come on, Nick. The fifth of your conclusions. What is it?"

"How am I doing, Sarah?"

"Pretty good." She moved across and hugged her husband.

Before getting to the fifth conclusion can I say that I don't trust Saleem. He's one of the plotters so why is he talking to you? I accept that Rashid's abusing of his sister is a serious matter but he knows that if his indiscretion is discovered he will disappear in agony beneath a truck-load of concrete. We must not trust him at any time Sarah.

She nodded in agreement but urged Nick on.

"Please. The fifth point. You've worked something out haven't you?"

"I wish I had." He drank some coffee. "I've realised that we have both been missing the biggest clue of all."

Sarah stood up. There was nothing in Nick's report that she had not thought of and she'd had the advantage of her detailed conversation with Detective Superintendent Khan. 'The biggest clue of all,' she thought to herself. 'What has he spotted that we've all missed?'

"Let me ask you a question. In fact, two. Firstly 9/11. The eleventh of September two thousand and one. Al-Qaeda launched four attacks. How many people died that day?"

"Too many, Nick. I can't recall exactly. Perhaps nineteen hundred. Does it matter?"

"Yes. It does. It was about three thousand people."

"So how does that help me?"

"It doesn't, Sarah. It's the second question that matters."

"Which is?"

"How many victims did they expect to kill?"

"Nick. Slow down. You've watched too many episodes of '24'. Come on Jack Bauer, let's get back to Islington."

"They launched four attacks but the one aimed at Washington did not even get there. It crashed into a field." He drank some more coffee. "They hoped to achieve a mass slaughter, which they did, but they could not have known that three thousand people would die. They did not say to themselves 'let's kill three thousand people'."

"Nick. Stop it, please. You're going overboard. Perhaps this was not such a good idea. You go back to being a headmaster and leave policing to me."

"What did you ask me, Sarah? How many glasses of wine had I drunk? Every bit of information matters."

DCI Rudd stood up. "Thanks for the lecture. I'm going to bed."

"How do they know that they are going to kill four hundred people?"

Sarah sat down on the sofa and dropped her coffee cup.

"Not five hundred, not three hundred. Saleem told you they are going to kill four hundred people. That might be a church but attendances vary. A department shop? Probably not. A tube train? They vary in length and there's no way the planners, who are rather careful, could be sure of the exact numbers on board. It is inconceivable that they would state the number without being certain. A plane? That's possible but security is so tight these days that it's unlikely. And again, how could they be so certain about killing four hundred people? Numbers of passengers in planes vary." He paused for a few moments. "A boat? A cruise liner? I just don't see it." He stood up.

"Why have you not mentioned a train?" she asked.

"I thought about that, Sarah. There are several reasons why anything travelling on rails would not work. How can you be sure that four hundred people would be on a train? How do you bomb the whole of a train which you need to do if you are to be certain of killing all the passengers? How do you hide the bombs in all the carriages? Now I come to think of it, how do you stop a train?"

"The Great Train Robbers stopped a train at Bridego Bridge fifty years ago, Nick," she suggested with half a smile.

"Sarah, in a few days or several weeks ahead, Saleem and his mates are certain that they know where four hundred people will be and how they intend to kill them."

She looked at her husband. "Nick, that is seriously worrying."

"But there's a third question, Sarah. Answer this one and I think you'll be able to find the terrorists."

"I've got to work out where four hundred people will be."

"Yes and no."

"Nick, please, I can't take much more of this."

"Four hundred people. Yes, you have to find them but the solution lies in the most important question of all."

"Which is what?"

"How can they be so certain that they are going to kill them all?"

* * *

A week had passed since it had been apparent that Amanda Adams-Smythe, the producer of the film 'Six Weeks in Summer', had disappeared. It was now certain that the £6 million less commissions, which had been sent from the solicitor's client account to the company's account, had immediately been transferred on the instructions of Osama Al-Kabal, to a bank in the Middle East. The finance director had, quite openly, flown back to Abu Dhabi telephoning Richard Rochards to say he was fixing up the initial payments for filming to start in early October.

"As a matter of interest, Caroline, did the funds from Osama Al-Kabal ever arrive?"

The solicitor flared.

"I can see this is a personal inquest, Matthew. Can we put on record that you were pressing me hard to send you the £400,000 commission Silverside Brokers were due under the loan agreement? If I recall you insisted I remitted the funds the same afternoon the loan proceeds were received by our bank. If I also remember rightly you sent me a beautiful bouquet of flowers."

Matthew Buckingham was sitting at his desk in the offices of Silverside Brokers. Caroline Pennington was opposite him. It was a damage limitation meeting.

"Let's keep our knickers on, Matthew, although, in your case, that goes against your instincts." She sipped some water. "Will you please order still aqua next time? Fizzy water affects my skin. The money is not yet missing. We have clear evidence that it is under the control of Osama Al-Kabal who is a director of the company. Neither of the other two directors, Richard Rochards nor Martine Madden, have contacted us. I received legitimate funds from the Pretty Fund's bank. That indicates they were happy that the legal formalities had been completed. It is true that Debra White and I have a few matters to resolve."

"You mean, who is Osama Al-Kabal?"

146

"They have a bank account with Coutts and Company in the Strand. They will have carried out rigorous checks on the directors."

"Let's cut to the chase."

"Do let's," replied Caroline.

"Where is Amanda Adams-Smythe?"

"Who cares? She's had doubts about her forthcoming wedding and is keeping a low profile. Happens all the time."

"If, for the sake of argument, the money has disappeared, who is liable?"

Caroline suggested they went and shared a bottle of wine at Corney & Barrow off Old Broad Street. Fifteen minutes later they were together in a dark corner. Matthew was strangely nervous in her company. Who was the politician about whom it was said 'there is something about the night about him'? She had a simmering allure but not one which was obviously sensual. He suspected that she played games with people.

"You've been with Mark Patterson-Brown for some years? He's twenty years older than you," he said.

"I'm beginning to ask myself the same question, Mob. I love Mark but he's ageing and his wife is getting suspicious. She must know what's happening but she's like so many of them. They just hope it's a passing phase."

He was surprised that she should reply so freely. He sensed that she wanted to talk.

"Are you a passing ship in the night, Caroline?"

She laughed.

"A long night, Mob. As you so bluntly put it, we've been together for ages."

They both drank their wine.

"Can I let you into a secret, Mob?"

"If you must."

"Perhaps there's been the odd indiscretion but I've been with Mark for so long I've lost the ability to create new relationships. If I lose him I'll have to put in some training."

She put her hand on his knee and laughed.

"Perhaps I'll see if you're available although I suppose Erica is taking your attention."

147

"Her name is Jessica. Why would I want to turn my back on a stunningly lovely, intelligent and committed woman for the mistress of an old-age pensioner?"

"Ouch."

She hesitated. Caroline had often struggled to anticipate a man's reaction to her. She decided to continue the banter.

"Because, Mob, you can't resist me. You've always wanted my body. Just look at you now: you're aroused like hell."

The problem facing Matthew was that she was right. It was just that she had never been available.

"You're sounding a bit desperate Caroline," he said. "You've been attached to Mark for far too long. You're out of practice and I agree with you. Any suitor worthwhile could be beyond you."

"Yet you find me attractive, Mob."

"I've always felt something and probably always will. It's just that I'm no longer available. Jessica and I will be together forevermore."

"That's what Adam and Eve said."

He laughed and changed the subject.

"Caroline. Something smells about Six Weeks in Summer Production Limited. Are you worried?"

"Yes, Mob. I can always cope with a puzzle but we now have three of them."

"Three?"

"Amanda Adams-Smythe is missing. We do not know where the five and a bit million pounds is."

"There's a third, Caroline?"

"Osama Al-Kabal is not the finance director: he's non-executive. He's not even a signatory on the bank account. The other three directors can each sign on their own authority. If Amanda is missing and Osama couldn't sign, who did transfer the funds and why?"

* * *

Jessica collected Matthew from Leighton Buzzard station at around nine o'clock. She thought that he looked rather weary. She told him her news, the most significant part of which was that she had persuaded the mortgage company to allow Matthew to let his flat in Covent Garden.

"I'm going into London tomorrow, after dropping Olivia off at school, to remove your personal items and to meet with an agent who will handle the tenancy agreement and all the formalities." She stopped while she negotiated the turning on to the ring road and round to Ledburn.

"The income will be more than your repayments: you negotiated an excellent deal, Mob."

"I know that we discussed it but I have been wondering if having a flat in London is not such a bad idea."

She looked in her rear mirror and indicated that she was turning right.

"I've just been told that my share of the film commission is £40,000." Matthew had a satisfied smile on his face.

"On which you'll have to pay income tax at 45 percent," she replied.

She stopped the car in the drive. They went inside and heard Olivia enter the kitchen from the direction of their neighbour's house where she had been staying. She sat at the table and chatted away. Eventually, after kissing her father and hugging Jessica, she moved towards the door.

"Olivia, did you feed Rustic?" Jessica asked her.

Olivia turned round and grinned.

"Sure did, Jess". They both laughed as she climbed the stairs.

"Jess?" asked Matthew.

"Kids always shorten names. That's Olivia's creation for me."

They went into the lounge and Jessica put on Mahler's 'Symphony No 2'. She thought that the petulant music might reflect Matthew's state of mind. It was the composer's most popular work and rather long at nearly ninety minutes. It was known as the Resurrection Symphony and focused in part on the afterlife.

Over the next hour she tried to find out what was weighing Mob down. She covered all aspects of his work, his health, her, Olivia, money and much more. In the end she gave up and went to bed.

Matthew sat there and continued listening to the Mahler composition.

He had not noticed Jessica creeping back into the room.

"Mob," she said. "I've something to tell you."

He stood up, turned on the side lights and turned down the music. He watched as she pulled up a stool and sat down in front of him.

"I've had a call from mother. I wish she'd have asked me to go up to Stratford to see her but she always does it in her own way. It was as if she was reading a medical report."

"Her health," said Mob. "She needs an operation?" He looked at her quizzically.

"It's gone beyond that. Being my mother she refused to go to see the doctor. She's been having backache and thought it was muscular. When she finally made an appointment they took her straight in, opened her up and put her back together again. She's full of cancer. She's refused all treatment although she's being helped with a pain management programme."

"Do we know… ?"

"Hold on, Mob. They are saying six to eight weeks. She must have been in agony lately."

"They'll keep her in hospital?"

"She's insisting on dying at home." Jessica paused. "There's something else. She has asked me if I'll look after her until she dies."

"Six to eight weeks when we are trying to convince the authorities that we're capable of caring for Thomas."

"If you speak reasonably to my mother she responds in kind. I explained all that to her."

"Is she having nurses brought in to look after her?"

"No. She's adamant that I'm there and caring for her."

"How is that 'reasonable' to use your word?"

"Because she's coming here. Her doctor has spoken to ours here, and it's been agreed. She arrives by private ambulance tomorrow."

Matthew put his arm around her and they snuggled together on the sofa. Soon after they both began to slumber. Suddenly Jessica shot upright.

"Mob, I hate myself for saying this but my mother is wealthy. We'll inherit a rather large sum." She paused. "£2,600,000 after inheritance tax. This excludes the house which she's leaving to the Shakespeare Foundation.

"She's worked it all out then?"

"To the last penny."

"What about your father?"

"She's spoken to him but he was drunk on a fishing boat off the Algarve coast."

Matthew pulled her close to him and hugged her.

"Are you able to handle this, Jessie?"

"I've always known that she would go one day and we're not close. She's somehow made the best of a bad job and she's certainly practical." Jessie paused. "She said a strange thing to me, Mob. She said that her greatest ability was to think the unthinkable. What did she mean?"

Matthew never replied because she had climbed the stairs and gone to bed.

He sat down and picked up his phone. He sent a text to Jessie's mother:

*If I must die*
*I will encounter darkness as a bride.*
*Complete and source. Mob x*

He sat back in his chair and wondered if she was well enough to reply. The red light pulsated on his phone. He picked it up and pressed the 'receive' button.

*And hug it in mine arms.*
*M for M. Good luck Mob. Mrs L x*

At ten o'clock the following morning the rigid body of Jessica's mother was found by the police who had been called in by a neighbour. She had taken an overdose of sleeping pills after drinking half a bottle of brandy. Jessica received a phone

151

call and immediately asked Matthew if they could afford for her to book a taxi to take her to Stratford-upon-Avon.

It arrived within half an hour and she was quickly on her way. Matthew had already told the headteacher that Olivia would be arriving late. After the vehicle had departed with Jessica he drove his daughter to the school gates and watched her run happily into the playground.

He hated himself for thinking the way he did but he could not rid himself of the knowledge of over two and a half million pounds. Jessica had committed herself to him before she knew about her inheritance. He could not be accused of marrying into money although that was exactly what was now happening.

It was her inheritance. There was no reason why they should share it. But that is exactly what he thought she might do. He already knew his partner rather well. She would see it as removing the last uncertainty to her having her own baby.

Mob was slow to turn on his phone having decided to take a day off work.

He realised there was a text message waiting for him.

*You take my life when you do take the means whereby I live.*
*The Merchant of Venice and Mrs L x*

# Chapter Twelve

The Borough Commander, Detective Chief Superintendent Max Riley, wanted his team sitting in the order which he had stipulated. To his left was Superintendent Moses. She was looking over the massed ranks of many of the Islington police team and making certain that she did not make eye contact with one of her senior officers. Even now she could not bring herself to accept that a fluke event in The Mall warranted the Queen's Gallantry Medal. Monica Moses was certain that the officer had tripped over and was lucky.

To the Commander's right-hand side was Detective Superintendent Majid Khan. At either end were the two Detective Chief Inspectors. DCI Percy Attwood was 'old-school' and, because he had similar looks to David Jason from the television crime series 'Frost', was known as 'Freezer'. At that moment in time he was a worried man. At the other end was DCI Avril Flemming, an Oxford-educated fast-track 'I'm on my way to the top' police officer who was talented and popular with her favourites.

DCI Rudd should also have been seated alongside the senior team but she usually chose to mingle with the other ranks and nobody objected to that. She had her own aura and was, as far as the Commander was concerned, a 'one-off'.

She was also dealing with personal conflict. She knew far more about the previous evening's events apart from the senior officer who she strongly suspected was the mole. She was keeping watch on that individual and she was trying to work out why there was eye contact with one of the other constables.

Commander Riley summed up the situation.

"You will all be aware that at about eleven o'clock last night there was an explosion at the shop run by Sultan and Namina Mohammed in Essex Road near to the Old King's Head public house. It was clearly arson although Forensic Services are asking for time on that. We found two badly burnt bodies which we believe may be the owners. We are treating the incident as a murder inquiry."

He paused and looked round the packed room.

'And you are probably going to find out that both the victims were dead before the fire was started,' Sarah said to herself.

She already knew that the Mohammeds were being threatened and that their three children, Mia, Ava and Talim, had been sleeping with friends for the past week. DCI Rudd had reported to D/Supt Khan that there was increasing tension in the community and DCI Freezer Attwood had also registered his concerns.

What Sarah had not been able to do was to identify that Mr and Mrs Mohammed were possibly under threat. She had no specific evidence for that and it would have alerted the mole to her suspicions. Was she gambling four hundred lives against two? Her professional dilemma continued. She knew that her career might be in the balance.

The Commander went into great detail about the plans now in force to try to calm the streets of Islington. There were regular meetings with community leaders and an increased visibility in public areas. Uniformed officers were everywhere but, with the budget cuts, Commander Riley knew that he could not maintain the overtime costs for too much longer. He had argued against the halving of his community support officers but financial priorities had won the day.

When it came to questions from the floor a young constable asked whether the Commander had any idea why the incident should have happened now? August had proved to be pleasant weather-wise: people were relaxed. Even though the Middle East was again making news in Syria and Egypt, in Islington, as far as he could sense, people were just going about their business. To add to the tension in the room the questioner did not accept the answer given that they had to be alert at all times.

"I'm sorry, Sir. I don't get it. I appreciate we don't have all the facts but this was obviously a racial attack and it has come completely out of the blue. Surely somebody, somewhere knows something?"

At that exact moment DCI Rudd was watching the suspected mole. There was eye contact and she swung round in her chair. At the back of the room was a recently recruited police constable who had already made her mark. Constable Gillian Pepper had quickly been nicknamed 'Spray'. In the male section she was given more lurid names as her uniform merely served to highlight her physical attractions.

The meeting broke up and DCI Rudd decided to walk out onto the streets of her territory. She had already debriefed with D/Supt Khan and was instructed to continue her undercover work. She was looking for Saleem and Rashid but she was still not sure who they were. She had possibly identified the terrorist's mole but she knew that she had no evidence and accepted that Saleem might have been using diversion tactics. She had just watched the suspected officer making eye contact with a young constable.

She was also going round and round in her own mind with Nick's key question.

*How can they be sure that they'll kill four hundred people?*

She set off for the Community Centre and passed a doctor's surgery which displayed a notice informing that it was a 'Yellow Fever Centre'. She decided to sit down on a park bench. She reasoned that she should tell D/Supt Khan all she knew and yet that could immediately alert the delinquent officer. In turn that could warn the terrorists who would simply move their base into another territory.

'If so,' she thought to herself, 'the chances of finding them before four hundred people are killed would be diminished.'

DCI Rudd realised that she was gambling with the odds that she was right and it was not her job to do that. Her text messaging service bleeped and she was ordered back to see D/Supt Khan.

She arrived back at the station and reached her boss's door. Her knock was immediately answered.

"There were two bodies, Sarah which we assumed were Mr and Mrs Mohammed," he told her as he waved her to sit down.

"We are sure that one is Mr Mohammed. He had been doused in petrol and set alight before the explosion but a ring on his finger survived the heat."

He paused and looked concerned.

"Our problems lie with the other body. It was a male and we now know that Namina Mohammed was visiting her sister in Haringey."

"Any possible identification as yet, Sir?"

"That's what's worrying me, Sarah. We know exactly who it was. Saleem Singh who lived in Camden Town. He was on the watch list and had just returned from Saudi Arabia. He's a convert."

"Excuse me asking but how can you be so sure?"

"He was wearing a bracelet with his name on."

The two officers looked at each other. There was no way that any terrorist would wear anything that would allow him to be identified.

"Whoever did this, Sarah," continued D/Supt Khan, "wanted us to know that Saleem Singh had been executed."

"Us, or the community, Sir?"

As she left the office DCI Rudd decided that she needed to up the pace of her investigations. She asked some questions and established that Constable Gillian Pepper was due to start night duty the next day and would be walking the streets of Islington. Sarah knew that it had to be carefully planned. The following night she went out late looking for trouble.

Two Afro-Caribbean youths were congregating outside a public house. One peed in the gutter and the other abused a passer-by. The usual approach would be to make her presence known and then chat to them. On this occasion she challenged the teenagers and told them that she was going to search their pockets. She received a torrent of abuse and a lecture on their rights.

"Hey. Bitch. Ain't you the one who won the medal? My brother and me don't want trouble. You're alright."

He was therefore surprised when DCI Rudd shoved him into a hedge. She reached for her mobile and called for assistance. The second officer to arrive was Constable Gillian Pepper. The leading constable, who was rather large, shouted "leave 'em to me, Spray," and cornered the two youths.

"Let them go," instructed DCI Rudd. She gave them a lecture and told them to behave themselves.

"But bitch. We daint do nothing."

The policeman followed them down the street leaving DCI Rudd and Constable Gillian Pepper standing together.

"Are you alright Ma'am?"

Sarah smiled.

"Thanks for coming so quickly. Funny, those two are usually drunk but peaceful. You can feel the tension on the streets. Sorry. We've not met. DCI Sarah Rudd."

"Constable Gillian Pepper and it's a privilege to meet you, Ma'am."

"Fancy walking?"

They covered several streets and two all-night cafes. At the second they purchased burgers for themselves.

"Bang goes the diet," laughed the junior officer.

"My husband likes the wobbly bits," responded Sarah.

They were together for nearly thirty minutes chatting away until Constable Pepper was called elsewhere.

"Thanks again for the help," called out Sarah.

She watched her run off. In their time together Gillian Pepper made no reference to men. She did not comment on her nickname. She did not refer to any other officer. She did not talk about her boyfriend. Her interests were in food, fashion, TV and cinema.

Sarah Rudd could see that she was rather attractive.

DCI Rudd was also pretty certain that Gillian Pepper preferred women.

* * *

The funeral of Estieve de May Lambert was brutal.

It was held on an overcast morning in the private chapel of the cemetery outside Stratford-upon-Avon. The order of service was dog-eared, the vicar was bored and the pall-bearers impatient.

157

Jessica was accompanied by Matthew and Olivia who had insisted on being with 'Jess'.

The chapel was bare but for the coffin, a cloth and some flowers.

There was an organist who played Bach rather badly and the whole of 'The Lord is my Shepherd' as a solo because nobody wanted to sing the words. Half-way through the short ceremony the rear door opened and a man in a white suit and a hideous shirt entered. He sat at the back.

The minister said something and closed with a reference to the Holy Trinity.

As the coffin was placed on the rollers Matthew took out his mobile and pressed 'send' so that as Mrs Lambert entered the furnace she was accompanied by the Bard. It was from 'The Tempest':

*He that dies pays all debts.*

Jessica exchanged a few words with her father who refused to acknowledge Matthew. He did however kiss Olivia and took out from his pocket around £1,000 in used notes. He thrust them into Jessica's hands.

"Any point in coming to hear the will read?" he asked.

"None at all," replied Jessica.

"Where's the pub? Think I'll fly back home tonight."

Jessica, Matthew and Olivia drove to the solicitor's office and confirmed the details of Mrs Lambert's will. She had changed it two weeks before she died.

"When she went to see the doctor she was already sure about her condition. She instructed that the moment they found anything inside her they were to sew her up immediately." Mr Parsons turned to Jessica. "As you know your mother spent her last ten years collecting antiques. She became particularly successful at it which is why, when all the formalities are completed, I'll be sending to your bank account around £2,600,000. The house goes to the Shakespeare Foundation and, at the last minute, she bequeathed all her furniture to the local hospice. She did decide to go there but changed her mind. He smiled. "There is also a bequest of £25,000 to the local cats' home."

"She was going to come to Ledburn so I could look after her," said Jessica.

"No," said Mr Parsons. "She never intended doing that. She just wanted to die knowing that you would have done so. You deserve credit Jessica for your willingness to help her."

Then it was all over. Estieve de May Lambert went to heaven, her husband was arrested at Birmingham Airport for molesting a stewardess and Matthew, Jessica and Olivia prepared to travel home.

Matthew, however diverted the car back towards the town centre, parked over the bridge and asked them to walk with him along the banks of the river until they were facing the theatre.

"Jessie. It's time to say goodbye to Mum. Your life is now with us in Ledburn."

Olivia squeezed up as close as she could get to her.

"It's not very original and it's all about the meaning of life. For some scholars these are some of the greatest words that Willie wrote. They come, of course, from 'Hamlet'."

He took her hand and held it tightly.

"To die, to sleep; To sleep: perchance to dream: ay, there's the rub;

For in that sleep of death what dreams may come."

As they meandered back to the car Jessica wrapped herself around Matthew with Olivia at her side.

"Mob. One promise please."

"Anything, Jessie."

"When our baby comes can we give it, as a middle name, 'Estieve'?"

Matthew smiled and ran his fingers through her hair.

"Only if it's a girl, Jessie," he laughed.

\* \* \*

Caroline Pennington refused to accept that she was beginning to enjoy her increasing contact with Matthew. She knew that he had deliberately put them in the boardroom at Silverside Brokers and had declined her suggestion that they have an early dinner together. She noted the bottle of Chablis, two glasses and some nibbles.

She was seething as she reflected on recent events: Sildenafil Citrate. Secretively. The row was volcanic. She was humiliated. She had realised that she needed to work harder in recent weeks but the double whammy came out of the blue. Mark Patterson-Brown, after nearly six minutes of self-masturbation, heaving and shoving, collapsed on the bed. At first Caroline thought he might be in trouble but he then made the mistake of blaming her.

"Well, old girl, perhaps you need to lose a few pounds."

That, in itself, was fair play. The good life was catching up with Caroline. Her increasing workload, as she became more senior at Christie Simpson, was restricting her visits to the gym. Her upper inner thighs were showing signs of cellulite. But she knew that she was as good as ever, perhaps even better since she had searched the internet and invested in a set of Ben Wa balls. She had used them for over five weeks to strengthen the walls of her vagina.

He fell off the bed and headed for the bathroom.

"Don't you dare you relic," she hissed to herself.

It was then that she noticed that he'd left his jacket on the chair. She leaped up and felt inside his pockets. She discovered a packet of Viagra pills. She went and lay back on the bed, naked and exposed. Mark returned wearing a towelling robe.

"Mark. Sit down."

He followed her instructions but stayed at the end of the bed.

"Does my body still excite you? Please have a look. It'll save you buying those DVDs from Charing Cross Road."

"Caroline. This is rather distasteful."

"Distasteful! My body?"

"No, no, no. Sorry darling, I'm not myself today. One of my horses…"

"I'm not 'Darling'. That's your wife. I'm your mistress. I have a beautiful body. You leer at it and I do things to you. You become erect. You then enter me and bring me pleasure. Except, Mr Patterson-Brown, you're losing your libido. Do you know what Viagra does?"

"Er… it increases a man's passion. I'm quite capable of…"

160

"It makes the blood flow into your penis so that you become more excited. You are struggling to achieve your full erection. While we're on the subject you are getting a drinking pot and losing your healthy looks."

"Nonsense. The girls still respond to me. It's you who is losing it."

She took out the capsule holding the Viagra pills and waved it in the air.

"Have you thought of increasing the dosage?"

He looked aghast and turned round to check his jacket and then back to his mistress.

"I'm already taking the max… er… Caroline, please. We've been together now for… I don't want to lose you."

They cuddled together and went back to bed whereupon Mark fell asleep.

Matthew tapped on the table.

"Hello, are you with us?"

Caroline looked up and realised that he was asking whether she would like a glass of wine. Silly question.

"Let me bring you up-to-date, Caroline. As far as we can establish Osama Al-Kabal is in Abu Dhabi with the Pretty Pair's five and a bit million pounds. The company's bank has refused to try to recover the funds because they are saying it was a correct transfer. I'll come back to that. We understand that Osama is starting to shoot the Middle Eastern parts of the script. Richard Rochards, the director, came into our office yesterday and seems to be completely in the dark. That's partly because he has been sent his whole fee of £200,000 and told that he is not wanted. He seemed more worried about his reputation than his profit share. The money and dismissal came from Osama. This means we are left with three questions which, as far as I can, I'll try to answer for you."

Caroline was drinking quite quickly and so Matthew poured her some more wine. She declined the nibbles as the words of her lover continued to resonate around inside her head.

"Amanda Adams-Smythe remains missing. She has contacted her family and broken off her engagement. What are her intentions?"

Matthew smiled as she began to relax. Caroline was not her usual self-confident self.

"The second question to be answered is that the transfer of the money was authorised, quite correctly, by Martine Madden. To add to the intrigue she left Heathrow Airport this morning for Baghdad. She has refused to answer my calls. What is her role in all this?"

He paused, stood up and walked over to the window.

"So we know that Amanda is missing, Richard is laid off, Martine is on a plane to the Middle East and Osama is making a film," summarised Caroline. "What other question needs answering?"

"Why are you being ignored?" asked Matthew.

She put her glass down on the boardroom table.

"You're the main conduit between ourselves, the Pretty Fund and the directors of the company. Yet you're being excluded."

For some unaccountable reason, at that moment, a thought flashed into the mind of the corporate solicitor.

'Stress can affect a man's libido,' she said to herself.

\* \* \*

"Nick, why do men watch lesbian pornography?"

The headmaster remained calm and poured some more tea into both their cups. They were in their kitchen awaiting the arrival home of Marcus who, as always, was testing their tolerances. Sarah continued with her line of chat.

"I don't have any desire to watch two men doing whatever homosexuals do but you love watching women together. Do you remember when we looked at the films on offer in the Watford Hotel? I think they call it room service. You thought that I was asleep when you subscribed for 'Millie gets a friend'. No wonder you were so keen to pay the bill the next morning. You didn't want me to see the items listed."

"She was quite a girl, was Millie," laughed Nick.

"So I noticed the next morning Nick. I've wondered about buying you your own copy!"

They laughed together and heard a sound at the door.

"That was our son who's just put his head round the door to say 'goodnight'," said his father.

"Is he…?"

"He's fine. He's thinking ahead to his exams next year. Have another chat with him: you were rather effective last time."

Sarah went upstairs, exchanged a few words with her son, told Susie to turn off her light and returned to the kitchen.

"I'll have a sherry please, Nick."

As he placed the glass in front of her he said, "Lesbianism, my favourite subject, especially at this time of the evening."

"It's a bit more serious than that, Nick," said Sarah. She recounted the events of the last two days and focused on Constable Gillian Pepper.

"I've asked the odd question where I can and there's no doubt that she's attracted to women: she may be bi-sexual."

"This you have deduced from eye contact in a briefing session?"

"I'm a detective, Nick. I know from Saleem who told me who the mole is."

"But you can't tell me."

"There are two senior female police officers. Superintendent Monica Moses, who hates me and who is desperate for a man. I sometimes think that she should wear a placard around her neck, 'Man wanted: apply within'."

"She does not sound like a lesbian to me," he said.

"Try the other one. Superstar DCI Avril Flemming from Oxford University."

"Whoops. Mrs Jealous is in full throttle."

"She's so ambitious, Nick and she uses her sex all the time. I sometimes worry about the Commander's blood pressure."

"Is she a lesbian?"

"Could be. It's hard to tell."

"Sarah. Why are we talking about lesbians? Who's the mole?"

"I don't know, Nick. All I have to go on is what Saleem told me and the rumours within the station. You'd be mad to put any emphasis on those. That lot would have Elvis Presley hiding in Islington."

"It would help if you'd tell me what Saleem said, Sarah."

"I'm in so much shit it won't make any difference I suppose." She paused. "It was not so much what Saleem told me but the way he spoke the words. He believed them."

"Did they cost him his life?"

"Meeting me probably did that but he was going to go anyway. He was so worked up about Rashid and his sister that he was certain to give himself away."

"So who did he say was the mole?"

She looked intently at her husband.

"Detective Chief Inspector Avril Flemming."

"Did he say all that?"

"No. He just said 'Bitch, Flemming'." She looked down at her notes. "Here we have a problem, Nick. She's known to be a racist. She's been imposing increased 'stop and search' targets and the troops don't like it. You must remember we're proud of our multi-cultural community."

"Who made eye contact with Gillian Pepper?"

"Need I tell you?"

"Sarah. This is getting heavy. DCI Flemming would have to be connected with the Muslims. That makes no sense. Saleem was setting her up."

"That's the logic." She yawned and announced that she was going to bed.

"What's not the logic, DCI Rudd? Please tell your husband everything."

"Avril Flemming has a five-year-old son who nobody knows about. She's unmarried."

"She wants to keep her private life to herself."

"I received a hand-written note. It was pushed under the door of my office three nights ago."

"Saying…"

"The father of her child is Mahmoud Bashman."

"Who is he?"

"He's a disgraced superintendent in the Met who was dismissed last year for fiddling his expenses. There were more serious issues but that was the excuse used."

They went upstairs to bed and soon fell asleep. At three-seventeen the next morning they were together in the kitchen, both unable to sleep.

"This is running away from you, Sarah. I can't rid myself from the thought that your life is in danger. Do you have any idea who put the note under the door?"

"An insider."

"How do you know that?"

"They avoided the CCTV camera. All our corridors are covered."

"Who was it, Sarah?"

"I simply don't know, Nick."

"But it might have been this Pepper girl?"

"You mean Constable Pepper. That assumes DCI Flemming is the mole and that she made eye contact with Gillian. We are taught not to rely on assumptions."

"So what are you going to do, Sarah?"

"It's time for Detective Chief Inspector Rudd to start being a detective," she said.

# Chapter Thirteen

Sarah Rudd wrapped her sweater around her shoulders in an attempt to keep the September winds off. The light was fading and, as she heard the planes taking off from Heathrow Airport, she felt a pang of envy of those lucky enough to be departing for the warmer climates of the southern holiday resorts. She was facing possibly the most crucial challenge of her career, Nick was deep into his responsibilities as a headmaster and Marcus and Susie were both showing some signs that they realised they faced examinations in the New Year. Her son seemed to be over his drugs problem and was talking to her.

They had all enjoyed their summer break and the occasional adventurous weekend compensated, to some extent, for the lack of the traditional two week break. She would long remember their trip up the Grand Union Canal and the discovery of Bridego Bridge where The Great Train Robbery had taken place. That was tucked away in the memory bank and there it would stay.

She wanted to go indoors, kiss Nick goodnight and go to bed early. But she couldn't. She had to decide her plan of action. She must stop a group of Islington-based Muslim terrorists killing four hundred people. She realised that her career was almost certainly over. When D/Supt Khan understood that she had not divulged all she knew she would be suspended and a long internal process would see her sacked with the possible loss of her pension.

Nick's conclusion was the definitive clue. She must work out how they could be certain that they would kill exactly four hundred people. Hardly a waking hour passed without her going over this question time and again. But she was now fairly close to finalising an alternative strategy.

The now deceased Saleem had told her that there was a

mole. He had named the person as DCI Avril Flemming. The note pushed under the door of her office had informed her that she had a son whose father was an ex-superintendent in the Metropolitan police. Sarah had established that they had worked together. She now concentrated on who had written the note.

Saleem had said there were two moles and one was scared. DCI Flemming had made eye contact with Constable Gillian Pepper. Sarah had engineered a meeting with 'Spray' and suspected that she was a lesbian. The note had been produced on a computer. There was no way she could send it to the laboratory for testing.

Sarah was fairly sure that the senior officer had started a relationship with the constable, they had talked in bed, Gillian Pepper was scared, she had met Sarah and realised it was her chance to escape her dilemma by telling all in the note pushed under DCI Rudd's office door. All Sarah needed to do was to prove her theory. She could then secure Islington Police Station by going to D/Supt Khan and exposing DCI Flemming. Her hunch was that the officer would cave in and lead them to the terrorists. If, however, DCI Flemming became aware that her cover was blown, she'd tell her control and the terrorists would disappear from their patch. Even worse four hundred people could possibly lose their lives.

Like all the best plans it was so simple. Sarah decided she would invite DCI Flemming, Constable Gillian Pepper and Detective Constable Zola Bahrain (to provide reassurance to the other two) to have coffee with her in the canteen. While they were together she would send an anonymous message around the station that Special Branch were about to arrest some foreign nationals. The moment DCI Flemming heard the warning she would excuse herself so that she could warn her contact. DCI Rudd would arrest her and the terrorist threat would be thwarted. She would do what she could for Constable Gillian Pepper but she suspected she would shortly be walking the streets as a civilian.

It was perhaps fortunate that she and Nick had been to the cinema to see the Oscar-winning film 'Argo'. Although it was dominated by the brilliant acting of Ben Affleck, the aspect that most caught their interest was the meticulous planning by the Hollywood moguls of the 'make-believe' film. It had to fool the Iranian officials and it did – just.

Sarah laughed as 'Argo fuck yourself' rang in her ears.

She applied that lesson to her strategy of getting the three officers to have coffee with her. She had to decide upon an issue that would bond them together. It was low risk in the sense that if it did not happen she could try again. It was high risk because DCI Flemming might sense a trap.

It required three days of intensive preparation which started with her reading a published best seller. She was almost embarrassed when she went into her local Waterstones to purchase it and she only just managed, later in the evening, to hide it from Nick. She absorbed it from cover to cover and gasped at some of the things the girl was asked to do.

Sarah then selected a chick-lit book from the latest reviews. *Emma: A Latter-day Tale* by Rebecca H. Jamison told of a woman, or, as the Americans would say, a 'chick', studying to be a life coach. In her spare time she was looking out to do good deeds. Sarah discovered that the genre was as much about family and friends' relationships as it was about romance.

Then came the hard part of her plan. She needed to write around two thousand words of her own book. She toiled away and discovered that, as her central character became more real, the prose flowed. The first few paragraphs occupied her for far too long. She could not remember what a woman of twenty-one years of age wears. How high were her heels and what about the length of her skirt? Would she be taking soft drugs and did she listen to Adele?

Once past the opening pages the words began to become clear and the tale unfolded so that after four days and nights (she changed duty times forty-eight hours into the task) she decided she was ready to put her plan to the test.

Her first instructor at Hendon College had a saying: 'When in doubt go back to the most likely.' Her point was that time and again officers missed the obvious because it seemed too easy. She would not make that error. She read again the personal letter she intended writing to her three colleagues. She knew exactly what would bring them all together.

**Personal**

*Dear... ... ... ... ...*

*I write in confidence for reasons I am sure you will all understand.*

*Whether or not we are prepared to admit it we know that we have all read 'Fifty Shades of Grey.' I loved Ana but not HIM!*

*I've always wanted to have a go at writing Chick-lit and I've started my first book: 'Emily's dream man comes home'. I've just finished the first chapter.*

*Now the truth! I'm scared of making a fool of myself.*

*Would you be willing to meet with me next Tuesday at 6.00 p.m. in the canteen to read through the early pages? I'll be able to tell from your comments whether I should stick to the day job! I've looked at the duty rosters (not that those are reliable) and it might fit with your schedules. I do hope so.*

*Please keep this private and please try to come.*

*Sarah aka DCI EL James.*

She would deliver the individual letters in the morning.

\* \* \*

Jessica was adjusting well into her new life in Ledburn. Her London flat was on the market and the estate agents were confident that they would find a buyer. She decided, against their advice, to vacate it immediately. She spent a weekend packing boxes up and selecting a few items of furniture she wanted to keep. She then arranged for them, together with her personal items, to be transported up to Bedfordshire. The remaining furniture was removed by a clearance firm and, as far as she was concerned, that was that. The manager at her bank met with her and agreed that she could leave immediately. She forfeited some of her entitlements but secured all her pension rights. She visited Stratford-upon-Avon and spent the day with the lawyers and executors of her mother's estate. She accompanied them to the house where she removed a few artefacts and photographs. After completing and signing a number of forms she confirmed with them that she had met all her responsibilities. She would leave it to them to file for probate and do all that was necessary. She then prepared to leave her mother's town for one last time.

There was one final task to undertake. She went to the town centre and to the Avon. She asked a motorboat proprietor to run her up river and to stop opposite the theatre. She stared at the bank where she, Matthew and Olivia had stood together a little time ago.

She took out the funeral urn and the piece of paper which Matthew, at her request, had given her that morning before he had left for the station. She scattered her mother's ashes on the water, looked down at his writing, and read the words he had given her:

*If I must die I will encounter darkness as a bride,*
*And hug it in mine arms.*

She gasped as, yet again, Mob had used his mate Willie (as he called the Bard) to capture the moment. He had also explained that *Measure for Measure* was known as a problem play because the comedy, for many, spent more time dealing with pride and humility.

"Bye, Mum," she said quietly. "One day soon I will be holding my baby and calling it 'Estieve'."

She arrived at her new home to find that Olivia was already hard at work in the animal sanctuary. Rustic was following her round as she chased after the two mongrel puppies that they had acquired the previous weekend from the Chilterns Dog Rescue Society near to Tring. They had an appointment with the vet in an hour's time for the second round of inoculations and to discuss the fitting of their identification chips.

Olivia finally climbed into bed at around nine-thirty and missed the arrival home of her father by an hour. Matthew smelt of alcohol and was clearly exhausted. Jessica was going to tell him that the letting of his flat in Covent Garden was almost finalised but decided to give him space.

He poured himself a scotch and settled down in the lounge.

He asked if the words had been appropriate and she reassured him that her mother was now settling in well in heaven.

Jessica also filled her own glass with whisky and dry ginger and sat down.

"Mob. We are not discussing this. Please understand what I am saying. There are no conditions, no obligation and no pressure." She sipped her drink. "Much of my mother's wealth was pretty liquid in government securities and so on. Mr Parsons told me today that he expects to be accounting to me for the final sum within ten to twelve weeks."

"I really am pleased for you Jessie. Can we go to bed?"

"The final amount will be nearer £3 million. There were two paintings that he thinks even my mother had not appreciated."

"Wow! Bed?"

"I want to put £250,000 in trust for Olivia. She'll get it when she's twenty one."

Matthew looked at her in complete surprise.

"And I'm going to open an account with the same amount of money for our baby."

"Our baby! You're not… ?"

"No. I'm not. But you do agree that it's now time we tried to…"

"But we want Thomas back. We agreed we'd write to the authorities at the weekend to put our case."

"I've made several calls. John Sneddon is in the prison hospital and is reported to be recovering from a break-down. Your ex-wife is still in a clinic and I managed to ascertain that she was found drunk again. We don't know where Thomas is but the papers are arriving tomorrow to secure you visiting rights."

"Can we talk about this at the weekend, Jessie? I'm bushed."

"You'll be tired then, Mob. I know that you are working long hours and you have serious worries. At least money is not one of them."

"It's your legacy, Jessie. Not mine."

"It's ours. We are living our lives together now."

He paused as he began to panic that her new found wealth might undo everything they had achieved so far.

"I'll take Friday off. We'll see if Olivia can stay with her friend. We'll go and find some old buildings to look at."

Jessica reacted to this.

"We can't drag her away from her animals? We also have to make sure there is a responsible adult to look after the live-stock".

"We'll walk locally then, along the canal, towards Milton Keynes," suggested Matthew.

"I want to start trying for our baby. I'm thirty-eight years old."

He sobered up and looked across the room.

"I think we should secure Thomas back first, Jessica."

"That's not how I see it, Mob."

* * *

On the following Tuesday at 6.00 p.m. the four female police officers met in the canteen at Islington station. Gillian Pepper had initially written to decline but, as Sarah was to learn later, had been admonished by Avril Flemming who told her to write again to Sarah accepting her invitation.

Zola Bahrain never stopped talking. She had read all three of E L James's best-selling books and was keen to tell her colleagues how her sex life had improved.

"Rammie and me never realised what you can do with a pair of handcuffs," she squealed.

Sarah went red in the face. She quickly admonished her own lack of attention. The message to the station would be broad-cast in sixteen minutes' time. She would be watching Avril Flemming and preparing to arrest her.

The three officers quickly read Sarah's first chapter. Secretly she'd been quite pleased with her writing. There were eleven minutes to go.

"Oh fantastic," cried Zola. "Just wait 'til I tell Rammie about that!"

"I think this sex thing can be overstated," said Gillian. "Surely what we women want is passion. We want to be loved."

"Speak for yourself," said Zola. "I enjoy sex. Forget all this

173

love stuff. I'll worry about that when I'm old. Sarah. Oh, I'm so sorry. DCI Rudd."

"Sarah."

"Fab. When Hercules gets home Emily's fully clothed."

Eight minutes to go.

"She'd be wearing stuff she could strip off so lover boy could take her upstairs."

Seven minutes more. Sarah was watching Avril apparently reading the copy carefully. Gillian Pepper was also watching DCI Flemming."

"Think about it. What does Emily want most? She'll be gagging for it. He's been in Afghanistan for five months."

Four minutes to go.

"Wrong, Zola. It doesn't happen that way." They all looked at DCI Flemming. "She'd want reassurances about their relationship and she'd talk all round the matter."

"Hell, she's cool," Sarah said to herself.

"Couples don't throw themselves into bed. It takes time to regain their intimacy. They'd go to the pub. Don't forget Sarah's written into the story that they are not married so there's no children. That makes all the difference."

One minute to go.

"No," said Gillian. Sarah's..." She looked at her superior and checked with her eyebrows that it was in order to use her Christian name. Sarah smiled indicating that she could. "Sarah's got it spot on. They'd be upstairs in an instant."

The Duty Officer burst into the canteen.

"Just to tell you that we think there may be a raid in a few minutes' time by Special Branch. Something to do with a bomb. No need to get involved. Just telling you."

Sarah had both her hands on the sides of her chair.

'Move a muscle and I've got you,' she said to herself.

"Gillian. I don't know you that well but couples don't do that," said Avril. "My Brendan got home last night after a week at a Paris conference and I'm still waiting," she laughed.

Sarah stared from the one to the other. Avril was calmly reading the chapter. Her boyfriend was called Brendan. The Duty Officer reappeared.

"Sorry. False alarm. Back to your coffees."

"Sarah. I'm loving this. When can we have Chapter Two?" asked Avril.

As DCI Sarah Rudd reached home and entered the lounge Nick was reading some papers.

"Good day, darling? Caught your mole?"

"Argo fuck yourself," she said.

"I'll take that as a 'no'."

Sarah told Nick about her plan and how it was foolproof except that all it proved was that DCI Flemming was not the mole."

"What about Pepper Spray?" asked Nick laughing at the nick name.

"There's something between them: there was some body language. I wonder if they might be bisexual."

Nick walked round the room. He looked at his exhausted wife.

"How did you pull off the bomb announcement?" he asked.

"I called in a favour, Nick. The duty sergeant owes me one and I persuaded him it was in the interests of internal security. I told him that I wanted to test the reaction of several of my fellow officers. He was dead against it but I managed to talk him round. The problem was that he was so nervous that he rushed in to make the second announcement far too soon. But, by then, I knew that DCI Flemming was clean."

"You did well, Sarah. Bed?"

"It's left me with two problems, Nick."

"Two?"

"I don't know who the mole is and…"

"Go on, Sarah. What's the other?"

"I've got to write the second chapter of *Emily's Dream Man Comes Home*. They loved it and made me agree to meet with them next Tuesday."

\* \* \*

The meeting was tense from the outset. The attendees were served with tea or coffee and each had a glass with bottles of still and sparkling water nearby. It was nine o'clock in the morning and the traffic in King William Street was heavy. The Governor of the Bank of England was suggesting that the economic recovery was real and that the Monetary Policy Committee should be able to keep interest rates low.

None of this mattered to the nine professionals seated around the meeting room table on the third floor of the offices of Goodlove, Green and Partners.

Stuart Green opened the proceedings by introducing himself and his colleague as partners in the law firm and their role, which was to represent the two partners of The Pretty Fund. Jonathan Pretty simply looked daggers and Roger stared down at his papers.

"Matthew, thank you for attending and I think you've brought with you…"

"Debra White is our compliance officer and Sabina Morina is one of our dealers."

Jonathan looked up. They had met for one evening only. She asked him to slow down on the charm and when his hand invaded her privacy she slapped him rather forcibly. There was still a slight blacking of his eye where she had caught it with her finger.

"Caroline," continued Stuart. "You are, of course, representing the company which we know as Six Weeks in Summer Production Limited."

"Yes. Thank you Stuart. I also have with me Gerry Wales who is our litigation partner." He waved a hand in the air.

"Where's our fucking £6 million?" snarled Jonathan Pretty.

"You will understand, Mr Buckingham, that our clients are exceedingly worried that the funds they provided only a few weeks ago have disappeared. But let's try to understand what has happened. Why is there no director here?"

Caroline coughed and offered to provide the answer to that question.

"There are, or were, four directors when the funds were advanced."

"Our money!" shouted Jonathan Pretty. His solicitor put an admonishing hand on his arm.

"Amanda disappeared and then returned to this country. She has broken off her engagement and is staying with her parents. To confuse matters even more we understand she has accepted an offer to produce another film. When it was announced that the company had raised its finance there was a lot of interest."

"Is she still a director of the company?"

"She is saying she has submitted her resignation but, as yet, we have not received it and she's still showing as a director at Companies House."

Both Roger and Jonathan Pretty shook their heads and Sabina turned grey.

"Richard Rochards has also gone?"

"Yes," said Caroline, "he was dismissed by the two remaining directors."

"So we have left Osama Al-Kabal and Martine Madden and it was she who transferred the money in the bank account to Abu Dhabi."

"She's now in the country and is emailing us with regular messages. We hope to hear soon that the film is being made. She is saying that they have a new producer and a director will be flying out from the United States in two weeks' time."

"You realise that there has been gross misrepresentation?" contributed the litigation partner.

Matthew looked at him closely.

"By whom?"

"By your firm Silverside Brokers, Mr Buckingham. I trust that you are keeping your regulator fully informed."

The threat of his rhetoric hung in the air.

"I have advised the Financial Conduct Authority fully," said Debra White.

"Our relationship with our regulator is nothing to do with you, Mr Wales unless, that is, you are trying to threaten us?"

He picked up his papers.

"Let's look at the Information Memorandum you produced, Mr Buckingham. On page sixteen, paragraph six, it states…"

"Stuart, did your client read and understand the risk warnings in our document and did you advise your client fully on the risks?"

"Risk warnings do not excuse gross incompetence, Matthew. Our clients have, in good faith, advanced £6 million basing their decision on your documents and the presentation made by Sabina Morina."

The trader was wearing a business suit and no make-up. She had a pendant around her neck. She coughed and put her hand up.

"Mr Buckingham. I wish to submit my notes of the meeting with Mr Jonathan and Mr Roger Pretty. They were made within twenty-four hours of my attendance at their offices. I ask that they submit their records in the same way."

Debra White had no idea that Sabina was going to make this move. She smiled at the representatives of The Pretty Fund and their legal advisers.

Stuart Green had seen it all before although the circumstances of this action was unusual.

"Miss Morina. It's not your place to tell others what they should do," he said. He turned back to Matthew.

"Can you please confirm that the eleven conditions my client imposed were satisfied before agreeing to advance the money?"

"Ten of them were but I'm concerned that you, Caroline, did not provide us with the details we required of Osama Al-Kabal."

Caroline coughed. She paused and drank some sparkling water. She then pushed it away. It affected her skin. She pulled the bottle of still aqua towards her.

"I accept there are still two documents outstanding but as Coutts and Co had registered Mr Al-Kabal as a director for the purposes of the bank account, it was mutually agreed to proceed."

"Stuart. Can I please make a point? We accept that these are unusual circumstances but Six Weeks in Summer Production Limited is a properly registered business with two directors who are making the film in Abu Dhabi. As yet, and within the terms of the loan, they are not in default."

"So Roger and I can tell our backers that all is well," sneered Jonathan Pretty.

"There is nothing astray at the moment."

"So we just sit here and wait."

"No. As soon as Sabina reaches Abu Dhabi and makes contact she'll send us a report."

They all looked at the trader.

"Her plane leaves Heathrow at 11:20 tonight," said Debra.

\* \* \*

Matthew had finished telling Jessica about the day's events. She could not understand why Sabina had been chosen as the representative to go to Abu Dhabi.

"It was her suggestion. She's worried about her City reputation and it was clear from the attitude of the Pretty's lawyers that they won't hesitate to take legal action."

"Can they win?"

"There's no default yet, Jessie. That's the daft thing. It could be that Sabina reports positively and all's well. I've given her my authority to stay out there as long as she feels she should. She's smart and I've real confidence that she might sort this out for me."

\* \* \*

Sabina Morina stood up on hearing that her flight number had been called. She was travelling with hand luggage only as she wanted to exit as quickly as possible through customs at the other end. The twenty-four-hour world of Heathrow airport swirled all around. Her intention was to reach her destination, find Martine Madden, confirm all was well and return to London as soon as possible. She had watched Jonathan Pretty leering at her during the meeting. There were better men than him out there. And she knew how to get them.

179

# Chapter Fourteen

The Planner, using his role as a cleric, met with the mole a long way away from Islington. It was only the second time that they had physically talked to each other, usually preferring to use disposable mobiles to communicate. Both parties were angry as the informer snatched the bag of money away from the radical preacher.

The Planner looked at the man he so despised. He needed his knowledge of police movements. It gave him an added level of protection. He had been so easy to recruit such was the extent of the man's bitterness. He recalled that evening, earlier in the year, when his brother had heard this infidel in a drunken rant against the Commander, the time spent checking him out and the discovery that he was in trouble with a 'Pay-Day' loan company.

He took a chance and met with him: that had been easy to arrange as the man seemed to be spending more of his time in the local pubs. As the resentment surfaced the target became evermore willing to provide information believing he was helping community liaison. He blinked as the Cleric told him of the hatred of the police that existed within the Muslim world. He persuaded him that if the officer could forewarn him of police raids and other activities, he, the Cleric, could work from the inside and preserve calm within the streets of Islington.

It is doubtful that the policeman really believed this façade but he was already seduced by the bag of money which had been placed at his feet. He could only guess at the amount but, judging from the protruding fifty-pound notes, it was sizeable. He was to go home and replicate the scene from the ending of the original film starring Robert Shaw, 'The Taking of Pelham 123'. This was where the crooked Tube driver Harold, played by Martin Balsam, is left with most of the money and lies on his bed making love to the dollar bills. Despite having influenza he yells with happiness.

Later that evening, having collected the money from around his kitchen, the police officer counted it into piles and added them together to reach an approximate total of over £6,000. It was enough. He would pay off his short-term debts and visit his wife who was staying with her mother. He wanted her back: he was lonely. In his euphoria he decided to ignore a nagging doubt, beating around in his brain, that this was an awful lot of money to spend on community harmony. He should, perhaps, have remembered that Harold Longman, the felon full of cold, was shortly to be arrested by the New York police.

Initially the mole was unaware of the dangers that lay ahead. He would receive calls from a person whose voice he did not recognise. He was able to report that there was no evidence that the police were following up on local intelligence. There were the usual raids returning absconded prisoners to jail, keeping minor drug pushers in check and the hated domestic violence where knives were used.

It was after the bombing of the Mohammeds' shop and the discovery of the two bodies that the atmosphere changed. As he had listened to the Commander's words, he started to understand that he was in far deeper than he had realised.

"You are lucky I am giving you that," the Cleric said. "Tell me more about this bomb alert."

"It was a false alarm. An officer wanted to test the reaction of her colleagues. The duty sergeant allowed himself to be browbeaten. It has been hushed-up."

The public house in Highgate shook as, far below, the Northern Line Tube train hurtled towards Edgware. The Cleric shook a finger in the air.

"One more setback and you will die."

'Setback'. The word shook the informer to the core. The truth was dawning.

"This is nothing to do with community liaison is it?" he said.

"You do not ask me questions."

He looked at the bag of money at his feet. He did not understand what was happening. His wife had again returned to her mother's home accusing him of lying to her. He had paid off the short-term loans only to find that he was now being hounded for outstanding interest. He could not meet with the lenders personally and dreaded the harassing telephone calls. He needed another £2,000.

"When do you move? I can't hope to keep things secret. Why did you have to bomb the shop and kill Mr Mohammed and Saleem Singh?"

He stood up and went to the bar to order himself a third pint of real ale. He bought water for his companion. The Cleric smiled: he needed this kafir for several more weeks.

"You are asking too many questions. You are nervous. Please pull yourself together." He allowed his words to hang in the air. "But I will tell you. Today is the last Wednesday in September. We will commit our service to our brothers in three weeks' time. After that you will be a free man. We will not contact you again."

The police officer drove to his empty home hating himself. How had he fallen so low?

As he poured himself a large gin and tonic DCI Sarah Rudd was in her office at Islington Police Station.

She reviewed the list written down in front of her:

*Commander Max Riley*
*Superintendent Monica Moses*
*D/Supt Majid Khan*
*DCI Percy 'Freezer' Attwood*
*DCI Avril Flemming*

She decided that it simply was not possible that the Commander was the mole. She also ruled out DCI Flemming who had sent her, in a plain envelope, her copy of *Emily's Dream Man Comes Home* with copious comments and suggestions. She thought that the title needed spicing up and offered *Emily's Afghanistan Dream*. She wanted more passion and wrote a discourse on the subject. She then proposed that as 'chick-lit' is about relationships perhaps Emily should have filled the months alone with a female friend.

Superintendent Monica Moses was due to appear before an annual assessment board and Sarah judged that she was the most unlikely informer in the station. She rarely socialised and

183

it did not seem possible that she could have links with Muslim extremists.

She narrowed her search down to three colleagues. The person she knew best was her own boss Detective Superintendent Majid Khan. He remained in contact with her over the phone calls: he was a clever actor if it transpired that he was the mole. This left her friend Percy. 'Freezer' was David Jason through and through and she often chided him for eating cholesterol-laden bacon sandwiches in the canteen. She had been seeing more of him of late as he worked even longer hours. He had made various suggestions as to where she should wear her medal. In Percy's case it was never crude although several of his ideas were inventive. Lately there had been less humour as the full horror of the bombing affected the local force.

Sarah took out another sheet of writing. It repeated the question posed by her husband: *How do they know that they'll kill exactly four hundred people?*

Freezer was still drinking and was looking at a calendar. He had the information from the Cleric: Wednesday 16 October. His clock chimed midnight. Twenty days to go. He googled the date and registered two events taking place. Micky Flanagan would be making people laugh at The O2 Arena and Tony Hadley would be singing the hits of Spandau Ballet at The Royal Albert Hall. Even the Planner could not blow up either of those two locations.

\* \* \*

She looked down at the toilet bowl and gave a silent cry of dismay. For the third month running she was not pregnant.

Jessica had the world at her feet. She was desperately in love with Matthew. As they were together more so they became closer. Matthew's libidinous nature was turning into tactile care. She adored picking him up from the railway station, driving him home, making him comfortable in their lounge, putting on a Mahler symphony, pouring his whisky and sliding in front of him a plate of toasted nibbles. This was after he had hugged Olivia and visited Rustic and the two puppies. He did not like the geese which followed him around the paddock trying to bite his heels.

Olivia never asked about her brother. She had willingly agreed to visit her mother with her father. That turned out to be a mistake as Anne Buckingham was incoherent. Matthew had exchanged sharp words with the senior nurse who had challenged him to find a way to prevent alcoholics from finding drink.

His daughter was edging closer to her 'Jess'. She had now started to ask if she could have a brother or a sister: she did not mind which.

Jessica had received a letter from Mr Parsons in Stratford-upon-Avon informing her that it was expected that a sum nearing £3 million would be sent to her bank account by the end of October. She had received a letter from her father which had been forwarded to her by her mother's executors. It was full of self-pity and how proud he was of his daughter and could she lend him £10,000 because there had been a fire at his bar. She noted the Iberian bank account details, tore the letter up and remitted him £1,000.

Unbeknown to Matthew she had been to a private clinic for a full medical check-up. She was thirty-eight years old and getting fitter. She devoured the female pages of the newspapers. She placed herself on an almost vegan diet and had lost nine pounds in weight. She went to the gym every day and, for her, the treadmill became the Yellow Brick Road. She was Dorothy running towards the Emerald City hoping that the Wizard of Oz could help her.

Mr Rudy Van Meyer produced his best consultant's smile.

"I was going to call you, Jessica."

"Cool."

"'Cool'. My daughter uses that word. What does it mean?"

'Clever,' thought Jessica. 'He's getting me to relax.'

"Move on doc. I'm calm."

"You've already asked me three questions."

"I'm paying the bill."

The American doctor laughed.

"You want a baby."

Jessica went quiet and the atmosphere changed.

"In the States I guess we'd shorten Jessica to Jessie," he suggested.

She smiled and the room radiated with her personality.

"I'm Jessica. Mathew calls me Jessie and Olivia insists that I'm Jess."

The next few minutes passed with a discussion on who was who, the domestic situation and her medical history.

"I'm a gynaecologist, Jessica. That means I understand your reproductive tracts. An obstetrician delivers your baby."

"So you can help me have my child."

"I wish I could."

She looked at the professional sitting on the other side of the desk. He was in his early forties and dishy.

"The most I can do is to tell you if you can have a baby. We have blood tests, scans, x-rays and the questionnaire that we completed together."

"Can I have a baby please, Mr Van Mayer?"

"You are supremely fit and all the working parts seem to be in order."

"So I can have my child."

"You're as near ideal as I can diagnose." He paused.

"Do you know that my job is easier if I have to give bad news?"

"Come again?"

"Just think about it, Jessica. If we were sitting here and I told you 'sorry, we've found something. You can't conceive', job done, you pay the bill and I move on to the next patient."

"I'm lost."

"You want certainty and I can't give it to you. There is no reason on earth why you can't get pregnant. You're under forty and even that does not really matter. You're wonderfully healthy and, of course, not that this has anything to do with it, you're an attractive woman."

'Medical ethics out of the window,' thought Jessica as she lapped up the flattery.

"Can you do anything to help me get pregnant please, Mr Van Meyer?"

"No."

"I read an article suggesting that pantothenic acid can help. Should I be taking it?"

"You are. It's to be found in many foods we eat. It might help your hair grow more quickly but it will add nothing to your fertility."

"What do I do then?"

"Get a hobby. Take your mind off things. The body works best when it's left alone. You need to make love with Matthew without thinking about babies."

She wondered about telling him what they did together the previous night but decided it was not suitable for the clinic.

"A hobby?"

"Research local history. Where do you live?" he asked turning over his notes. "Leighton Buzzard." He paused. "Surely many things have happened there."

"To be honest, Mr Van Meyer, I'm told that it has been a peaceful domain for centuries." She paused. "Although I was reading in the local paper recently about a train robbery."

"There you are, Jessica. I prescribe that you become an expert on train robberies."

"Will I get pregnant?"

"Hope so. You'll certainly become one hell of a party bore!"

"Your account, Mr Van Meyer? I like to pay my bills on time."

"In the post, Jessica. Good luck."

She laughed.

"That's rather English for an American!"

"Bonne chance, ma petite. My wife is French."

She returned to Ledburn and destroyed all her vitamin pills. She went into the town and replenished their fridge with meats and packets of frozen chips. She visited the library and downloaded the newspaper reports of the train robbery. She tried to borrow the latest book on the subject but it was out. She returned home, changed into shorts and walking boots, and decided to start by locating Sears Crossing.

She had two hours left before she'd collect Olivia from her friend's house. She wanted to have at least one hour of daylight remaining to clean out Rustic and exercise the puppies.

She ploughed through the fields down to the railway line. She watched the Virgin train rush towards Euston Station. She sat down and thought about her meeting with the baby doctor. She was aware that success in pregnancy depended on a number of factors. She thought she was healthy but it was reassuring to hear his confirmation of the fact.

She liked that chat-up line. Somehow the events of recent weeks had dampened Matthew's libido which was usually pre-empted with outrageous suggestions, most of which concerned her anatomy.

She had enjoyed being flattered.

All she needed to do now was to become pregnant. It was time that Jessica Lambert had her baby. Quite what that had to do with the 16.24 Euston to Northampton commuter train, which was coming to a halt at Leighton Buzzard station, she would leave to the wonders of modern medicine.

How the Great Train Robbers could help her become pregnant was simply beyond her.

* * *

Sabina Morina flew by Etihad airlines from Heathrow into the capital of the United Arab Emirates, Abu Dhabi International Airport, landing at Terminal 3 early in the morning. Her cab driver took the E10 and eventually the E22 motorway which led into Sheikh Rashid Al Maktoum Street and on to the Crown Plaza Abu Dhabi hotel. She settled in, showered, changed and headed for the Corniche business centre. She was looking for Osama Al-Kabal.

Over the next three days she searched everywhere but she never found him. She went to the bank where the £5 million had been transferred and they flatly refused to speak to her beyond the initial pleasantries. There was no account in the name of Six Weeks in Summer Production Limited and they were unable to comment on the name of the individual for whom she was searching. She visited all the central hotels and asked for Osama himself and Martine Madden and again drew a blank. She returned to the airport and attempted to access

188

passenger lists over the last few weeks but she realised herself it was a futile exercise. She visited the British Embassy in Khalid bin Al Waleed Street and spent nearly an hour reading about the UK Department of Trade and Investment's initiatives to create closer trading links, and admiring the picture of the Foreign Secretary before being advised that there was nothing the officials could do for her.

At night she sat quietly in the bars of the hotel and attracted regular approaches all of which were rejected. She tried to establish if there was a dedicated film centre but the whole atmosphere was one of mystery and secrecy. After three days she flew back to London and a day later found herself in Matthew's office together with Caroline.

She delivered a full report and handed over a written version. Neither of her listeners could fault her application and their discussion moved on to whether they should appoint a firm of international solicitors who might be able to use their network to find Osama Al-Kabal.

Sabina disagreed with this strategy.

"The whole time I was there I felt this shroud of secrecy," she said. "We are foreigners. Outwardly they welcome our sportsmen and women and our boats. But beneath the surface there is an impenetrable shield. We'll only locate Osama Al-Kabal if he wants to be found, which seems unlikely."

"What do you suggest we do?"

"We must concentrate on Martine Madden."

"We can't find her, Sabina. She has a flat in Fulham which is unoccupied. Her parents live in London as well but will not speak to us. We gained an impression that their daughter is not welcome at home. We can't report her missing because she's unmarried, has no children and is twenty-six years old. We've spoken to Amanda who is simply not co-operating and has left for her new project."

"How on earth did we allow this to happen?" said Matthew.

"That's rather what the solicitors for the Pretty Fund are asking," said Caroline. "The problem is that we don't have an answer."

* * *

The Planner was reading the newspaper headlines with intense satisfaction. He was being kept informed about the situation but he wanted to confirm for himself what the self-satisfied infidels in England were reading. He was pleased with what he saw: *Islamist mob parades nuns in Cairo*. He liked the fact that al-Qaeda driven rioters were targeting Christian teachers. They were hated by the hardline Islamists because they were teaching Muslim children the wrong things. Churches, homes and businesses were being attacked. Since the Arab Spring had driven President Mubarak from power in 2011 the Planner had encouraged his Middle Eastern brothers to greater violence. The local Muslim Brotherhood party pleased him: nearly nine hundred people had died in the last four days of violence.

It was not enough. America was withdrawing from world politics with President Obama relying more on rhetoric and less on co-ordinated action. They were also watching the oil situation carefully because the process of fracking had already reduced the United State's dependency on imported fuels by 40 percent. Their forward projections foretold of a weakening of power in the Middle East.

The key weapon in the hands of the terrorists was fear. The Planner knew that politicians collapsed in the face of violence. They would spend billions they did not have trying to placate their voters. He was on the verge of delivering one of the most outrageous atrocities ever experienced in the Western world.

This was because of the simplicity of his idea. He thought of the four hundred people who would be thinking about their wives, husbands, lovers and mistresses, their children and homes, cricket and the football season, the TV schedules, their credit card debts, their health, their latest cholesterol readings. Perhaps some would be thinking about politics and ponder as to whether they should switch to the UK Independence Party.

They would die horribly. The second round of gas tests in the desert near to the Iraq border had been filmed. It had taken a man of two hundred and ten pounds just four minutes to die a screaming death. The Planner watched it again and again. He loved the ending where a yellow liquid poured from his mouth. He realised that the individual's muscles were cramping and he could see moisture being forced through the pores of the skin. He turned the volume up as loud as possible so he could relish the cries of agony. He then viewed again the death of a naked woman. It ended by her body seemingly being lifted in the air. Her screams were wonderful.

He reviewed his meeting with his informer. The decision to give him the date of Wednesday 16 October was taken in the belief that it would relax him a little. He was showing considerable stress and they reasoned that the panacea of the cash would not last long. He was finished anyway because Ahmed had already been instructed to kill him immediately after the event.

There was no way that their mission could fail. Despite that, they were all to meet that evening and go through the schedule hour by hour. The man replacing Saleem had been vetted and would be there. The two engineers had returned from Yorkshire where again they had been sent to try out the explosions. They filmed the rock fall for the Planner who asked endless questions. He would insist they met night after night. This meant that Rashid was restricted in his efforts to meet with the deceased Saleem's sister.

DCI Sarah Rudd was getting nowhere and yet she still rejected the thought that she should inform D/Supt Khan of her latest investigations. Much to her relief DCI Avril Flemming had been taken off her normal duties and seconded to Camden Town. No reason had been given. She'd only be away for a week and she asked that the next meeting of the 'chick-lit' group was delayed until her return.

She simply had no idea who was the mole. The previous evening Nick had suggested that she marked them all out of ten only to find that her own boss, D/Supt Khan, scored the highest points. He then recommended that she concentrate on the outstanding question of how the terrorists could be certain that they would kill four hundred people.

"Nick," pleaded Sarah. "I've no idea. If they try to attack a ship how do they place the bombs to ensure a fast sinking. Modern boats stay afloat. It can't be a plane. There is absolutely no indication that the airports have increased security ratings. We know that the planning remains within Islington even though there was the scare over my meeting with Saleem Singh."

The outpouring became a torrent.

"Nick. I will certainly lose my job and our pension before this is all over. But it will be worthwhile if I can stop the carnage which we believe will happen. I don't know how long there is to go. Nick, I don't know what to do."

"Do you remember when you rescued the kidnapped child in Ealing?"

"Of course."

"How did you do it?"

"Do what?"

"Work it out."

"I sat in my office and re-read the files."

"What do you think you should do, Sarah?"

The front door shut a few minutes later. It then re-opened as Sarah returned to tell her husband that she loved him. He heard her car being driven away and within an hour she was in her office tidying up her files before starting to review every single piece of information. She had, beside her, a piece of paper.

Two hours later she was still looking at a blank sheet.

Detective Chief Inspector Sarah Rudd was at a complete loss on how to solve the coming terrorist attack. She had to go and see D/Supt Khan. But he was possibly the mole and all that would do would be to move the terrorists into another district.

For the sake of the lives of four hundred people she had to provide answers and find them soon.

# Chapter Fifteen

They had spoken late last night and were now in a small office at the back of Silverside Brokers, fully committed to implementing their agreed strategy. There was no body language, an absence of innuendo and a commitment to talk openly. There was a table and four chairs of which two were not required. On the table there were bottles of still and sparkling water and two note-pads each with a pen placed on the top sheet.

Matthew looked at Caroline and confirmed the purpose of this private meeting.

"As we discussed, we'll start by listing all the parties."

"Agreed, Matthew. You talk. I'll write."

"One. Six Weeks in Summer Production Limited. It's the corporate body which has accepted the loan of £6 million from the Pretty Fund."

She registered this detail quickly and nodded her head.

"Two. The directors of the company. When the loan was made there were four: Amanda Adams-Smythe, Richard Rochards, Osama Al-Kabal and Martine Madden."

Caroline completed this section and then went to say something. He held his hand up.

"You should make a note here that subsequently, as far as the official records are concerned, Amanda and Richard have either resigned or have been dismissed. There is the question of whether Amanda's leaving or Richard's sacking are legal: please add that as an addendum to this section."

He poured her a full glass of still water and pulled the bottle of sparkling aqua towards himself.

"Three," he continued. "The advisers to the company. There's your law firm, Christie Simpson, which means you. There's Maidstone New Issues which is Mark Patterson-Brown and, of course…"

"Silverside Brokers which is you, Matthew," she stated as she continued penning her notes.

He moved on rather too quickly.

"The loan came from The Pretty Fund."

"It's actually a limited partnership, Matthew," she said as she wrote. "As far as we are concerned it's the same as a limited company. The two partners are Jonathan and Roger Pretty and there are twenty-two investing members."

"They are represented by Stuart Green of Goodlove, Green and Co, City lawyers."

"Nasty people, Matthew."

"I think we should add Coutts Bank to the list, Caroline."

"Definitely," she concurred. "I'm going to write down the Financial Conduct Authority and the Law Society. Obviously we and Stuart Green are regulated by our own body and you and Maidstone New Issues are covered by the FCA."

"What about The Pretty Fund?"

"They answer only to their shareholder partners. It's a private equity business."

She looked down at her notes.

"A cast of many," she said.

"Six Weeks in Summer Production Limited has received a loan of £6 million from The Pretty Fund. The finance was to be used to make a film. Coutts Bank transferred the net balance, which it received from your firm, to a Middle Eastern Bank. The two remaining directors have disappeared and Sabina could find no trace of them in Abu Dhabi."

"Caroline. Who's to blame?" asked Matthew.

"Wallets," she replied.

"What does that mean?" he said.

"We agreed last night that we'd look at this purely practically. I can probably make out a case that everybody has some culpability but whether that's judgemental rather than legal will keep us here to the early hours." She drank some water. "I think the important question is who is likely to move first."

"Who do you think?"

"Goodlove, Green and Co and the Financial Conduct Authority."

"The regulators arrived this afternoon. Debra has been keeping them informed and two inspectors came in and confiscated our files. They are coming back in forty-eight hours' time."

"What does Debra think? She's street-wise and smart."

Matthew raised his eyebrows. "You spend most of your time berating her."

"That's the game we play, Mob. She's good, I promise you."

"Debra called in our own lawyers a week ago and they have audited our processes. As a result she's more confident that we might survive."

"That's a bit dramatic, isn't it?"

"As far as the FCA is concerned we're guilty until we can prove that we are innocent."

"Well, that's outside our control. The question is whether The Pretty Fund will make a move. It's a relatively small business. Their balance sheet stands at around £80 million. Roger Pretty is successful. He'll take risks and is prepared to wait for his return. That's why he argued so fiercely for a higher percentage share of the profits from the film. On the projections of revenues of £20 million, the fund might have received over one and a half million pounds as well as their interest and repayment uplift. Remember, they were due to be the first to be repaid and would have gained a 50 percent amount on top of their £6 million."

"What part does Jonathan play in this?"

"He spends most of his time with the shareholders. He's working out, I guess, whether he can get away with a mistake or if he needs to spend big sums on legal action."

"Will they stand any chance in the courts?"

"It depends who they sue, if they do. The guilty parties are the directors. They have committed gross misrepresentation. They said they'd make a film and they haven't. Two have gone and two have disappeared. So Stuart Green will then target my firm. We dealt with satisfying the eleven conditions on the loan. Any lawyer worth his salt would find something amiss."

"So you might be in trouble, Caroline."

She laughed. "Not a chance, Matthew. We rarely sue each

other and we know all the tricks. Ask yourself: "why am I a corporate finance partner? Answer. Because I don't get it wrong. My files are watertight and Stuart Green knows that."

"So who is vulnerable? Maidstone New Issues?"

"Rather. Except that Mark Patterson-Brown has no money and he's facing a costly divorce." She held up her hand. "No. Before you ask, we are still together. Just. Mrs Patterson-Brown has had enough. Simple as that. She's just turned sixty and she's been reading all these articles in the *Daily Mail* about the retired brigade starting their lives again. That's what she's doing. She's moving to France and she's taking the lovely Mark to the cleaners. He's already sold three of his racehorses and only secured enough to pay off the bank loans."

"And Stuart Green knows that?"

"The governor of the Bank of England probably knows that. Mark is drinking far too much. Alcohol makes him rather garrulous."

Matthew looked at Caroline.

"That leaves Silverside Brokers, doesn't it?"

"If I were Stuart Green I'd already be preparing the action. He knows that you haven't much money but he'll have checked and read your professional indemnity policy. My guess is that your insurers will try to settle at around £3 million and if I were acting for the Pretty Fund, I'd accept it."

"Where does that leave us?"

"You have an action against all four of the directors of Six Weeks in Summer Production Limited."

"What are our chances?"

"Barring a miracle, nil." She frowned. "You'll not be able to renew your professional indemnity insurance cover because no other company will take you on. The FCA will give you three months and then suspend your permissions."

"Close us down?" He was horrified at the thought.

"More complicated than that, but, in a nutshell, yes."

"What do I do, Caroline?"

He paused. His divorce from Anne had been bloody and the building up of Silverside Brokers was his penance and his dream. She temporarily shattered his self-confidence but he rebuilt and regained his self-respect. Once he'd started even the recession could not stop him.

"Do you have a big garden, Mob?" she asked.

* * *

There were fourteen days to go. The Planner lifted himself off his prayer mat and ordered his brothers to sit round him. They were to disappear out of circulation meeting in twelve days' time at a location just off the M1 motorway. The only exception was Rashid who would be guarding the gas containers. He would continue to walk the streets of Islington until he made his move.

The Cleric began an hour-long rant against infidels. He evoked the teaching of Mohammad and the greatness of Islam. He knew that the seven terrorists believed every word. Each would perform their tasks to perfection. The bombs would explode and the trap would be set. Rashid would let out the gas and die a martyr's death. The others would be out of the country, some within hours. The Planner would remain in Islington and preach his sermons of hate. Ahmed would kill the mole. They would allow the second officer to live because they had no knowledge of these events.

The Cleric tried to envisage four hundred bodies. Many would have a family and, in many cases, children and ageing parents. The authorities would attempt to censor the press but the rescue services would use their mobiles and earn fortunes from selling the photographs of the agonised faces to the media. The helicopters would quickly appear overhead but the explosions would create dust clouds which might take days to disperse.

The police and ambulance services would be overwhelmed and the army would be called in. Then it would be discovered that the cuts had been so savage that the generals would consider calling up the reservists. The hospitals, already nearing crisis levels, would be overtaken by dead bodies, collapsing relatives and stressed rescue workers.

COBR, the Cabinet Office Briefing Room in Whitehall, would

197

be occupied by senior politicians and their advisers. The media would call it COBRA by adding an 'A' (the number of the room) and using it to mean the Prime Minister and his inner circle. He would begin by evoking the spirit of Tony Blair and justifying every mistake they would subsequently make by the justification of a war against terrorism. It would not be long before events overtook the political process. The media, itching to retaliate against the Leveson Inquiry, would launch a blame game as never before.

The Cleric also knew that eventually the British people would take over. They would bury their dead, they would suffer within their estates, the community leaders would fight to hold onto the multi-racial progress being made and the police would regroup and regain their authority.

But it would take months, if not years, for Britain to recover. There would be a huge commercial consequence as transport systems ground to a halt, airport security became a nightmare and government debt spiralled out of control.

The strength of the Cleric was that he knew all that. He would not allow his brothers to exaggerate their task. It was simply one battle in the war ahead. The Cleric knew that he had to break the British people. To achieve that he had to undermine their belief in the system. The politicians were long discredited. The real power lay with the police and the legal system. Most people believed that they were safe and that the courts dispensed fair justice. This was backed up by the dedicated schoolteachers, the doctors, nurses, the fire services, the paramedics, the council workers, refuse collectors and the voluntary sectors. This was their way of life.

On Wednesday 16 October 2013 the Cleric and his brothers would commit an atrocity so devastating that the whole fabric of British society would come under threat.

He was now becoming excited. He dismissed the terrorists for the last time and decided to watch the films. He concentrated on the yellow liquid coming out of the man's mouth as he died his agonising death. The naked girl then was shown twisting and convulsing. He turned the sound up to its maximum volume. He thought he detected the word 'please'.

He let his mind roam to a place in England where, in two weeks' time, four hundred people would die in the same way. It was his offering to Islam. He would achieve veneration because his plan would not fail and one of the great single act killings of non-believers would take place. He could not be stopped.

He was Islam's servant. He would not fail. His place ahead in Allah's paradise would be secure.

\* \* \*

Deep down inside her Caroline Pennington was a pussy cat. She did not want to have sex with Mark Patterson-Brown but she felt sorry for him. She was looking forward to her Threadneedles Hotel shower and she had purchased a bottle of expensive perfumed body-wash for the occasion. Before she was able to enjoy that she had to lie there while he huffed, puffed and groaned. She started thinking to herself about his condition. Despite the excessive alcohol intake he led an active outdoor life and was careful with his diet. He probably consumed too many shell-fish but that went for a considerable number of activists in the City. He was utterly relieved by the imminent departure of his wife to France and was pleased, in one way, to rid himself of his horses.

He had decided to sail around the world. He already had an ocean-going yacht which was moored on the south coast but now he was going to fulfil his dreams of global exploration. They did not even talk about it any further because he knew that Caroline was not prepared to make up the crew. There was the girl he had met in the local pub who seemed quite inter-ested and she had a twenty-two year old body.

Caroline waited for the moment of satisfaction and she waited and waited. He suddenly rolled off her with sweat pouring off his face.

"Have you taken the Viagra, Mark?" she asked.

"Double dosage. Must have something on my mind."

This was rather what Caroline was thinking as, to her relief, the hot water started pouring down over her skin. She sus-pected that Mark Patterson-Brown was a worried man and his divorce was not the most significant part of his stress. Through-out their passionate relationship he had, until recently, shown a remarkable virility. That was a key reason why Caroline had stayed the course.

Now he was struggling and yet physically he'd not changed. The poison was inside him.

Mark Patterson-Brown was a very worried man.

* * *

Detective Chief Inspector Sarah Rudd made her first real break-through when at the bottom of her garden thinking about things. Nick, Marcus and Susie were all at school and she was on late duty.

Initially the idea she had was radical.

From the outset she'd been told that there were two moles inside Islington Police Station. One was a senior officer and the other was scared. This was why she had pursued the idea that it could be DCI Flemming and Constable Pepper and she now realised that her lesbian theory was stupidly wide of the mark.

She was diverting her thinking from the mole to the second person and her idea was most certainly original.

'What,' she was thinking to herself, 'if the word was not 'scared'? That implies intimidation and perhaps threats and she had no evidence for that. Was it possible that she had mis-understood the speaker? What if she had not heard 'scared'?'

She looked at the elms which marked the boundary of their garden. What had Nick made her do when she was strug-gling to find the kidnapped baby? She had to think about the obvious. It was then that it hit her. She played around with the notion for some minutes and decided she did not care what time she arrived at work. She thought about a word which had completely thrown her off the track. She heard the sound again and then she reached a crucial conclusion.

'What if the word was 'scarred'?' she asked herself.

She looked at her watch and again decided to delay changing for work.

'Scarred,' she repeated.

She tried to work out the exact meaning. It could refer to physical injury or to mental damage. She could only think of one officer who qualified for those two descriptions.

Her mind went back to The Mall and she shook as she recalled the assassin's bullet hitting her armoured vest. Even now her doctor was concerned about the healing process. She had lost her libido and regained it. She was going through the menopause. She had let down her son. She had mishandled the meeting with Saleem and perhaps caused the death of two people. Each day she was agonising as to whether to confess all to Majid Khan. Or was he the mole?

Sarah recalled Marcus's joke which he had told at breakfast time: "I'm in two minds whether I'm a schizophrenic."

'Not bad,' she'd thought before ruffling his hair.

She lingered on in the cool air.

'Am I in charge of myself?' she asked herself. 'Have I really thought this out? Am I justified in believing that my way is the only route to stopping the atrocity?'

"Or," she exclaimed, "is DCI Rudd physically and mentally damaged?"

"Oh God!" she cried out. "Am I scarred? Am I the other mole?"

\* \* \*

Jessica was late.

'This Mr Van Meyer knows his stuff,' she laughed to herself. She wondered about rushing into Leighton Buzzard and buying a pregnancy testing kit but decided it was too soon.

Olivia was at school and her worried partner was in London with an overnight case as he faced meeting after meeting with his staff and the lawyers. She knew that tomorrow he would be hearing the judgement of the regulators.

She was beginning to enjoy her life-style. Each morning she cleaned for two hours. It was a large house and there were the animals to feed and their various shelters to clean out. Olivia was a great help with this at weekends and after school. She then took the dry-cleaning into the town and collected various items waiting for her. The gardener came three times a week and pottered around rather effectively. She was beginning to understand how lawns grew although the October weather was bringing this to a halt. She cleaned out Rustic and played with the ever-growing puppies. The geese squealed at her and she shouted back at them.

She had now researched the financial advisory sector and met with four different groups in Milton Keynes.

The accountants started by listing their fees and were rejected almost immediately. The private client stockbroker was immensely impressive but then told her he was retiring. His offer to introduce his partner did not survive. The Independent Financial Adviser blamed the compliance regime and told her she must fill in several pages of forms so that he could categorise her 'risk' level. She turned down the opportunity!

She met Fiona in Starbucks. There were only two chairs vacant and so they found themselves sitting together. They started talking. While not giving much away Jessica mentioned her search for financial advice.

"You could try my partner," said Fiona. She went on to explain that she was in a three member tax advisory firm and she'd be pleased to make the introduction. "There will be some form filling I'm afraid but we serve lovely biscuits."

They talked on and then Jessica asked, "What sort of things will your partner ask about?"

"The only questions that matter to us are the ones you ask. We find tax efficient solutions, Jessica."

Two days later Fiona Wilson became the financial adviser to Jessica. She was later to become her confidant due to her integrity and professionalism. When she found out that her client was about to inherit nearly £3 million she stayed up all night structuring a financial strategy which she submitted to her other two partners. Her senior colleague was authorised to give investment advice. "I'll make the profits, you save the tax," he laughed as he congratulated her.

Jessica was becoming increasingly interested in local history spurred on by her fascination with The Great Train Robbery. She did not deal in half measures. She was minus twelve when the event occurred and she decided she wanted to understand the environment and social aspects of the locality in which it took place. She read the archives in the library and several of the many books written about Leighton Buzzard.

It was the period when the post-war 'golden age' was slowing down. The April 1963 budget took 3.75 million people out of taxation and reduced the rate on the first £100 of earned income to 20 percent. The cry was for faster wealth creation as the middle class began to emerge. The felons, mostly from London (apart from the mysterious Irishman), shared a similar hunger for wealth but chose different methods.

Jessica wanted to know about the world in which they existed. The Vietnam War was underway and President Charles de Gaulle vetoed the United Kingdom's entry into the European Economic Community. She wondered whether to write him a personal letter of thanks. The Beatles recorded their debut album. Even now she played 'Please Please Me' on her CD. Dr Beeching was damaging the railways by closing down some stations. She could remember her mother saying how much he was hurting rural communities. The Aldermaston marchers protested against nuclear weapons.

She thought about this. Jessica had never felt strongly enough to protest against anything. The Alabama race riots occurred and again this made her think. She understood that some commentators believed that in his time Tony Blair had contributed to Britain's race problems by liberalising the country's borders. Back in 1963 Bob Dylan released 'Blowin' in the wind': perhaps one of her favourite tracks of all time. Back to race: President John F. Kennedy promised a Civil Rights Bill. She decided to read more about this. Valentina Tereshkova achieved a first. She tucked this away and decided to ask Matthew what she did. Kim Philby defected to Moscow. She struggled to understand this because for her 'The Cold War' meant nothing.

Jessica read the words and unashamedly started to cry: 'I Have a Dream' catapulted Martin Luther King Jr. into greatness. Christine Keeler went to prison for perjury having brought down John Profumo. She read all the details as she loved scandal. Alec Douglas-Home became Prime Minister.

Who was he... a Liberal? Malcolm X appealed in the States to the 'Grass Roots' and now she stopped in her tracks.

22 November 1963. President John F. Kennedy was assassinated. She closed the pages. She could read no more. 1963 was a bloody year.

She was on a hillside looking down at the railtracks. She was beginning to understand the world in which the robbers and their victims lived. When she first read about the unguarded mail train and the crude manner in which it was stopped by using a black sack to cover up the lights, she was disbelieving. She quickly appreciated the national outcry when it became known that the thieves took away around two and a half million pounds.

'No wonder the judge locked them away for so long,' she thought.

She had viewed Bridego Bridge and imagined the thieves humping the sacks down the incline before loading them into the waiting vans. One Sunday, when Matthew had taken Olivia to Milton Keynes, she went back and scrambled up the slope so she could watch a train pass through on the slow line. The Intercity Virgin expresses went too fast. She was perplexed that Bruce Reynolds, the mastermind, thought that they could stop any train.

But they did. Violently and brutally. Not quite as the newspapers claimed which they did by exaggerating the physical abuse of the driver Jack Mills. The police and railway officials were nowhere to be seen and it took a passing train driver to convey messages.

As she read on she yet again applauded the British spirit. When eventually the police went into action they pursued the robbers around the globe and caught virtually all of them. She decided to return to the scene of the crime again. She was planning to go to Glasgow and retrace the whole journey.

But for one final time she needed to absorb the atmosphere as the train reached Bridego Bridge and the post office sacks were plundered. She knew for certain that it could never happen again.

# Chapter Sixteen

Her lips lingered on his far longer than was usual. She also took the unusual step of illegally parking her car on a set of double yellow lines and walking with him to the platform. She watched as he threw down a coin and picked up a copy of *The Times*. She was surprised when he went into the toilets: they'd only left Ledburn twelve minutes earlier. She looked up at the travel information. The train from Northampton was on time and due in at 6.14 a.m. The station clock showed that there were three minutes to go before the eight carriages pulled in to collect the Leighton Buzzard commuters.

They were standing around, humourless and quiet. The odd group of regulars laughed at the jokes which they told each other every one of the five days they met. There would be fewer of them on Friday as the more senior civil servants usually began their weekends with their families on Thursday evenings. It was simple to pick out those commuters who would be travelling first class: they had an air about them. The annoying cyclists, decked in their sweaty lycra outfits and using their 'I'm good for the ecology' label as an excuse for pushing and shoving their metal pieces into already crowded bays, took no prisoners.

Jessica was usually amused by their antics. Today, her thoughts were purely for Matthew. He had tossed and turned all night long as he prepared for his interrogation. The future of his business was at stake. The travellers began to shuffle into position. They knew where the driver would halt the carriages and they wanted to be first on in order to secure one of the few remaining vacant seats. Matthew could relax because he always travelled first class and was guaranteed a place. His compartment would not be full until they stopped at Watford and collected a few more London-bound executives.

The announcer signalled the arrival of the 6.14 a.m. to Euston. The fight to board was underway. They were ready to leave. The buzzer sounded, the doors closed and hundreds of Britain's key workers, packed like tins of sardines, began reading their newspapers and prepared to spend just under forty minutes doing so until the train pulled in to Euston station on the north side of the London congestion zone. Jessica had spotted a rather pregnant woman climbing on board. Her mind began to play silly games. She wondered what would happen if the expectant mother needed the toilet. Could she reach the tiny cubicle in time? They were all, effectively, London Midland captives until 6.50 a.m.

She wandered back to her car after buying her own newspaper. She was thinking about her partner. He was probably not reading *The Times*: his thoughts would be on the meeting ahead.

This began in the boardroom of Silverside Brokers in the City of London at 9.30 a.m. There were three officials from the Financial Conduct Authority who throughout would refer to themselves as the FCA. The senior inspector, Carol Sixsmith, did most of the talking. Her junior, Andrew, supplied regular papers and references and the third visitor was a lawyer who did not speak throughout the whole event but who did make copious notes.

Matthew opened the meeting courteously by introducing Debra White, Craig MacDonald, Ashtella Khan and Sabina Morina. They had decided not to ask their lawyers to attend because they felt it would send the wrong signals to the FCA. It was irrelevant because if they had been present the regulators would have ignored them.

Much to Matthew's surprise there were no further introductions. Andrew plugged in a machine and nodded towards his boss. Carol Sixsmith said that she wanted to play a recording of a telephone conversation between Zabo Brooks, one of the brokers, and his client.

"I want you to listen carefully to this recording. Here's the investment story which was approved by Debra White." She smiled as she handed out the papers. "We, at the FCA, know Debra well."

'As the judge said "You'll be given a fair trial, then hanged",' thought Matthew to himself.

The telephone conversation lasted eight minutes. There was a balance between Zabo's explanation of the sale of shares in Six Weeks in Summer Production Limited and the questions posed by Mrs Florence Courtney, a widow living in Sussex. She wanted to understand how the film could generate £20 million in revenues.

"Debra," asked Carol, "why is Mrs Courtney categorised as being eligible for high-risk shares?"

"She's a former Treasury under-secretary, she's wealthy, she invests regularly in higher-risk shares but she limits her exposure to 10 percent of her total portfolio."

The inspector indicated that she was not completely satisfied with that response.

"She's a widow living alone. Do you not feel she is vulnerable to high pressure sales techniques?"

Craig gripped the edge of the table and received a stern warning stare from his boss.

"Ashtella," continued Carol. "You challenged this call when you reviewed it. Why?"

"I thought that Zabo talked too much. He kept to the script and Mrs Courtney is well able to assess the strength of the investment. I wanted her to be given longer to consider the details. The sale was closed quite quickly."

"She wanna t' buy the bloody things," snapped Craig, only to find Matthew's hand on his arm.

"Mr MacDonald," said the inspector. "We are well aware that your job is to sell shares to your clients. We authorise you to do just that. Please be patient with us. It is in your best interests to allow us to follow through our process."

"Zabo forgot to send the risk warnings," said Ashtella. "We corrected that immediately."

The senior FCA inspector found a list placed in front of her. She nodded and returned it to Andrew who ran an orange felt-tipped pen across one of the lines. An hour later there were eight orange streaks on the sheet as Debra, Ashtella and Craig were taken through call after call. The inspector called a break in the proceedings. Matthew dashed downstairs and into the fresh air. He texted Jessica. *Hell. Pure hell. Mx.*

Carol Sixsmith was ready, when they returned, with a fresh pile of papers.

"I want to review the Information Memorandum which was produced to sell the shares. It was compiled by your analyst, approved by Debra and signed off by you, Mr Buckingham. Please will you turn to page eighteen, line six."

They were looking at a passage wherein the document explained the filming process.

"The word 'accommodation'. It has two 'c' and two 'm' letters in it. You have spelt it 'accomodation'. It really does annoy me when you advisers cannot even get your basic English correct."

Matthew wondered if he was losing the will to live. Debra was furious with herself. That was down to her. Craig was planning to set a world record for the lunchtime consumption of pure malt.

"We'll now read all the 'risk warnings'. Andrew, please."

These were two pages in length covering all the eventualities that might occur that, as dictated by the regulations, should be brought to the attention of the potential investor.

"Andrew," ordered the inspector, "please read out number seventeen again."

*"The directors cannot guarantee that the film will be made on time or within the budget set. They will be taking out appropriate insurance to cover these two eventualities."*

She turned to her colleague. "Thank you, Andrew. Debra, why did you not insist that the insurances were in place before signing off this document?"

The compliance officer of Silverside Brokers gulped and hesitated.

"She tried to," intervened Matthew. "Debra picked this up and I overruled her. I instructed that no monies were to be taken until the policies were received."

Carol Sixsmith glowered.

"Do you often tread all over your compliance officer Mr Buckingham?"

"My job is to assess risk. I believe I made a correct decision. You will understand, Ms Sixsmith, that I'm here to provide leadership and make decisions."

She smiled.

"Forgive me reminding you, Mr Buckingham, but, as you put it, you're here while the FCA continues to grant your permissions to perform the roles for which you are currently authorised."

"Quite," said Matthew.

There was a further break, another text to Jessica containing a single expletive, a return to the room and a fresh pile of papers.

"Ms Morina. We have read your report on your visit to the two partners of The Pretty Fund. At the start you give their address but you have omitted the postcode. I'm not happy with that. It's careless."

"I wrote up the report early the next morning and I did not have all my papers to hand."

She was actually in the lounge of the man from Muswell Hill, who was snoring away in the bedroom, wondering where his wife was.

"Andrew here is going to read out your paper. Andrew, please."

Four minutes later the inspector from the FCA asked Craig MacDonald what he thought of Sabina's summary.

"Utter perfection if you wanna have it straight."

"I agree with you, Mr MacDonald," said Carol Sixsmith.

Matthew looked on in amazement. He'd been wondering about becoming a Buddist monk.

"Five minutes please," said the inspector.

Another text, another expletive and they were back in the room.

"Mr Buckingham. You will understand that we, at the FCA, place the highest importance on investor integrity. We accept you have to make a living and…" she smiled at Craig, "I do know the cost of a single malt but nothing excuses the exposing of your clients to unacceptable risks."

Matthew was now wondering if there was a direct flight to the Himalayas.

"Andrew, please." She was handed a set of papers which she distributed around the table.

"In reviewing this case we have identified twenty-three areas which require improvement. Debra. Andrew will be visiting you in two weeks' time to review this list and your progress in their implementation."

"That's it?" asked Matthew.

"The FCA is particularly pleased with the results of our work. Silverside Brokers are adhering to high standards. Of course there is room for improvement but these are difficult times. We know Debra well and I look forward to working with you in the future. Ashtella, your role is vital. Please maintain your excellent vigilance in monitoring the brokers' calls."

She paused and closed her files.

"Mr MacDonald. You won't listen to a word I say but please try to curb your colleagues' worst excesses. We know they have mortgages to pay but you must offer your clients the highest standards."

She stood up and asked Matthew to walk out with her. As they reached the street she hailed a taxi, turned to him and smiled.

"Where's the £6 million Matthew?" she asked.

"In Abu Dhabi somewhere," he replied.

"Serves them right. These private equity funds think they're God. I look forward to their shareholders suing the Pretty Brothers to high heaven. They should have controlled their money much more carefully. I'd have sent one million to start with and then applied strict monitoring. Cheerio."

Craig and Debra had now caught up with him. She'd been crying and was aching from an avalanche of Scottish hugs.

"Mob. Silly… er… whatever. Does she really think I'd drink a single malt?"

Jessica did not understand the text message she received.

*Have cancelled the flight to Tibet. Oodles of love. Mob xxx*

* * *

The Planner landed at King Khalid International Airport and was quickly taken the thirty-five kilometres into Riyadh where he joined five and a half million other Muslims. He settled into his hotel, was taken to the mosque, prayed and then found himself in a room with three unnamed al-Qaeda officials. There was an understanding that no names would be used. He ignored the bowl of dates but allowed himself to partake of the coffee which he sipped.

He was instructed to give the names of the six brothers who would achieve the destruction and the single member who would die. He knew that they had all this information. They asked many detailed points about the suicide brother. It was, as they all understood, the highest risk of the attack. All too often al-Qaeda had been undone as the will to live overcame the belief in Islam.

"The train will arrive at the entrance at six twenty-two," explained the Planner. "It will be travelling at sixty-six miles an hour. Just before it enters a brother will run onto the line waving a red flag. The driver will apply the brakes but will not be able to bring the train to a halt until the eight compartments are in the tunnel. Our brothers at the southern end will have already exploded the four bombs. The rocks will crash down and the exit will be sealed. Before this happens a brother will have gone one hundred yards into the tunnel and set up a charge which will blow the rail lines. They will buckle and if the train is still moving it will derail. At the other end our brothers will wait for the last carriage to enter and then they will set off the four bombs which will close the passageway. The four hundred infidels will effectively be in a tomb. At this point our brave brother will explode the gas canisters: he will die immediately. Some gas will escape through the airways and bricks but it is so deadly that there will be a toxic cloud in the whole area within minutes. There is simply no way anybody will live. We have tested the gas many times."

The film he had brought with him was now shown.

In answer to further questions he explained that the brothers would be taken northwards towards Wales and Holyhead where they would cross to Ireland.

211

The Planner was now asked about the mole.

"He continues to have money worries. He is scared. He will not talk and if there is a leak of any information he will tell us immediately. Of course he will die."

Their debate moved on.

"We have dealt with the famous police officer well. We had no idea that she'd return to full-time duties and we decided she might be dangerous. We started the phone calls and she reacted in exactly the way we thought. When Saleem betrayed us we had no choice but to kill him and the shop owner. We thought she'd concentrate on trying to discover the informer. She was sidetracked by the note. She spent too long believing it was a female officer. Our informer tells us she is quiet and subdued. She can now be ignored."

\* \* \*

Matthew wanted to get home. He longed to climb down onto the Northern Line platform at Bank Tube Station, travel round through Moorgate and Angel to reach Euston, then dash to platform eighteen, the fast commuter train to Leighton Buzzard, hug Jessica, get home, play with Rustic and Olivia, then supper and bed.

But Caroline wanted to hear about the FCA visit and insisted on meeting up. She gasped as she heard the inspector's closing comments.

"Please, Mob. Take me through it again. You're saying that the FCA is ruling that Silverside Brokers have a clean bill of health and that they suggest the Pretty Fund shareholders sue Jonathan and Roger?"

"The inspector said that privately to me and I doubt if it's their official line."

"But if that happens Goodlove, Green and Co will slam in a legal action against me."

"I suppose it would help if we could find the £5 million," said Matthew, not realising that the funds were already further depleted.

Caroline stormed off without a further word being exchanged between them. She reached the Threadneedles Hotel and went up to the room which Mark Patterson-Brown always booked for them. He was lying on the bed naked. She went to the cocktail bar and poured herself a drink. She took off her clothes and put on a towelling robe. She lay down besides him.

"Where are we going, Mark?"

He remained silent.

"Do you want it?"

"Up to you."

She realised that he'd been drinking heavily. His clothes were everywhere and never before had he left his wallet and two phones so exposed. She also realised that he was now asleep.

A few minutes later the red button on the one mobile began to pulsate. She checked that he was snoring soundly, picked it up and went into the bathroom. She sat on the seat and pressed the 'receive' key. She read the text message:

*Four left. Sent to Belize account. Luv u Dad. M.x*

She returned to the bedroom and then retired to the lounge. Mark appeared an hour and a half later wearing a towelling robe.

"Better?"

"Vaguely."

"Who is 'M', Mark?"

"'M' who?"

"The 'M' who sends you text messages with kisses."

"Can't you guess, Ms. Big Shot lawyer."

"I'm too old and too tired for silly games Mark. Who the fuck is 'M'?"

"My daughter."

"What daughter?"

He went over and poured himself a large vodka and tonic.

"The daughter my family do not know about Caroline."

The talking stopped as she thought carefully about the question she should ask next.

"How old is this daughter?"

"It's not 'this daughter', Caroline. She's my favourite child. She has none of her mother in her."

"So who is the other parent?"

"She's long gone. Lives in Africa somewhere. We only knew each other for a few weeks. She came back with my child. We completed tests and I had her adopted. I looked after her and as she grew up we became close."

Caroline began to think deeply.

"Hang on. 'M'. Martine?"

"Yes. Martine Madden. She's my daughter."

"And she's in Abu Dhabi with the Pretty Fund's money."

"I'm not sure where she is. She flew out to meet with Osama and pay him off. His take was one million." He refilled his glass and sat down again.

"She's been trying to find a way of getting the money back to England." He paused and looked tired. "There's only £4 million left. Remember Silverside Brokers had £400,000 as their commission and we took some fees." He sighed.

"The last few years have been very difficult, Caroline, and Maidstone New Issues was already heavily indebted in 2008 when the recession hit. I've remortgaged my house and the stables and now my wife has found out. I told Martine last year and she'd read a script which gave her the idea of 'Six Weeks in Summer'. I'm staggered that nobody spotted how weak Richard Rochards and Amanda Adams-Smythe are, or were. It amazed me how easy it was to fool the Pretty brothers. The reason is there's so little business around that idiots like Jonathan and Roger are willing to believe anything."

She decided to let him have another drink because, at that moment in time, she did not care a jot if Mark keeled over and died a horrible death.

"So what's happening now, Mark?"

"Martine can't get the money back to the UK. The banks are too security-minded."

He went to his phone and read the text message.

"Ha. It's in Belize. I hope Martine will enjoy spending it."

"Belize?"

"I have an account there. It's a good place to become accepted in being a Commonwealth country. My office is in Belmopan. Flights to central America are easy."

"Surely the lawyers will apply to have the money returned to the UK?"

"They have to prove a crime. Martine is still a director of the company. It won't be easy, and anyway, she'll have moved the money on."

Caroline thought about what he had said.

"Aren't you joining her?" she asked.

"I'm joining the legal system, Caroline." He laughed. "I've allowed myself to get involved with a share scam. One of these wind farm frauds. The government is rather generous with its payouts."

He drank deeply.

"There are some rather heavy gentlemen chasing their money. I'm meeting my lawyer downstairs at eight o'clock. We'll then go to the police station. It's the only way that I can stay alive."

"And us?"

"You can see me if you wish, Caroline. A pretty girl is always welcome. I think there are such things as conjugal visits."

"So that's what I am, is it Mark? A fuck."

"A very enjoyable fuck, Caroline. But don't let's get too emotional. I've taken you from nothing, taught you how to make love, shown you the financial world, wined and dined you, given you the self-confidence so that you're now a partner in your firm and, perhaps more than anything, made you something in the City."

"So that I'm known as Mark Patterson-Brown's mistress."

"It doesn't work that way Caroline. I've told you many times. This place has no morals whatsoever. Everybody's on the make. The only God is money and preferably other people's. The City of London is a con trick. Fund managers pay themselves vast salaries, have index-linked pensions, six weeks' holiday, offices, women, the lot. That's all before the investor stands any chance of getting any return on their funds. Do you really understand what fraud pensions are? Level after level of charges are taken by the managers and there's no accountability. The regulators are the best paid and achieve fuck all."

He was sitting on the side of the bed. His thighs were open and she could see his penis and testicles. She'd read somewhere

215

that women facing rape should try to kick the assailant between the legs. If she could crush the sex organs the victim might experience an indescribable pain and possibly face surgery.

He seemed transfixed by the lifting of the weight, now he had told her the whole story.

"Would you like some good news?" he asked.

"Try me."

"There's no way Goodlove, Green and Co will sue Christie Simpson. There's no case to answer and Stuart Green knows it. The FCA inspector was right. The Pretty boys were careless. You're off the hook, Caroline."

She put her clothes back on and checked that her shoes were firmly on her feet. She rubbed her right ankle. She looked over at him again. His legs were open and she shuddered at where she'd once gone. She walked towards him and he looked up at her. His eyes were vacant.

She turned away and went over to the door. As she shut it behind her she spoke quietly to herself.

"Caroline's story. End of Part Three: 'shagged to death'. Part Four begins here: 'tomorrow the world'.

As she entered the lift she laughed.

"You're right, Mark. The City is a façade and I'm a bloody good player in it."

* * *

The truth was beginning to dawn on Detective Chief Inspector Rudd. This whole episode had been, from the beginning, far too obvious. She recalled the first call to her mobile, the discussions with D/Supt Khan, the 'chick-lit' adventures with DCI Flemming and Constable Pepper, and, far worse, the meeting at the Mohammed's shop and the subsequent deaths of two people.

They were playing games with her and she now reasoned that they were scared.

She was scarred. She accepted that. But they were worried. They had their mole and yet she posed a threat to them. This was surely the clue she'd been seeking. What was so special

216

about her? Was it her profile as a medal winner? She was a hero but why would that disturb the terrorists?

She sat in her office and yet again read her files. There was something that she either knew or might do that could upset their plans. She tried to get into the mind of the Planner. There would be one and he'd be local. Probably a cleric. But there were over fifteen of them in Islington and too many to investigate individually.

DCI Rudd reached a conclusion that she hated. Was it possible that her high profile and career to-date simply scared them. Her fellow police officers were the best of the best but their role, in the context of draconian financial cuts, was to maintain order in their community. They were letting crime after crime go undetected and fiddling the statistics because that is what the Home Office really wanted. What they did do was deal with the major incidences very well indeed.

But she was different. She was not fazed by authority. She did not always follow the party line. Perhaps that was what really concerned the Planner. Was she, DCI Sarah Rudd, capable of achieving results against the odds?

Now she had to prove herself as never before. She was concerned, perhaps more than at any other time in her career.

*How were they certain that they would kill four hundred people?*

# Chapter Seventeen

Commander Max Riley looked at his colleagues but did not smile. His voice then conveyed his inner concern.

"We have absolutely nothing on him," he said. "DCI Attwood please, your comments."

Freezer liked the limelight. He could put aside his personal financial problems and his ever-present resentment of graduate appointees and demonstrate that his old-style policing methods were the most effective.

"Soleim Sarringh is a fanatical Muslim cleric but he's clever. We've monitored his preachings and that, in itself, is not easy because he moves around. He has an address but he's never there. He has no other means of support, no family that we can identify and no woman, which is not a surprise because he's a fundamentalist and a strict interpreter of the teachings of Islam. As we all know that means he despises any liberalisation of females. You may recall that we had a spate of attacks on prostitutes and it's possible he was behind those."

"What we do have," continued the Commander, "is a report that he recently travelled to the Middle East and back again in three days."

Monica Moses looked up from her notes. "And he travelled first class no doubt."

"No," responded Freezer. "They don't do that."

"What's your point, Superintendent Moses?" asked the Commander.

"Air flight is not cheap, even economy seats. He's well financed and he can afford to fly to the Middle East and back for what can only have been a meeting."

"That's my conclusion," said Max Riley. "What we do need is to find out what the meeting was about."

"We're getting carried away here, Sir," said DCI Attwood. "If every time someone flies to Riyadh we press the panic button policing will grind to a halt."

"Percy. We have an obligation to follow up on all intelligence. I expect you to support me on this."

"Of course, Commander. We'll be on the streets today, tomorrow and every day. But we all have to manage our resources and I'm concerned that we might be over-stressing this one piece of intelligence."

DCI Rudd was listening to every word rather carefully. The meeting lasted a further four minutes and, as they exited the Commander's office, she found herself alongside DCI Avril Flemming.

"Buy you a coffee?" suggested Sarah.

They settled down in the canteen. She looked at her colleague's trim figure and groaned as she devoured her chocolate éclair.

"How was Camden Town?" she asked.

"I've no idea, Sarah. I was there a whole week, I arrested some drunks, told the drug pushers to hop it, and I booked a French lorry driver for getting stuck on a yellow box junction…"

They stopped and laughed.

"Who needs UKIP?" she said. "We'll get rid of the French on our own!" She finished her glass of iced water and began drinking a black coffee.

"One a day. That's what I'm allowed. Now, my chick-lit friend, how is Emily getting on with her returning soldier?"

Sarah laughed. "I've left them in bed." She stood up, straightened her skirt, and sat down again.

"The cuts are hurting, Avril. The hours my team are working and then I get a reprimand for exceeding overtime budgets. If something serious happens we're dead in the water." She wiped her mouth and tried to justify another cake. "The Commander seemed agitated today don't you think?" asked Sarah.

"The Arab Spring stuff continues I think. It's pretty horrible what's happening in Syria. The use of gas is nasty. What Max is really concerned over is the fear that some fanatic might try to replicate it over here."

"I thought that Freezer seemed to be trying to rub the boss up the wrong way."

"Certainly not himself. Several people have commented recently that he seems distracted."

"Perhaps he has a girlfriend," laughed Sarah.

"The chick-lit at work," grinned DCI Avril Flemming.

As they walked back to their offices Sarah decided that her colleague was not quite the hot shot she thought she was. DCI Rudd reasoned that she had missed an important clue in today's meeting with the Commander. She decided she wanted to be with her husband who, unaccountably, had taken a day off work.

She arrived home and put her phones on the side-table. Nick was drinking a bottle of lager.

"Stop there, Sarah," he ordered. "I've got some news for you and I sense you want to talk to me. Who goes first?"

"I know my place, Nick. Tell Auntie Sarah everything."

He began slowly and then it simply poured out. Nick Rudd had been approached by a firm of London-based headhunters. An educationalist in London had managed to secure millions of pounds of backing for the establishing of a national network of private schools. Each would cater for foreign nationals with the emphasis on Commonwealth countries.

"This, Sarah, is the clever bit. Their real attention is not on Oxbridge but on our legal system. We provide the best training in the world. A newly-qualified barrister coming out of Grey's Inn will walk in to a top government position back in their own country."

He took her through his two interviews and three meetings about which she had known nothing. When he mentioned the salary, and that was just the start, she gasped in surprise.

"How many schools, Nick?"

"They're buying two existing establishments in the Home Counties and they've already started building their flagship base."

"Where is that, Nick?"

"Just outside Northampton."

"What are you saying to me please, Nick."

"We'll have to move home."

"Marcus and Susie will hate that."

"Yes, I know. And you Sarah?"

"I've always wanted to be a village bobby." She drank some tea. "Nick, which school will you be head of? This flagship I imagine."

"No."

"So?"

"They want me to be chief executive of the whole group and I'll get 10 percent of the shares."

"Fantastic!"

They decided to go for a walk. They had two hours before getting back to greet Susie. They reached the park and Sarah began telling her husband about the morning's events. She took three calls and said that she'd be at the station by six o'clock.

"Interesting," said Nick. "It feels as though things are happening. How do they know that they'll kill four hundred people?"

"I've identified the mole, Nick."

"DCI Avril Flemming, our dumb blonde?" he laughed.

"She's not as smart as she thinks she is."

"How do you justify that? You told me that she's on her way to the top."

"She missed it," said Sarah.

"Missed what?"

"The mole gave himself away in the meeting."

"He was wearing dark glasses."

"He knew where the Cleric had flown to. He mentioned Riyadh. The Commander only referred to the Middle East."

"Who knew, Sarah?"

"DCI Percy 'Freezer' Attwood."

Sarah Rudd let her thoughts wander. She had two options open to her. The first, and the correct one, was to immediately seek a meeting with her boss D/Supt Khan. The second, and the one she'd decided to take, was to engineer a chat with Freezer.

"I'm getting a bit concerned about the time I've taken off recently," said Nick. "To add to it they want me to attend a dinner in Northampton next Tuesday evening to meet the investors. It's going to be heavy and they've booked me in for the night. I'll travel back on the Wednesday morning. There's a train at 5.46 a.m. to Euston. I'll come home and still be at school on time."

"Or you've got a mistress and this is a remarkable cover story," laughed Sarah.

He turned and hugged her.

"Oh boy, have I a mistress. She's called 'Mayfair International Schools. Chief executive: N. Rudd BA and nothing else."

"Except a new job, marvellous salary, pension and perks, a loving wife, two adoring children and unlimited sex," laughed Sarah.

"Can you bring the handcuffs back with you tonight please, Sarah," he asked.

* * *

Caroline paid the bill and stood up.

"One for the road, Mob?"

They had enjoyed an early evening wine bar meal and were now wandering around the streets of St. James's. They decided to go into the Ritz and they were soon seated with vodka and tonics in front of them.

"That's an extraordinary story, Caroline. Mark's under caution and the process will put him in jail?"

"You know how the system works, Mob. Once the shit hits the fan more and more comes out. He has debts all over the place. He'd plundered his own pension fund. His wife is lucky that she has two sons to look after her."

"And Martine?"

"We think she's still in Belize. The two law firms met together today. Stuart Green was rather impressive. It was agreed that there would be no legal actions between us on behalf of our clients. We're concentrating on recreating the path of the funds and seeing if we can find weaknesses. We might have a go at Coutts Bank although I can't see it myself. The mandate was properly completed and I can't believe they've done anything wrong. Of course once we reach Abu Dhabi it becomes much more difficult."

223

"What is Martine's situation?"

"We think she might be scared as she now knows all about her father. We are proposing to send someone out to Belize to find her. She does have, we think, £4 million. How are things at Silverside Brokers?"

"The FCA is due in to check their 'to-do' list but Debra is born again. The atmosphere is so improved and she and Craig are organising several broker training evenings. They are bringing in real clients who seem all too keen to help."

"The lovely Sabina?"

"She's been promoted to Head of Institutional Sales and rumour has it that Jonathan Pretty has a huge smile on his face."

They re-ordered their drinks and slowly the atmosphere changed.

"Caroline?"

"Go on, Mob. Get it off your chest. You've been playing with me all evening."

"Where are you going? The whole City knows that you were the mistress of a discredited fraudster. Do you have regrets?"

"None whatsoever, Mob. Mark helped me grow up. The City is not what he thought. I believe there's an underlying integrity beneath its skin. A majority of the professionals I work with are the best in their field and they have, if rather expensive, decent standards. Buy me another drink and I'll tell you that some politicians are rather nice people."

"No more drink, Caroline. I'm off home."

"To the lovely Jessica?"

"Yes. We have a future together and now matters at work have settled down, I can begin to enjoy my home life."

"Oh! Another man off my list."

"That's one problem you'll never have, Caroline. You are a stunningly lovely woman."

"Can we meet again, Mark?"

"Always available to you. You know that."

"If only that was true," she said to herself.

* * *

224

When DCI Rudd returned to Islington Police Station she noticed that the light was on in the office of DCI Percy Attwood. She opened the door and went in.

"Sarah," he exclaimed as he covered up his notes. "This is a rare honour."

"Reprimand accepted, Percy. I must try to circulate more."

"Sit down. What's this book you're writing? We all want to read it. Lots of *Fifty Shades of Grey* in it I hope."

"Percy. It'll make EL James seem like Enid Blyton."

"I grew up on the stories about Noddy and Big Ears. But tell me Sarah. How do you know about all this stuff?"

"Stuff Percy. What do you mean?"

"Bondage, whipping, that sort of thing."

"I have a vivid imagination." She smiled. "Changing the subject I thought you were rather impressive in the meeting today. The Commander tends to over-react don't you think?"

"He'd have us looking for terrorists twenty-four hours a day if he could."

"He didn't mention terrorists, Percy. Is that what you think?"

"No. Of course not. It's just that these preachers are so dangerous."

She poured herself some water in the plastic cup on his desk.

"Are you feeling well, Percy? You look a bit under the weather."

"Nothing more than usual, Sarah. Long hours, no thanks, colleagues who take jollies to Camden Town."

"Yes. You mean DCI Avril Flemming don't you?"

"I walked the beat for years to learn my trade. She comes in on one of these schemes and I'm pushed aside. They all talk about community policing but unless you have me and my kind out there, it means nothing."

"You don't feel appreciated. Is that what you are saying, Percy?"

"My bank balance is most certainly saying that, Sarah. We try so hard to budget but our fuel bills go up and up."

"Well Nick and I have two salaries and we struggle," said Sarah.'Although not for much longer,' she thought to herself.

"I have a friend who got himself in a muddle with these pay-day loans. I've been helping him out."

Sarah realised that he was referring to himself. He was the mole and they'd converted him with bribes. She knew that Percy Attwood would almost certainly end up in prison. But she needed to know more about the planned attack.

"I've read that the rates of interest are scandalous, Percy," she said.

He wiped his mouth with his sleeve.

"It's the phone calls. I mean to say that he tells me they phone him all the time."

"Are you helping him as a police officer?" she asked.

"Nope. That's against the rules and I've my pension to worry about. I've lent him some money."

"Even though you are struggling yourself, Percy?" said Sarah. "You'll have to excuse me. I'm very busy. You heard what the Commander said."

Sarah stood up and then looked down. The papers on his desk had moved and, reading upside down, she was able to detect, written on his pad in large, scrawling writing, *WED 16 Oct.*

DCI Rudd had uncovered the mole and now had the date of the attack: Wednesday 16 October. She wondered about seeing D/Supt Khan but Freezer had become suspicious. She would give herself a little more time. She then stopped in her tracks. There was very little time left: today was Wednesday 9 October and it was almost over.

Of even greater importance was her inability to answer the most important question:

*How were they sure that they were going to kill four hundred people?*

\* \* \*

Mark Patterson-Brown smiled at his solicitor.

"Walter. That went rather well, don't you think?"

"I estimate two years, Mark. A year off and an open prison. Write your memoirs and make a fortune."

"And I've got rid of my wife."

"Not my territory, Mark. My partner is handling your divorce. My bill. How will it be paid?"

"Martine's managing to filter some funds back unless you would like it paid offshore?"

"A cheque will be fine," he laughed.

The accused looked down at his mobile phone. There was a text from Caroline.

"You're in the past," he said to himself as he pressed the 'delete' button without reading it.

She was wishing him all the best for his future.

'After all,' she reasoned to herself, 'the sex was rather good, and those showers… .'

\* \* \*

Jessica was marvelling at the coincidence.

She was shortly to inherit a little over £2,900,000 and, if the Great Train Robbers had not ignored the Scottish and Irish notes, that was roughly the sum of money they'd have netted. She realised that in today's money, fifty years later, their take was rather more, but, even so, two and a half million pounds is a lot of money.

She looked again at the pregnancy testing kit. She'd given in and was ecstatic at the result. She'd decided to cook Mob a special dinner and she had bought an expensive red wine to relax him. She'd then break the news. It was the perfect way to end the week together. She so wanted to tell Olivia but she knew she must wait for that moment. She contented herself by sharing the news with Rustic who passed wind.

Now she had her project ahead of her. She had decided to set up a media company specialising in current documentaries. She was paying a firm of business advisers in Milton Keynes to identify a small company which she could purchase. She was willing to commit up to a million pounds to that. She wanted youngsters with energy and vision. It was they who understood social media and apps and everything technical.

It was when she had been researching the year of 1963 that she began to realise that there was a wonderful story to tell.

Even now she had only managed to write a vague thesis. At the heart of her story was the parallel nature of man. She wanted to trace the physiological passage of a person born in 1963 through all the stages of his life: from birth, through infancy, childhood, puberty, teenage years, the twenties, thirties, forties, fifties, retirement, geriatric years and death. She decided to standardise events: masturbation, sex, partnerships: marriage, children, divorce, retirement, grandchildren and death. She would overlay that with the history of the world from 1963 to 2040 when the man could expect to die.

How much would historical events distort the life of the man? War was the event that immediately came to her mind. Since 1946 he'd not had to fight a conventional battle apart from those members of the armed forces, a few caught up in Korea, Iraq and Afghanistan. The motor car: she'd always considered that its greatest impact was the splitting up of families due to global mobility. Radio and television would play a big part but, of course, the Internet had created a seismic change to the whole world. Improved medical treatments were extending life but we were all suffering the same illnesses. Influenza was influenza.

One of the biggest changes that she picked up from the biographies of the train robbers was in housing standards. Several had to flee to Brazil to find a better life where they could live without the fear of arrest and deportation.

She looked at her watch. It would soon be time to collect Matthew from the station. She was glad that the fishmonger had suggested the fresh Dover sole. Mob would complain that she'd not selected a white wine but she wanted him as relaxed as possible.

As she drove to the station, with Olivia singing happily in the back of the car, she pondered again about her media company. She was looking at several possible businesses and had a pile of DVDs to watch. There was one comprising mostly females. It was promoted to the top of the list. She was now reading *The Times, The Daily Telegraph* and *The Daily Mail* every day and watching *SKY news* every hour. She wanted to understand better their ability to select the right stories. She always listened to the *Today* programme on Radio Four and now was becoming a fan of a range of other stations: *Three Counties* was a particular favourite.

But she knew there was a long way to go and her background as a banker came into play. She sent an email to the girls asking for an up-to-date cash flow analysis. To her surprise she received it by return.

'Of course,' she thought to herself, 'there might be the largest crash ever on the M1 motorway about which to make a documentary. But that,' she thought, 'was rather unlikely.'

\* \* \*

The Planner insisted that they try a mock attack on the Sunday evening. The traffic was lighter and most people would be in their homes, suffering from Sunday lunch excesses and hangovers and thinking about the week ahead.

The journey took them an hour in their two vehicles. They were ordered to follow every speed limit and not to take any chance of being flashed. They parked without difficulty and split into two groups of three. The ones attacking the southern end were delayed by a woman and her two dogs who sensed something but she was eager to get home and they moved on. Several trains passed through but that was of no concern. The terrorist with the responsibility for buckling the railway lines with a small detonation ran into the tunnel, counted to fifty and ran out again. He was told to repeat the exercise and again achieved the required timing. They had checked the train timetable to make sure there was a gap long enough to do this exercise.

The team at the northern end were worried about the speed at which the train would enter the tunnel. They were concerned that the pre-placed bombs might be dislodged. By coincidence a local train passed through and their fears were realised. They decided to place the explosive after the train had gone through the opening. This would add three minutes to the schedule and the Planner was not happy.

229

They argued for over forty minutes until it was decided to place two bombs inside the tunnel and, when the train was fully in, they'd explode further detonations to seal the gap.

The Planner wanted four hundred people to die as nastily as possible. He was not prepared to allow one infidel to be spared. His service to Allah must be complete. He set down his prayer mat and gave homage to his God. He asked that his brother, who would set off the gas canisters, would enter Paradise as quickly as possible.

They returned to Islington as slowly as possible. They were dropped off individually so that there was no obvious traffic movement to attract the attention of the security services. The Planner knew that his trip to Riyadh had been registered as he had expected but he also knew from his mole that the Commander was guessing wildly. He had asked about the problem officer and did not understand the answer that he was given.

What had 'chick-lit' to do with the truth? He was, however, satisfied that this police hero posed no threat to his moment of greatness. His time was approaching and the British establishment were about to be destabilised in a way that no other terrorist group had ever managed. He also knew that he had the media on his side. They would show every possible twisted and agonised body that they could because it would be construed as being in 'the national interest'. The Prime Minister would give speech after speech promising everything, delivering nothing, and simply waiting for his government to collapse. The likely outcome would be a national Government of unity. In the communities the Cleric would continue the war. Morale would be high. The converts would flood in. Everybody backed winners.

# Chapter Eighteen

Gordon Panting always wore a white shirt and tie when, as he had done for the last eighteen years, he was driving his train. He arrived at the Northampton depot and telephoned Bletchley to clock on for his eight-hour shift. He collected his job card which was faxed to him by the supervisor and which told him his journey details: Rugby 5.16 a.m., Long Buckby 5.25 a.m., Northampton 5.46 a.m., Wolverton 5.58 a.m., Milton Keynes Central 6.02 a.m., Bletchley 6.07 a.m., Leighton Buzzard 6.14 a.m., Watford 6.33 a.m. and Euston, London 6.50 a.m. He checked the up-to-date notices: there were no engineering works which could delay his progress.

The irony of the punctuality issue never ceased to amaze him. It was the responsibility of the conductor to keep to the time-table: he just drove the train using speed changes to help the process. There were, of course, safety limits for him to follow. The modern phenomenon of 'delay attribution' dominated attitudes. There was a variety of people from London Midland and Network Rail trying to avoid financial penalties for late running either by ensuring the timetables were met or by blaming the other side.

Many commuters thought that the announcement 'we are sorry to report the cancellation of the 9.53 a.m. to London due to signalling problems at Watford' probably meant that there were no staff, the train was in the wrong place, the station was closed for staff training or some other reason.

Nevertheless, and despite his cynicism, Gordon put safety at the top of his personal agenda. He was taken by taxi to Rugby where he met his conductor. They inspected the eight carriages from front to back. He entered his cab and locked the door: the conductor was allowed in but the practice was not encouraged. He was cocooned in his own world with only the Cab Secure

Radio for outside contact. His personal mobile phone was switched off and would remain so for the whole journey.

He inserted his metal master key, turned on the electrics and switched in to Area 61: Rugby. He coded in '4147' which meant he would leave from platform three. The conductor buzzed twice and Gordon prepared to take his train out of Rugby on the slow line to London. He liked Arnold Numanga: he was fair to the customers. He, like everybody else, needed the commission from ticket sales to feed his four children, but he tried to be polite at all times.

The driver checked the signals which offered green, double yellow, yellow and red. The green light was showing. He was clear to leave and was soon on his way to Long Buckby. It was a dark and stormy start to the day and he needed his wipers on at full speed to ensure good vision. There was a loud clap of thunder which failed to make any impression on his steel chariot.

He was a proud and satisfied man. He never forgot that his prime responsibility was to get his passengers to their destination safely and, with the help of Arnold, on time. It would take an earthquake to stop Gordon Panting from doing just that.

\* \* \*

The car crash happened completely out of the blue.

Sarah had decided to drive her husband to his dinner in Northampton. For Nick, and his future with Mayfair International Schools, it was an important occasion. She had nearly driven him to total distraction as she pressed and repressed his two suits, insisted he wore white shirts and cleaned his two pairs of black shoes for him. Marcus and Susie were staying with friends that evening. Having driven up the M1 she left her nervous husband at the hotel at around lunchtime. After smothering him with kisses she checked the time on her watch, read several messages on her two mobile phones, and decided to use the afternoon to divert back westwards across the southern side of Bedfordshire. She crossed over the A5 and stopped to check her map.

She had read and, unusually for her, re-read the story of The Great Train Robbery. She accepted it was an extraordinary event but the aspect that most captured her imagination was the police action in capturing the robbers and securing the tough prison sentences handed down to the criminals. She accepted that the world had moved on but DCI Sarah Rudd was not alone in believing that criminal tolerance had reached a point where it was threatening civil unrest. Private housing estates were just one example of how the wealthy classes were protecting themselves because the police were unable to control their communities.

The Great Train Robbery exposed the laxity of the system of transferring high value packages using the railway system. New and more sophisticated methods were almost immediately introduced and there were few serious incidents on the railways after that date: 8 August 1963.

Sarah wanted, for one last time, to revisit the scene of the robbery, to relive those events which she now understood so well, then put the book away to concentrate on her policing duties and her support of the chief executive of Mayfair International Schools. She became lost in her thoughts: she knew that she was wrong to delay revealing her suspicions over DCI Percy 'Freezer' Attwood but she was concerned that she'd simply move the planning of the terrorist attack away to another location and prevent any chance of its detection. In her heart of hearts she doubted if her career would survive and she paid particular interest to the areas around Northampton. She might, before too long, be starting a new life as a housewife.

She thought again: there was one day to go. She made an impulsive decision: she'd phone D/Supt Khan and expose her colleague. She decided to pull her car over as she left the southern edge of Leighton Buzzard. She'd drive to Bridego Bridge. She thought it was fitting that her call should be made from the scene of another catastrophic event.

The harvester was being driven by the son of a local farmer in a reckless manner. As he negotiated the corner the vast amount of metal behind him swung out into the middle of the road. Sarah came round the corner and smashed straight into it. The rescue services were quickly on the scene and the paramedic insisted that she was taken to Milton Keynes hospital for a full check-up. The car was towed away and later condemned as a write-off.

She was kept in overnight as a precaution. She had a gash on her forehead and her right collar bone was bruised but not broken. She texted Nick and both her children but did not tell them of her situation. She said that she had been called in for night duty and that she'd telephoned Nick's parents who had agreed to stay on at their house until the next morning.

She discharged herself from the hospital at four-fifty on the morning of Wednesday 16 October: she needed to get back to work. She used a taxi to reach the station, bought her ticket and caught the 5.54 a.m. train to London. She'd have a last look at the scene of the robbery south of Leighton Buzzard as her train passed over Bridego Bridge.

\* \* \*

Nick Rudd was not far behind her as he caught the 5.46 a.m. train from Northampton which would arrive at Euston at 6.50 a.m. He was in a tired but upbeat mood. The previous evening had, for him, been a landmark occasion. He was starting to realise just how much he knew about educational practices and their application. As the discussions developed he contributed a professional appraisal of the standards the schools must attain if they were to fulfil the ambitions of the parents. The diner in the dark suit and cream shirt had said nothing throughout the debates. He was the investor whose millions of pounds were financing the venture. He listened as Nick returned time and again to the aspirations of the mums and dads. He had expected to be bored to death with discussions on examinations and marking standards and the policies coming out of the coalition government.

To him Nick was different. He realised that for their chief executive, the examination structure was a fact of life and they'd work within it. Nick talked about pupils and gave a number of

234

examples of where good teaching practice might change lives. He continually went back to the parents. He stunned the table by explaining his belief that the disadvantage of the single parent family was a myth.

"If I went under a train there is no way that Sarah would allow the education of Marcus and Susie to suffer," he said. "I have a number of kids in my school with only one parent which is usually the mother. They have stories to tell but many of them are phenomenal in their determination to give their children the best start in life that they can. In fact they are sometimes more focused."

The financier sat back and allowed himself half a glass of the burgundy. He was pleased with the progress being made. They had selected well and their chief executive was at the beginning of a rewarding adventure. He made a note to confirm the details of his salary package and his contract. Within a year the competition would try to poach him.

Nick sat back in his seat and opened a copy of *The Times*. Despite his best efforts he had indulged a little too much and regretted selecting the pheasant for his main course. As the train left Northampton he needed to find the toilet. He opened the door and pushed his way past a man with a rucksack on his back. He swung round in anger as Nick asked him to move. He felt a metal container inside the bag hit his shoulder. He gave the man a look: his eyes were vacant.

\* \* \*

They had been in place at the Berkhamsted tunnel since four o'clock in the morning. The Planner was in continual contact although he insisted that they use their communications sparingly. The three men had hidden themselves at the northern end of the tunnel and placed the two bombs inside ready for detonating immediately the train had passed through. They each carried guns. At the southern exit the explosives were ready for the one terrorist to run in and buckle the lines so that the train would slow as it crashed into the rocks. They were being hampered by torrential rain. The black thunder clouds had been building up from the Atlantic coast since the early hours and there were streaks of lightning across the western skies.

The group at the northern entrance to the tunnel were forced to return to their vehicle to collect additional waterproof covers which they used to protect their phones, guns and explosives. They allowed themselves bottles of water and nothing else. None of them smoked cigarettes. They were tense and thoughtful as several early trains from London in the south and from Birmingham, Manchester and the north-western side of the country on their way to London, rushed through the heavy storms. The temperature was around eight degrees centigrade which was comfortable for their fingers.

In Islington the Planner was thanking Allah for his blessings and promising to deliver a great victory. The deaths of four hundred infidels would secure his place in Jannah, the Islamic concept of Paradise. He had read, and re-read, every word of the Quran. His wish was to leave the garden and to reach Firdaws where the prophets, martyrs and the most pious dwell. He revisited his vision of the carnage and his belief that the government would eventually fall. He prayed for Rashid as his brother prepared to die for his cause: he was a martyr who Allah would embrace.

The disturbance occurred at around five-thirty in the morning as the first signs of daylight came in from the east. The Grand Union Canal followed the path of the railway line often being only a few hundred yards away. At the tunnel entrance it was actually within hearing distance as the waterway swung eastwards around a small incline.

Overnight a couple had moored their barge on the bend intending to navigate the Leighton Buzzard locks in the morning. They were partners from High Wycombe where they both worked in local government offices. They were taking a few days off in a late autumn break. They had borrowed a friend's craft on several occasions.

They had argued the night before about money. They shared their mortgage payments but could never agree on

236

the household bills. Before they left on the Sunday afternoon they had opened the week's mail and discovered an electricity demand that was well above the usual quarterly payment. She had wanted to pay monthly but he had objected. Their relationship was struggling and this latest minor tiff lit the fuse paper.

They had gone to bed well past midnight but the tensions re-emerged when he got out of the bunk and fell across the cabin floor. She awoke with a start and almost immediately started to shout at him.

"Bloody wake me up now!" she screamed. "I'm going home."

"It's dark outside and it's raining cats and dogs you ignorant bitch."

The three terrorists immediately registered the sound and located its source. The senior member moved around to the hidden side of the embankment and reported in to the Planner. He was given his instructions. He spoke to the two others and they split up. The first terrorist crept forward and settled about thirty yards away from the canal. The other two approached the boat, one from the north and the other from the Berkhamsted direction. The sound of shouting inside the barge did not abate at any stage. They edged themselves into position. The centrally-placed terrorist picked up a can he had found near to the entrance of the railway tunnel. He had slipped two pebbles inside and now rattled the container.

The sound stopped immediately as the couple sensed an intruder. The man came out of the boat and stepped onto the bank. He looked around him but was far too slow to prevent an arm curl around his chest and a hand cover his mouth. At the same time a knife was drawn across his throat and he died almost instantaneously. His body dropped to the ground. The second terrorist had now climbed down the five steps into the cabin and found the girl standing in front of him. She was wearing a t-shirt and her hand was up to her mouth. She was shaking her head. He did not hesitate as he bounded forward and sank his knife into her stomach. He twisted the metal to ensure that he inflicted as much damage as quickly as possible. Her face contorted in agony but her life lingered on. He picked up a towel and covered her face. He was forced to hold on to her for nearly sixty seconds until he felt her life ebb away. He lowered her to the floor and removed his weapon, wiping the blood-covered blade on the cloth. He checked her pulse one final time and returned to the railway line. He was forced to fling himself to the ground as an early morning Virgin train rushed towards Watford and on to London.

\* \* \*

He simply could not stop hugging her. Olivia had joined them in bed early that morning and they shared Jessica's news together. The announcement that his daughter would not accept a brother brought them great amusement. They moved on to the breakfast table and were soon ready for the trip to the railway station. Jessica would later run Rustic's owner to school and then have a telephone conference call with the two executives of the media company she was proposing to buy. She seemed as thrilled by her commercial progress as she was at becoming pregnant.

Matthew was feeling relaxed. The FCA had confirmed with Debra that Silverside Brokers were clear to carry on their activities and Caroline had stunned him with the news that she had made a personal decision to fly to Belize and find Martine Madden and the missing money. He thought it was an emotional decision rather than a sensible option.

He was looking forward to a period of consolidation: it was time to take advantage of the growing economic optimism and to build up his business so that he could retire in five years' time just before the next financial crisis exploded. He was experienced enough to know that it was all about economic cycles: good times, bad times.

Jessica drove the car past the taxis and stopped outside the main entrance of the station. Hundreds of London commuters were preparing to begin their journeys to their place of work. Many would reach Euston and then catch a Tube train on the Northern line to Bank station. Some would continue using the Docklands Light Railway to reach Canary Wharf. They generally ignored each other and some looked decidedly dismayed by the thought of the traveller facing them. They used routine as their shield. Every weekday they arose at the same time, followed the same procedure, said the same things to their bed partner, left the children alone, missed breakfast, got in their cars, drove to their parking place, locked their vehicles, walked to the station concourse, bought their morning paper or picked up a copy of the free distribution *Metro*, checked the information board and, with about two minutes to go, stepped out in the rain to make certain that they were standing on the same place on the platform. This ensured that they would get a seat. They'd store their cases and raincoats on the luggage racks, settle down and emerge thirty-six minutes later at Euston having completed the first part of their journey.

She gave Matthew a special maternal hug and told him how much she loved him. She noticed that there was a train standing stationary at the platform but she did not pay much attention to it.

* * *

Gordon was angry. He was stopped at a red signal. He telephoned his signaller and had difficulty in hearing his instructions. How many times had he told Control that good communications were vital and yet again he was struggling to maintain contact with his base. The weather was getting worse and visibility was down to less than fifty yards. Now he was being told that the train in front had developed a problem. The light on one of the doors was showing that it was not correctly closed and it had not been possible to correct the fault.

His train was stopped outside Bletchley and he was told that it had been decided to cancel the train in front. There would be a few minutes delay while the passengers transferred and then it would go on to Tring to be secured in the siding. He groaned and knew that the rest of the journey to Euston would be a stop and start affair. He called in Arnold who told their passengers the news.

Nick put his paper down and checked his watch. There was, as yet, no response to his text message to Sarah. He was also fascinated by the man in the space between the two compartments. When he had returned from his trip to the toilet the swarthy individual had deliberately moved well away from him in an exaggerated manner. He seemed to be mumbling to himself.

He checked the time again. He wondered about phoning her but he knew that once he started talking about the dinner there would be no stopping him. He was not to know that, at that precise moment in time, his wife was standing on the platform of Leighton Buzzard Station.

Sarah was utterly frustrated. She was still feeling bruised and she had a headache. She wanted to reach London, go home, change and get to the office of D/Supt Khan as quickly as possible. She was also excited about the evening ahead with Nick and her children. She sheltered from the rain as more commuters crowded onto the platform. She listened as the station officials were checking that the faulty train could be moved on. There were some cross words being spoken.

"Four hundred passengers to get to London and now this fuck up," shouted the more senior station controller.

She recoiled at the sound of his words. She pulled out her warrant card and shoved it in front of his face.

"DCI Rudd. Please take me to your office now."

The official reacted surprisingly calmly and led the way through the platform doors, down the steps and into the offices behind the ticket kiosks.

"You said that there would be four hundred passengers on the train," she said as they sat down.

"Approximately. There'll be more this morning because of the broken-down train."

"Is it exactly that number?" she asked.

"Most of our trains are packed at this time of day but the 6.14 a.m. is an early one and not completely full in First Class: so the answer is 'yes'. May I ask what this is about?"

"And if there was an attempt to blow up a train?"

"Out of the question. We have CCTV everywhere. We are

much more security conscious than you might think. You might set off one explosion but you'd need a number of bombs to damage a train and eight carriages."

He stood up and asked Sarah if he could see her warrant card again. He read it and handed it back to her.

"Are you special branch?" he asked.

She ignored the question.

"Of course," said the man in the corner who had been listening to their conversation. "There is another way to blow up the train," he laughed.

Sarah Rudd went over to him.

"How?" she asked.

"Blow up a tunnel and kill them all with the rubble."

"How many tunnels are there between here and Euston?" she asked. "Quickly. We have no time to waste."

"From here to Watford just two. But you'd never manage it there because although there is a long tunnel into the station they all divide into two and they're so busy that you'd never conceal your activities."

"The other one?" she snapped.

"Berkhamsted through the Chiltern Hills. It's smaller and shorter but it's also isolated on the rural side. You might reach it by the canal tow path." He paused. "But just thinking about it, after the first few trains passed through, the daylight would come up and any unusual activity would immediately be spotted. My guess is that perhaps the 6.14 a.m. just about to leave is the only sensible opportunity there is. It's the 5.46 a.m. from Northampton where it picks up many of its passengers."

DCI Sarah Rudd now knew where the attack would take place. She told the two railway managers to leave the office and to prevent the train from leaving. She called D/Supt Khan and was immediately connected with her boss.

"Sir. There's to be an attack on the Northampton to Euston commuter train at the Berkhamsted Tunnel. They are going to blow it up. There's a mole, Sir. DCI Percy Attwood has been turned. We'll need everything, Sir."

She rushed out as she saw that the 6.14 a.m. from Leighton Buzzard to Euston was leaving the station.

241

"I ordered you to stop it," she shouted.

"We tried. There's only two of us. The signal is green," blustered the station official. "The phones are down again. We're having trouble contacting the driver."

"You should have told the bloody conductor," yelled DCI Rudd "I wanted the train stopped."

"He's inside. He can't buzz the driver to go until all the doors are closed. We tried, I promise you."

She watched the train disappearing down the line and then suddenly it stopped.

Gordon was frustrated by the delays and wanted to get his train moving towards the south. He tried to use his phone to check with Control that he was clear to move on. He was not aware that back at the station there was pandemonium. Police cars were arriving and officers emerged on to the platform. A police helicopter appeared in the skies and circled around. The storms were increasing in their intensity and the rain was lashing across the countryside. There was a loud rumble of thunder in the distance. He had a green light and could go. He pulled his power break control (the PBC as it was called) towards him with his left hand to accelerate ahead.

His signaller contacted him again. He struggled to understand the message. He thought that he was being told that they'd decided to stop the defective train at Ledburn and move it across to the fast track and take it back to Bletchley. He was not to know that there was an argument going on because the day's schedule required this train back in service as soon as possible.

It was at that point in time that Sarah Rudd realised that her husband was on the train. He had been catching the 5.46 a.m. from Northampton. She texted him:

*Nick u r in great danger. There's a bomber on board your train. Get out now.*

She pulled a police constable over to her.

"Take me to the Berkhamsted tunnel," she instructed.

"Must be beyond Cheddington Ma'am."

They rushed to his car and he used his blue light to fight through the congestion ahead.

"We'll pick it up at Grove Lock."

Gordon Panting's sixth sense told him something was wrong. He called for his conductor who was involved in separating two women who were arguing over a seat where one had placed her luggage.

DCI Rudd was on her mobile to D/Supt Khan as they sped through the traffic and along the canal road towards Ivinghoe. She could see the train on the line travelling away from Leighton Buzzard. She could not understand why it was moving so slowly.

"That's Bridego Bridge ahead, isn't it?" she shouted.

"The Robbery bridge, Ma'am."

"Yes. Stop there."

\* \* \*

Ahead of them the terrorists were looking at their watches and peering through the torrential rain. They were wondering where the train was as it was now four minutes late."

On board the 6.14 a.m. from Leighton Buzzard, Nick Rudd had his eyes firmly fixed on the man standing in the adjacent compartment. He had taken his rucksack from off his back and had it opened at his feet.

The first class compartment had been declassified by the conductor and every seat was taken: there were still many people standing in the aisles. Matthew accepted the necessity of this action but silently hated this moment when his privacy was invaded by a mass of humanity. He turned his back on a mountain of a man who had slumped in the next seat making clear his joy at travelling in such luxury.

The police operation was now in full swing as the elite response unit left Hemel Hempstead and sped towards Berkhamsted. Local police forces were being mobilised, hospitals put on red alert and the government were already aware of the situation.

Commander Max Riley was red in the face.

"DCI Attwood. Now, who and where?"

He was shaking and crying at the same time. He looked at his boss.

"Sorry," he mouthed.

"Who and where, Percy? Tell me for God's sake."

Superintendent Monica Moses came up behind him and threw a glass of cold water into his face. He sat up with a jerk.

"Gas. They're going to gas them all," he spluttered.

One of the terrorists on the northern side had made a terrible error. The girl was not dead. Her body was riddled with pain but she had enough life left in her to try to drag herself up onto her feet. She fumbled with a box of matches and turned on the methane stove. As she struck the match it caught the fumes. There was an explosion and a gas ball lit up the whole of the area. Armed police were now arriving in numbers and searching for the terrorists. The three on the southern exit of the tunnel were preparing to set off their bombs before fleeing into the Chiltern Hills.

The Planner was getting angry as his channels of communication were seemingly closed down. His third phone rang and he answered it with a single word. The second mole within Islington Police Station told him that their cover was blown. He calmly closed down his operations, changed his clothing and exited through a concealed door at the rear of the building. He would soon be travelling north towards Scotland and then over to Europe before catching a plane to Saudi Arabia. He was forced to pray standing on his feet. He knew that whatever was happening back in the Chiltern Hills the fear factor would take over and the British public would demand to know how this whole campaign had been allowed to happen.

On the 6.14 a.m. from Leighton Buzzard to Euston, Gordon Panting pulled his PBC towards him and relaxed as the train gradually gained speed. The suicide martyr had his hands on the two gas taps. Nick was reading his text message and watching him like a hawk.

# Chapter Nineteen

Gordon Panting had decided to demand a meeting with his bosses. Too often when there were heavy storms, problems occurred with the communications system. He was late by a few minutes and his pride in his punctuality record was dented. The conductor was reporting an overcrowded train: he tried to radio back for further instructions. He could not see more than three hundred yards ahead as the moisture-laden atmosphere closed in around him. He increased the speed of the train cautiously but was happy to sense that he was making progress. He then had to slow down as the signal overhead showed a double yellow warning light.

Ahead at the Berkhamsted tunnel the three terrorists on the northern side were watching the canal boat sending flames up into the sky. There was a second explosion but the black thunder clouds closed in all around them. Their two explosions were ready to be detonated inside the entrance and they had the follow-up bombs ready to ensure that the tomb of the four hundred infidels would be sealed. At the other end the rails had been buckled by the first of the detonations and they decided to complete the closing of the tomb.

The explosions shattered the brickwork and the supporting frame collapsed as the rocks above cascaded down to seal the exit of the tunnel. As the clouds of dust and concrete merged with the rainfall the visibility reduced to under twenty yards. They started to run back to their escape van only to find themselves being hailed by officers from the firearms division of the Hertfordshire police. One of the al-Qaeda fighters put his hands up but the other two went for their weapons. The first was shot almost immediately. The other began to run away but took a bullet in his thigh and collapsed to the ground. He fell down on the grassy bank and lay still.

\* \* \*

The police constable was driving rapidly down the Ivinghoe road until he reached the turning. He swerved right into the lane and skidded on the gravel bringing his vehicle to a stop just before the brick columns holding up Bridego Bridge. DCI Rudd told him to stay with his car and report to his controller. She leapt out and began to scramble up the banks where, fifty years earlier, the Great Train Robbers had brought down their loot of high value packages.

She peered down the track towards Leighton Buzzard. Through the torrential rain she was certain that she could see the train approaching. She could make out two lights and realised it was not far away. It would quickly pass through and enter the Berkhamsted tunnel.

Aboard the train, Nick Rudd was becoming more fixated about the passenger with the rucksack at his feet. He had read his text message from Sarah. He seemed to be silently chanting and Nick could see beads of sweat on his forehead. It was at that point that the illogicality of his situation dawned on the headteacher. The man was carrying no rainwear. He was dressed all in black and had soft pumps on his feet. The stormy weather had been over the whole of the United Kingdom for the last forty-eight hours. He decided to wait for the guard to appear and then he would challenge the stranger.

In the first class carriage Matthew was getting irritated by the huge commuter sitting next to him who had taken out a meat pie and was relishing every noisy mouthful. He was dropping crumbs on the table which he was sweeping away with an exaggerated wave of his arm. He was unable to get both of his fat legs inside the space and was sitting with part of his body in the aisle. He had undone his top shirt button and allowed his bulging excess fat to hang out over his collar. He was reading the *Metro*. The headlines suggested an improving economy as retail sales increased by three percent over the last quarter and

246

the housing market responded to the Government's funding initiatives.

Matthew wanted to get to work. He wanted to share his news although he had promised Jessica that he would not yet tell anybody. Perhaps he'd take Craig for a celebratory lunch-time whisky. They had secured a block of shares in an online gambling platform out of Israel. The brokers were selling the investments fairly easily, Debra was happy and Ashtella was monitoring their calls. He looked down to read the text message from Caroline. He suddenly realised that he was really looking forward to seeing her again. Whether or not she had returned from Belize with any or all of the missing four million pounds he'd buy her dinner. He had to decide if he would tell Jessica about their 'date'. That decision could wait for the future. All he wanted to do now was to reach Euston Station.

Gordon Panting's phone was crackling with static as the signaller desperately tried to contact him. The visibility around his train had reduced further as the storm reached its zenith. He had not registered that there were no other trains running between Milton Keynes and Watford as the police closed in around the tunnel. He had to hold his speed because of the yellow light. He was approaching Ledburn.

At Bridego Bridge the constable had reversed his vehicle to the corner of the lane to provide a guide to the approaching vehicles. He could see their lights coming in from the southern side. He was constantly on the phone. He was asked about the police officer with him and he reported that she had now disappeared out of sight. He thought that she was up on the rail track.

Commander Max Riley was continuing to question DCI Percy Attwood. They were already at his house and examining his computer. His officers had sealed off an area in Islington and were frantically searching for a cleric.

"Why Percy, why?" asked the anguished policeman.

He rubbed his face with a towel.

"You!" shouted the accused. "You let these fucking educated children in to do police work. Out there it's my thirty years experience that keeps the peace. I watched as this sodding new Police and Crime Commissioner was elected. He's no idea about what I do as he gets his chauffeur-driven car, swanky offices and is treated like a god. Then he appoints his mates to all the jobs and my budgets are cut yet again."

He sat up rigid looking first at Superintendent Moses and then at the Commander.

"You're getting the police force you deserve, Max. You've betrayed us."

DCI Sarah Rudd was standing on the track just beyond the bridge. She could now hear the train approaching. Inside was her husband rushing towards his death in the Berkhamsted tunnel. She could vaguely see police lights down below but knew that she had to stop the train. How did they do it fifty years ago? They tampered with the lights. They crudely cut wires and used black paper bags to cover up the green signals.

It was at that point that she focused on the colour red. It was the only sign that the driver would recognise to indicate danger. Sarah realised that there was some of that colour available to her. She looked down at her saturated skirt and pulled it up to her waist. In one of those absurd moments, only achieved by human beings, she stared around her to make sure nobody was looking at her privacy. She lowered her knickers. They were bright red. She straightened out her clothing and squeezed the rain-water out of her underwear.

She could now make out the train coming towards her. She stood in the middle of the track and raised the red flag above her head.

Gordon Panting was staring ahead of him. The early light was coming in from the east and the electricity was lighting up the skies. Just for one moment he thought that he sensed movement ahead of him. His view was restricted and he could not see the blue police lights filling the roads around the bridge.

Nick Rudd was becoming increasingly concerned about the agitated gestures of the man standing in the compartment space. He was continually checking inside the bag at his feet.

The police were having difficulty finding the northern entrance to the tunnel. At the southern end the three terrorists were either dead or wounded and in high security custody.

There were frantic calls being made but the fire on the canal was diverting their attention. At the tunnel the three Islamic fighters remained ready to seal the site of the imminent death of four hundred British commuters.

Sarah remained rigid as she held her warning sign above her head. She was soaked to the skin and scared. She was now shaking with the cold. The train was getting nearer and she had no other solution to offer.

Gordon Panting peered ahead and his left hand moved towards his brake controller.

Sarah was thinking that it was all in vain. She was not pre-pared to step aside and let the oncoming train pass through. She thought about Marcus and Susie. What would they do without her? But she would have saved the life of their father and guaranteed their future.

There was a sudden deluge of rain and the skies filled once again with electricity. She made one last effort to stop the 6.14 a.m. train from Leighton Buzzard to Euston. She raised her arms up as far as she could manage.

There was a flash of lightning across the skies. It seemed to catch the material in her hands and she felt her knickers rever-berate. The tension surged down her arms and she collapsed to the ground falling just outside the rails and onto the gravel. She cried out in pain.

Gordon peered anxiously ahead of him. He was certain that he had seen the briefest flash of a light. There was no gantry at this point but there had been a red signal: he was certain of that. He used his left arm to push the power brake control as far away from him as possible as he instigated an emergency stop. The train came to a halt in a few hundred yards. The passengers were thrown around the compartments and throughout the passageways. The man sitting by Matthew was sick.

It was the final straw. He kicked him away and fought his way to the compartment linking the first class carriage to the rest of the train. Nick now made his move. He stood up, pushed aside two women and dived on the man. There was a violent struggle. He found himself being helped by another man. Their faces met. "Matthew, pleased to meet you," the stranger gasped.

There they stayed until, five minutes later, the police persuaded them to release their captive. The bag remained where it was before the bomb disposal unit took away the two canisters of deadly gas. Nick staggered out of the train and refused any help. The commuters were being treated for broken bones, bruises and shock. A pregnant woman had gone into labour. People were being led back down the track.

DCI Sarah Rudd was on her mobile to the Commander. She gave a full and coherent report. She said that she was unharmed. She refused all offers of help. She looked around as the full exercise swung into action. It was the British police force and rescue services at their very best. Further down the line the three terrorists had been captured.

Despite the crowds around her she felt alone. She stared ahead and realised that a man was walking towards her. The people seemed to make a pathway for her and she ran towards her husband. They clung and cried together. They wanted to get away. They scrambled down the slope of Bridego Bridge to the road below and started to walk down the lane. They were feeding off each other and beginning to return to their normal selves. They agreed to talk later.

As they reached the rescue services Nick turned to his wife.

"Sarah. You won't believe this. You know they talk about adrenalin being an aphrodisiac, well guess what?"

"You're feeling randy," laughed Sarah.

"Putting it bluntly, yes."

"Well, Nick," she said, "you might have a pleasant surprise ahead of you. It could be a lot easier than you might think."

\* \* \*

As the day developed the storm clouds cleared, the air temperature rose and the sunlight radiated out from the skies. The West Coast Main Line railway was closed completely for Intercity trains and the economies of Manchester and Birmingham suffered. From Northampton through to Watford the Railway Police combed everywhere. The 6.14 a.m. from Leighton

Buzzard to Euston was declared a crime scene and remained stationary just south of Bridego Bridge. The army had recovered the two canisters of gas from the carriage and were now taking them for testing at a secret location. At the Berkhamsted tunnel, on the northern side, the three terrorists were captured and taken away to Paddington Green police station for questioning. The fire on the canal boat was extinguished and it was later lifted out of the water and taken away for police forensic examination. Inside, the body of a badly burnt young woman was discovered and removed for medical inspection and identification. Nearby, a second corpse was recovered. At the exit of the tunnel army bomb disposal units had cleared away the rubble and checked for further explosive devices. It was to be established that the railway line was hardly damaged by the attempts of the Islamic fighters and the amount of brickwork dislodged by their bombs was so insignificant that the 6.14 a.m., from Leighton Buzzard, would have ploughed through and retained a momentum to reach the station ahead.

The Assistant Chief Constable arrived to take overall charge of the situation. At eleven o'clock he gave a press conference to the world's media in the park opposite Leighton Buzzard station. He started by giving out a telephone number so that worried relatives could establish the whereabouts of their loved ones. Many of the four hundred commuters were still struggling to reach home or work either by bus or taxi to London. He confirmed the basic attack on the railway system and the capture alive of five terrorists from the scene of the tunnel and one on the train which had stopped just after Bridego Bridge. He reported that there was one dead terrorist and two bodies had been recovered from near the entrance to the tunnel. He described it as a single attack by an unknown group who had yet to be identified.

Behind the scenes there was total panic. Downing Street called a meeting of COBRA and every police officer was called in to duty. The British Transport Police, assisted by army bomb disposal units, launched a checking of every tunnel which took three days to complete. The Prime Minister made a statement in Parliament calling for calm.

The British media saw it rather differently and immediately labelled the attack as the British version of 9/11. As The Great Train Robbery, fifty years earlier, had exposed the vulnerability of the railway system to theft, so the 16/10, as it was to be called, shook the public's confidence in the country's security services to its core. The immediate question being asked was why the Prime Minister and the Foreign Secretary should be spending their time on Middle Eastern politics when it was clear that the country's own safety measures were in need of urgent attention.

Then the blame game began almost immediately as the Labour leader and shadow Home Secretary began to raise the question of the budget cuts imposed on the police and the army. A panicking Prime Minister announced an immediate injection of £2 billion into the police budget, without consulting anybody, and making a mockery of the Chancellor's austerity programme. The value of the pound fell on the world's currency markets, interest rates rose and the Governor of the Bank of England found his promise to keep to a growth strategy under pressure.

* * *

At Islington Police Station Commander Max Riley retained the confidence of his bosses. Superintendent Monica Moses took over responsibility for community safety and, somewhat to her surprise, recruited DCI Avril Flemming to work alongside her. D/Supt Khan concentrated on the hunt for the relatives of the terrorists. A total of over thirty homes were searched and a number of weapons recovered. The church leaders worked closely with the authorities and normality returned to the streets quite quickly. An offer from the London Mayor to visit the area was politely declined.

DCI Sarah Rudd refused any medical attention and she and Nick reached their home late in the afternoon. She showered and then allowed him to check the bruises on her back where she had fallen on the railway track. Their brief moment of passion had passed and the reality of their situation was dawning on them. His parents agreed to continue to look after Marcus and Susie and police cars came to take them to Islington Police Station.

Nick gave a statement to an officer from New Scotland Yard. He told them of the man who had helped him and who had disappeared almost immediately the police had secured the terrorist. "His name was Matthew," he told them. He then received a visit from Commander Riley. They spoke privately together for ten minutes and then shook hands. Nick was desperate that there should be no personal publicity. He faced a media search for the man on the train who had subdued the bomber: when he was later identified the impact on his life was minimal.

Sarah had completed a seven-page statement which, by eleven o'clock in the evening, she had signed and handed over to the investigating officer. She now found herself talking privately to the Commander.

"You made an independent decision not to inform D/Supt Khan of the developments, DCI Rudd."

She took great care in explaining to Commander Max Riley her actions and why she delayed for so long. He confirmed that DCI Percy Attwood had been arrested and would go to prison along with a junior constable who he had blackmailed into helping him. The Commander wanted to understand how she had managed to stop the train. She told it to him as it was. He remained speechless. Although Gordon Panting was later to confirm that he thought he spotted a red light, it was never disclosed how DCI Rudd had stopped the train. He ordered her to go home and return for duty on the following Monday. He asked that she agree to have a medical check and she refused.

Her departure from the building was delayed by the arrival of D/Supt Majid Khan. As he reached her he stopped and stared. His face was drawn and his eyes dark.

"You do not realise, do you?" he said.

DCI Rudd immediately sensed his inner tension.

"I'm sorry, Sir. Realise what?"

"Yesterday was the day that Muslims celebrated the festival of Eid-al-Adha. It's when we commemorate Abraham's willingness to sacrifice his son to Allah."

"I had no idea, Sir. It was not on the annual list."

"It moves each year with the lunar calendar. That's not so important. What is special is the fact that it is the day we seek to improve the quality of our lives. Some Muslims will organise the sacrifice of an animal. Others dress in new clothes. We help our poorest families."

Her hand flew to her mouth.

"I had no idea, Sir."

"You are a friend to all of us, Sarah. You prevented our extremist brothers from committing an atrocity that would have wrecked the years of community building you see every day here in our patch." He took a step back. "There is so much to be done."

He moved past her and entered the station.

As they sat together in the back of the police car taking them home Nick squeezed his wife's hand and used his eyes to ask the question on both their minds.

"I wonder if there are any vacancies for traffic wardens in Northampton," she said trying to get closer to her husband.

\* \* \*

Mob reached London at midday and rushed to his office. The taxi had cost him over £100 but his company had taken in a line of shares which Craig and his team were now selling to their clients. Debra was prowling around the corridors and Ashtella was listening intently to the conversations.

The atmosphere at Silverside Brokers had changed following the FCA visit. There was a new confidence and suddenly the regulatory members of staff were being seen in a supportive way. The brokers themselves were raising their standards and they were making money.

"I'm tellin' y'u laddie, we'll clear a hundred on these."

Craig and Matthew were sharing an evening drink together and, much to his surprise, Craig was told that his companion had booked into a hotel for the night. He asked why he was not staying at his flat in Covent Garden.

"Tenants," he replied. "But that can change."

Matthew had spent a long time on the phone with Jessica who wanted to tell him about her media coup. They established that Olivia was watching every news broadcast and rushing out to inform Rustic on the day's events.

Caroline arrived at the hotel at ten that evening. She had landed at Heathrow the night before so missing the security clampdown. They immediately went into the restaurant and she began to tell him about her adventures in Belize. She had met with Martine and thought that there was a good chance that she might be able to recover much of the missing money. Martine knew she could not return to Britain and had already met somebody who was attracting her attention. She was dismissive of her father and blamed him for all her troubles.

Matthew had other things on his mind. He had never really liked living in Leighton Buzzard and the move back to Ledburn was beginning to stress him. When he had been packed like a sardine on the 6.14 a.m. train he suddenly wanted to get away from the fat man beside him and go to where he belonged. He was a man of the City. That last journey had seemed to trigger these thoughts. Jessica was now pregnant: that would change everything.

It was almost inevitable. They finished their meal and without a word being spoken Caroline followed him up to the bedroom. They went in together. Mob turned on the side lights and put on some background music. They kissed in the centre of the lounge area. She stepped back and began to undo the buttons of her jacket which fell away to the floor. She removed her blouse and Matthew gasped as, for the first time, he could stop imagining and see the real thing. Her skirt followed downwards: she was wearing suspenders and stockings and the effect was phenomenal. Her thighs glistened with her oily skin. They were sensational. He looked at her sex. He bent down and picked up her top, which he wrapped around her shoulders.

"Too soon, Mob?" she asked.

"Too soon, Caroline."

It was Jessica who was one of the first people to link the 16/10 incident to The Great Train Robbery. She phoned the girls at the media company in Milton Keynes and they immediately started work on a documentary programme. One set out to research the archives and prepare the background material from fifty years ago and the other sent her assistant down to Ledburn where she set up in a room in the house. It took her two hours to get through the police checks. She accepted an offer to stay the night and immediately was taken on a tour, by Olivia, of the animal sanctuary.

* * *

Nick Rudd gave his notice in and announced to his school that he would be leaving at Christmas. He signed his employment forms with Mayfair International Schools. He and Sarah spent many hours with Marcus and Susie who were devastated by the news and the moving to new schools. They spent the following weekend touring the town and surrounding villages but it did little to placate them.

Seven days passed and towards the end of October Marcus had identified, from the Internet, where he wanted to live and which school he would be attending. Susie claimed she was being bullied into decisions which she was not a party to and protested loudly. They visited the region yet again and slowly peace was restored.

They put their house up for sale and were surprised to find a buyer within days at the asking price. The government's attempts to stimulate the market were most certainly having an effect. Nick wondered if he might have to vote Conservative at the 2015 General Election but dismissed the idea as preposterous.

Sarah was having trouble sleeping and so she visited her doctor for a full medical check. He listened carefully to her latest adventures and nearly collapsed at the story of how she had stopped the train. The electricity from the lightning flash concerned him and he sent her for further tests. These proved negative and she was given a clean bill of health. The doctor peered over his glasses.

"I know that I'm wasting my breath, Mrs Rudd, but is there any chance you might find a more sedentary way of life? He laughed but out of respect for his patient who was so very different to the majority of his daily list.

The letter arrived and Sarah knew exactly what it would say. She handed it to Nick who gave it back to her. She used a knife to open the envelope. Inside the letter said that she was to attend a meeting with Commander Riley in two days' time, at 10 a.m. She was to come alone.

\* \* \*

The Planner arose from his prayer mat and went into the side room where three men were waiting for him. It was nearing midday in Saudi Arabia and temperatures were soaring. He contented himself by eating the dates and drinking coffee.

Their debriefing process was entirely satisfactory. The British Government had been destabilised and no amount of political rhetoric could hide from the public the reality that a catastrophe had been narrowly avoided. The media continued to speculate whether the attempt to kill hundreds of commuters could have worked. Security experts, by the dozen, earned generous fees from TV appearances during which they explained why the attack could never have succeeded. But few people were convinced.

The Planner explained that morale amongst his Muslim group was improving and converts were beginning again to appear.

He received the blessing of his brothers and began the journey back to Britain to continue his work. He would be identified as soon as he arrived at Heathrow but he had not committed any provable offence and there was an expensive firm of London lawyers, already in receipt of substantial funds, who would ensure his freedom and ability to continue his work for Islam.

# Chapter Twenty

The tension increased as Matthew and Jessica realised that they were not enjoying listening to one other: both of them wanted to do the talking. They both had so much to say but, unlike earlier times together, there was an unspoken battle for the centre ground. They were almost circling each other with verbal pincer movements. Finally Matthew took advantage of a brief lull as Jessica poured some more coffee.

"It was amazing, Jessie. There were police everywhere and nobody really knew what was happening. When we were allowed off the train we were told that we had to queue and register with a police officer. I managed to dodge that and I walked across the fields to the road. It was raining cats and dogs but I had my umbrella. I managed to hitch a lift because it seemed all the locals wanted to help."

He paused, went over to the cocktail cabinet and poured himself a whisky, and returned to his story.

"I managed to get a lift to Hemel and then a taxi to London. I booked a room at Threadneedles Hotel and used the bathroom to shower before going to the office. The atmosphere was electric. Craig had this line of stock and the brokers sold half of it by the end of the day. When they're making money they are different people, Jessie."

He paused again. "Debra is a changed person. The endorsement she received from the FCA has revitalised her. The whole process is so much more efficient and, do you know what, our clients are getting an improved service because we are dealing with the administrative matters better. Ashtella has only recalled two sales in two days."

"Did you have dinner on your own?" she asked.

"I drank too much malt whisky with Craig and then crashed out," he lied.

"I couldn't raise you on your phone."

"Sorry, Jessie. I left my charger in the office and when I reached the room it was dead." He stood up and went over to refill his glass.

"Jessie. The whole adrenalin in London is changing. The Conservatives are already starting the 2015 General Election campaign. It's the European Elections next year and they want a damage limitation result. They know that they'll be slaughtered but if the results are not as bad as forecast they'll call it a good outcome. Funny world politics!" He drank some more Scotch. "I want to raise something with you. This lease on my Covent Garden flat. I want to get out of it. I want my own place back. I paid £390 for the hotel room last night, and I suspect that if business continues as it is, I'll need to stay in London more regularly."

"But you'd also like to hear about my news wouldn't you, Mob?"

She gave him no choice in the matter. Over the next fifteen minutes she exploded with excitement as she told of how she had worked with the team from the Milton Keynes media company to cash in on the events at Bridego Bridge. Such was their response to Jessica's initiative that within two days a basic script had been agreed and the various sections allocated to their editors. She was following his rule: concept then detail. She had transferred £20,000 to the company's bank account from her personal savings with a building society. They had immediately taken on two graduates who were given the task of monitoring news channels so that they captured every development of the story.

"Mob. We are meeting next Monday for a full day's planning session. I've been asked to chair it."

Matthew's heart sank. He now wanted to move back into London and to City life. She was loving it in Ledburn and building up a serious business in Milton Keynes. She was rather strong-willed as he very well knew.

\* \* \*

260

Detective Chief Inspector Sarah Rudd sat in front of the Commander and was puzzled at why he did not serve the tea and coffee himself. He had picked up his phone and asked his personal assistant to come in and to attend to those duties. She was unable to resist the Bourbon biscuits and justified her decision with the knowledge that Nick continued to love her curves.

"Detective Chief Inspector. I have read your statement and discussed the whole episode in great detail with D/Supt Khan. Superintendent Moses has played an overseeing role. I now want you to take me through, in your own words, the series of events leading to your stopping of the train at Bridego Bridge. You are not to miss out a single fact. I'll decide what is relevant."

An hour later, and after several cups of tea, Sarah finished her story from the first of the phone calls, 'Watch Rashid', to the final outcome south of Leighton Buzzard station. The Commander did not move a muscle as she described waving her knickers in the air to stop the 6.14 a.m. train to Euston.

"Your husband showed great courage, Sarah, and yet I gather he's managed to snuff out any publicity. The gas in the canisters could have killed hundreds of people."

"He didn't know that. He just realised that something was wrong. He did what he did instinctively."

"And you, Sarah, did what you did. What you did not do was to inform D/Supt Khan of all the information you had to hand. Your single-minded approach could have led to the death of hundreds of people. You were playing God Sarah."

"With respect Sir I was fulfilling my responsibilities as a police officer. It took me so long to expose the mole. If I had divulged the facts that I had, I was certain that Freezer would hear and the Planner would have moved out of our community the same day. That would have meant we'd have given up the best chance we had to stop the atrocity."

"Please answer me a question DCI Rudd. What would have happened if you had not stopped the train?"

"I'd be dead, Sir."

"Pardon?"

"I had no intention of moving from the track until it did stop."

Their conversation continued for another twenty minutes but they both knew what was going to happen.

"Sarah. I'm afraid you've reached the end of the line". He then realised the impact of the metaphor he had used.

"Quite a ride, Sir." smiled Sarah.

He stood up and handed her a large white envelope embossed with the police crest. It was addressed as 'Strictly Private and Confidential. Mrs Sarah Rudd'.

As she was leaving the office she turned back and faced her boss.

"Did you make any mistakes, Sir?" she asked.

\* \* \*

There was, however, a hero. Amongst his fellow drivers, Gordon Panting had become a legend. The jokes never stopped: *"don't get your knickers in a twist today, Gordon"*, they would tease him.

He loved his period of fame. He may not have got his passengers to Euston on time but he achieved his over-riding aim: they were all safe.

\* \* \*

The former Labour Prime Minister Harold Wilson once said, during his first year in office (1964), *"a week is a long time in politics"*.

For the relationship between Matthew and Jessica it took far less than seven days for the crisis to arrive. Perhaps, they were to reflect later, it required less time, maybe hours or even a word of four letters.

Was it possible that up in Heaven Jessica's mother was sending Mob an astral text message selected from *King Lear*?

*Time shall unfold what plighted cunning hides.*

In a more modern age Pink Floyd confronted the same issue in their song 'Time':

*The time is gone*
*The song is over*
*Thought I'd something more to say*

262

*Home*
*Home again*
*I like to be here*
*When I can*

Although 'home' was not the word which pre-empted the crisis it was the underlying cause of Matthew's personal stress. He could not banish from his thoughts the moment when he had stood in front of Caroline and wanted, beyond desire itself, to possess her. It was not even the phenomenal landscape: her sensual skin, the curves, bulges and secret entries. It was not the usual macho need to conquer.

It was London, the financial City, the nomenclature, the brokers and their sale of shares, the bars, the hotels, the restaurants, the free distribution paper *City A.M.*, the rumours, the scandals, the making of money and the women.

They wore their business suits to tantalise their male colleagues. They played their trump card shamelessly and then feigned surprise when the offers came: the hand on the shoulder, the possibility of a drink together, the payment of a bonus, the suggestion of a meal, the false concern "It's too late to guarantee your safety on the Tube train", the hurried, and pre-planned, hotel room, the large vodkas and tonic, the music of Lloyd Webber and the conquest.

They would say *"I won't do anything that might affect your married life,"* before noticing that they'd missed the last train home from Waterloo station.

But the piece of the jigsaw that Matthew liked the best was the next morning. No questions asked. After the telephone call, and the lies to those at home, it was back to the making of money. There would be an exchange of looks and an answer to the unspoken question "Next week?". There would be further desires: fornication is addictive.

Matthew Orlando Buckingham was hooked again and wanted to rejoin. The markets were up, trading was improving, the commissions were pouring in: the City was alive. He wanted to live in his home in Covent Garden. He hated the train journey to, and from, Leighton Buzzard. He resented the intrusion into his privacy when 'First Class' was declassified and a fat bastard, no more than a stomach on legs, and eating a meat pie, sat down beside him.

He wanted the privacy that London offered. He wanted back in.

He loved his daughter.

The word that precipitated the collapse of their relationship comprised four letters: 'your'. It was used in a casual but fatal way. Jessica knew about Caroline. She did not know the name of the woman but she was street-wise, she could sense when Mob was lying, and he had a smell of guilt about him. She would have let that pass: many women gain a perverse sense of pride knowing that their partners are still attractive to the hunters. Providing the bills are paid and the house-keeping allowance hits the bank account every month, they may turn a blind eye while their loved ones 'mature'.

Jessica had gone on and on about her new media business and their first documentary. Matthew tried to show some interest but what The Great Train Robbery had to do with a terrorist attack on a commuter train outside Leighton Buzzard was beyond him.

"So if you get involved full-time, and as you are investing up to one million pounds that seems likely, what will happen to your baby?" he asked.

"Please say that again, Matthew." instructed Jessica as she pulled the kitchen table sharply away so that she could stand up.

"What I said was that if you are going…"

"I heard everything you said, Matthew. There was a word I did not like hearing."

She was repeating his full name: 'Matthew'. Her tone of voice was entering into dangerous territory. He looked at his watch and noted that he had forty-five minutes clear before he needed to collect Olivia from her music lesson.

"OK, Jessica, 'Mastermind' is over. What word did I use that you don't like?"

"I like it very much indeed, Matthew."

He looked to the heavens for Shakespearean guidance. Jessica, however, did not want to be interrupted.

"'Your', Matthew." She hesitated. "That's the word that tells me all I need to know." She poured herself a glass of water. "A baby, Matthew, should be created by the act of making love: it takes place between two people. Their affection for each other is transferred to the child. You have never made love, Matthew. You just crave sex. It's a totally different thing."

"Will you please stop calling me, 'Matthew'?" he pleaded.

"You stick it in, you pull it out, job done. What's on *SKY Sports*?"

"Jessica. It's your baby. I'm the father. I've given you all you've ever wanted. It was one of the first things you ever said to me: 'It's time I had a baby.' Remember?"

"I was quoting my mother actually but you're right. I told you I'd decided to have the baby and forget the man." She wiped her eyes.

"Now you will have the baby, Olivia, and the husband."

"I don't think so, Matthew. I'm not going to marry you."

He looked at her and grimaced.

"So what happens to me?"

She smiled and walked around the table.

"You're going back to London, Matthew. I've given the couple in your flat notice to quit. Strange really but my solicitor was surprised when I insisted on a monthly tenancy." She kissed him on the cheek and squeezed his shoulder. "I don't know her name but she's a lucky girl. I'll stay here for as long as I want: John Sneddon has agreed to sell it to me for £700,000. Thomas is to remain with his foster parents: they are asking to adopt him and that could possibly happen."

She paused and looked tired. Her bottom lip seemed to quiver.

"Your ex-wife is not in good shape: John's promising to look after her when he comes out of prison."

She stopped walking around the room and turned to face him.

"I'll bring up Olivia and you can come whenever you want. I suggest that you have a room here. I'll have my baby and you, of course, will have full paternal rights."

She paused and swallowed.

265

"We'll not fall out over the detail will we, Mob?"

She carried on talking.

"There will be a nanny. You are to keep lover-girl away for at least a year, if it lasts that long. We'll explain everything to Olivia: pressure of business and all that. She's been through so much she knows the ropes. She'll love the new baby and I'll make sure her schooling goes well. She'll get all the love she needs. You must make your visits regularly and special for her."

"And what if you find another man, Jessica?"

"The offers will come pouring in, Matthew, but I've a huge investment to look after. To be honest I've had enough of men."

\* \* \*

Caroline and Matthew had never stopped texting from the moment they left the hotel together. They were both frustrated by their aborted encounter the night before but they intuitively understood that their consummation was a matter of time. It felt right. She had been initiated by Mark Patterson-Brown into the City and its rules. He was now learning about divorce and its consequences.

They were both ready for the next stage of their lives which they intended to share. They had, perhaps, been coming together for some time. His flat would become vacant as the tenants had indicated that they would move out earlier than their notice period. She immediately agreed to move in with him. They were now sharing a meal together in a Soho restaurant.

"Do you really think that you have chatted me up enough, Mob?" she asked.

"Get real, Caroline. We've been summing each other up for what seems like ages."

"But we appear to have made some important decisions rather quickly," she said. "Not that I mind."

"That's how the City works, Caroline."

They decided, without saying another word, on how their evening should progress. They walked up Charing Cross Road and booked into a hotel. They went straight up to the bedroom,

266

locked the door, and exploded into each other's arms. The pent-up desire and emotion propelled them into bed.

* * *

They sat together holding hands. Marcus and Susie were both asleep upstairs.

"Come on, Sarah. Let's do the deed and plan our new life together."

"You read it, Nick. I'll start crying, you know that. I'm no good at reading my own obituary."

"You've had a fantastic career, Sarah. Let's open it and move on."

The former Detective Chief Inspector slowly opened the envelope. Nick had already run a knife across the top to release the contents. She took out a sheaf of papers. She carefully read the covering letter.

Sarah began to shake and then the tears came pouring down her face. Never before, outside the birth of their two children, had Nick seen her show so much emotion. She handed him the covering letter. It was from Commander Max Riley.

It was a long two pages. It reviewed recent events and explained that the police were keen to restrict any personal publicity that might accrue from her outstanding detective work in preventing what might have been a national tragedy. He spoke on behalf of the whole of the Metropolitan Police in commending her, yet again, for her outstanding bravery. He emphasised that this came from 'the highest level'.

He went on to explain that, after the most careful considera-tion, it had been decided that, for her own personal safety, she could not continue her police work in Islington. They there-fore wanted to recognise her outstanding career by offering her early retirement on a full pension. The generous financial settlement was explained fully. Nick's heart sank. It was the end of the police career for his wife. He looked up: the tears were still flowing. He turned over the page and was stunned by what he read.

The Commander set out, in some detail, a job vacancy for a Superintendent in the Northamptonshire Police Force. The position involved co-ordinating all the local sources of community information into a central function with the objective of improving the safety of the local people. It would mean a promotion and a minimum of five years more service.

Max Riley then explained that, because of the unusual circumstances, it had been decided, following legal advice, that on his personal intervention and recommendation, the position was to be offered to her subject to an interview with the Police and Crime Commissioner and the local board.

*You are entitled to assume that all the members have already been consulted, as has the PCC, and, should you wish to be considered for this important position, you can expect an enthusiastic welcome.*

The letter concluded as follows:

*I see the situation rather differently. My own view is that the Northamptonshire police force is extremely fortunate to be welcoming perhaps the best, and bravest, serving police officer with whom it has ever been my privilege to work.*

She looked at her husband.

"Can I say 'yes', Nick?"

"Any chance of me stopping you?" he laughed.

"I'm a police officer, Nick. It's what I do best."

"And a mother," he added.

"Yes. I'll never make that mistake again."

"And something else."

"What, Nick. What more can I be?"

"A lover."

She laughed, a sound of total happiness.

"Ah," he said. "I've been meaning to ask you something, Sarah." He pulled her towards him.

"When we were walking away from Bridego Bridge, and I told you the excitement was making me randy, you said it might be easier than I was thinking. What did you mean?"

Sarah looked at her husband.

"Nick. Are you serious?"

"Yes. I didn't understand what you meant."

She looked at him.

"Nick. Where were my knickers?"

The penny dropped.

"But you were soaking wet. There were people around."

"I was also rather willing."

Nick laughed and paused. He then adopted his provocative style.

"Superintendent Rudd?"

"Yes, Nick. I'll be Superintendent Rudd."

He grabbed at his glass of whisky and water.

"Not Detective Superintendent Rudd?"

"No. What point are you making? Do you want to show me off at your new school?"

"Superintendent Rudd will be back in uniform."

"I'll be walking the streets of Northampton in my full outfit, Nick. Is there a problem with that?" She stopped and put her hand to her mouth.

"Oh no! I've just remembered. A police uniform is an aphrodisiac for you, isn't it Nick?"

"How would you feel about driving back to Bridego Bridge and recreating the stopping of the train but with you in uniform."

"And wearing red knickers?"

"I'll provide the flash of lightning," he suggested.

* * *

The rain clouds over Ledburn delayed the arrival of the early morning light from the east. She had not slept. Her hand was on her stomach as her baby stirred within her. She was sitting at the kitchen table waiting for Olivia to appear. There were no more tears left.

It all made sense. He was a City man and he was relishing the life there, his business and the women: that was what he wanted. He'd be happy in his Covent Garden flat with his new girlfriend. He'd be loyal to her and he'd keep up his visits to see his daughter and their new baby. She had her new media business in Milton Keynes.

269

But it was not what Jessica really wanted. She wondered what her mother might say: was she trying to send her some thoughts from her heavenly abode?

*Get thee a good husband,*

*And use him as he uses thee.*

But for Jessica it was not proving a case of *All's Well That Ends Well*. She had been willing to have a liberal approach to their relationship. She'd have turned a blind eye to the odd indiscretion. In her heart of hearts she wanted the man with whom she had fallen in love with and who had given her the baby inside her.

She heard a noise. It was too early for the milk and paper deliveries. She knew that Olivia was still asleep. She stood up and wrapped her dressing gown around her. The door opened. He was soaked to the skin.

"No taxis," he said.

There was a red mark on the side of his face.

Jessica leapt towards him and took off his raincoat. She fetched a towel and started to dry him. She ran her hand over his facial injury.

"Caroline," he said.

A few moments later they were sitting at the breakfast table drinking coffee and sharing their thoughts.

"I'm crazy Jessie." He paused. "I was in bed with her and I suddenly thought that I'm soon to be a father."

"What happened?"

"I told her that I was going home to you."

"You used the word 'home' Mob. Is that what you really want?"

He stood up and moved round to her chair. He lifted her up and put his arms inside her gown. He squeezed her flesh and kissed her.

"Let me keep the flat in London Jessie. I can't do that journey every bloody day. But I'll always come home and I'm going to be the best dad in the world to our baby."

"And me Mob?"

He kissed her again.

"You Jessie, are going to be my wife."

270

For some crazy, perhaps romantic, reason he then took her outside and stood her in front of the animal enclosure. The rain poured over them as he took her left hand and placed a ring on her finger.

"Will you marry me please Jessie?"

She looked into his eyes and again felt his injury.

"Yes Mob, I will. For ever."

She suddenly realised that Rustic had come out of his stable and was rubbing his nose on her arm. He snorted.

After all, he'd seen it all before.

### The End

# Author's Note

The actual Berkhamsted tunnel lies just before the station and is no more than a few hundred yards long. For the purposes of this book I have moved it northwards into the Chiltern Hills near to the Grand Union Canal and extended it. The planned attack on the 6.14 a.m. from Leighton Buzzard to Euston is pure fiction. As a regular commuter into Euston station I am hoping it stays that way.

It should be remembered that they said The Great Train Robbery could never happen. On 8 August 1963 it did, at Bridego Bridge.

Lightning never strikes twice – or does it?

**Tony Drury**
**Leighton Buzzard**
**November 2013**

**Coming next...**

## *The Lady Who Turned*

*The Lady* magazine is under attack. The bedrock of the British establishment has been rescued in recent times by a family member. Now it was being coveted by a foreign oligarch. The publication "for elegant woman with elegant minds" is facing its gravest hour.

Away from its West End offices, and across in the City of London, there is a corporate financier who does not play by the rules. Brendan Howes-Wittingham loves good wines, money and women in no particular order. He has his own goddess – Margaret Hilda Thatcher. When a call comes from a solicitor contact asking him to help save *The Lady* publication, he invokes her memory and becomes determined to help. He will banish the predator. There are just two issues: firstly, he underestimates the enemy and is soon receiving death threats. He is not to know that within two months a contract will be put on his life and a femme fatale will start to close in.

Secondly, he falls headlong in love with Ester Somerset who works in *The Lady* offices. His second marriage has been in trouble for some months.

Brendan fights tooth and nail to save *The Lady*. He has to contend with a wife who is clinging on, the dazzling Ester Somerset who is starting to respond to the vibes, to the female killer edging nearer and to *The Lady* herself.

But he is never to forget the words of his exemplar:

"You turn if you want to, the lady's not for turning."

*The Lady Who Turned* will be published by City Fiction in Spring 2014.

# About the author

Tony Drury is a corporate financier based in the City of London. He is a Fellow of the Chartered Institute of Bankers and a Member of the Chartered Institute for Securities & Investment.

Tony has written extensively over the years and is particularly well known for his financial and political books. He blogs weekly for www.enterprisebritain.com – both in his own name and as his alter ego Mr Angry. He is chairman of Axiom Capital Limited, a London-based corporate finance house, chairman of Globe Capital, a business advisory company based in Hong Kong and a director of AIM-listed Alpha Records Group plc.

He is a member of The Romantic Novelists' Association. His first novel *Megan's Game*, which was published in the spring of 2012, is set to hit the silver screen. Accredited producer, Paul Tucker believes it will make a great feature film with international appeal! The screenplay is now written and principal photography is planned to commence early in 2014.

Tony is passionate about the economic value of small businesses. He has chaired a committee of City-based financial market practitioners which focussed on how to revitalise the SME sector. His paper was delivered in March 2013 to Greg Clarke MP at HM Treasury.

In October 2013 he became an Ambassador for HEART UK, which concentrates on the dangers of excess cholesterol.

*A Flash of Lightning* is his fourth novel.

**For full details of Tony Drury and his books please visit www.tonydrury.com. Follow Tony on Twitter @mrtonydrury.**